VIRAGO
MODERN CLASS
135

Elizabeth Taylor

Elizabeth Taylor, who was born in Reading, Berkshire, in 1912 and educated at the Abbey School, Reading, worked as a governess and librarian before her marriage in 1936: 'I learnt so much from these jobs,' she wrote, 'and have never regretted the time I spent at them.' She lived in Penn, Buckinghamshire, for almost all her married life. Her first novel, *At Mrs Lippincote's*, appeared in 1945 and was followed by eleven more, together with short stories which were published in various periodicals and collected in four volumes, and a children's book, *Mossy Trotter*. Taylor's shrewd but affectionate portrayals of middle and upper middle-class English life soon won her a discriminating audience, as well as staunch friends in the world of letters. Rosamond Lehmann wrote, 'she is sophisticated, sensitive and brilliantly amusing, with a kind of stripped, piercing feminine wit'. Elizabeth Taylor died in 1975.

Novels by Elizabeth Taylor

At Mrs Lippincote's
Palladian
A View of the Harbour
A Wreath of Roses
A Game of Hide-and-Seek
The Sleeping Beauty
Angel
In a Summer Season
The Soul of Kindness
The Wedding Group
Mrs Palfrey at the Claremont
Blaming

Short Story Collection

Hester Lilly and Other Stories
The Blush and Other Stories
A Dedicated Man and Other Stories
The Devastating Boys
Complete Short Stories

ANGEL

Elizabeth Taylor

With an Introduction by
Hilary Mantel

virago

F

TO
PATIENCE ROSS

VIRAGO

Published by Virago Press Limited 1984

Reprinted 1984 (twice), 1990 (four times), 1991, 1999, 2001,
2006 (twice), 2007 (twice)
This edition published by Virago Press in 2008
Reprinted 2009, 2010, 2012 (three times), 2013 (twice)

First published in Great Britain by Peter Davies Ltd 1957

A CIP catalogue record for this book
is available from the British Library.

ISBN 978-1-84408-307-7

Printed and bound in Great Britain by
Clays Ltd, St Ives plc

Papers used by Virago are from well-managed forests
and other responsible sources.

MIX
Paper from
responsible sources
FSC® C104740

Virago Press
An imprint of
Little, Brown Book Group
100 Victoria Embankment
London EC4Y 0DY

An Hachette UK Company
www.hachette.co.uk

www.virago.co.uk

INTRODUCTION

I must begin with a confession. Although Angelica Deverell is not a real author, I feel as if I have read her books; and indeed, as if I have come dangerously close to writing them.

When I was a schoolchild of seven or eight, half-dead with boredom and frustration, and required to write a 'composition' by Sister Marie, I decided to enliven my ink-spattered page by writing not 'it was a fine day' or 'the sky was blue' but rather, 'the sky was a perfect azure'. Sister Marie called me out to the front of the class, eyed me suspiciously, read out loud the startling phrase, and slapped me. It was for making blots, she said. But really, I believed, she slapped me because she thought I was getting above myself.

I now think 'the sky was blue' would have been better; or no doubt the sky could have been left out of it altogether. But I was right in one respect. Sister Marie was acting as a social commentator, not a literary critic. One day it's azure sky, the next it's red revolution. When, as a precocious schoolgirl, Angelica is begged by her mother and aunt to 'say something in French' she chooses a stanza of 'La Marseillaise'. A rebel from a back street – though in search of a revolution in self-esteem, not in society – she is raising the bloody standard against boredom; against the crushing low expectations of her milieu; against the threat of living an ordinary life.

When I try to work out where I had picked up such an affectation as 'azure', I can walk without hesitation up to the attic in my grandmother's house, where there was a little cache of books – in effect, the only books in the house – which I read at lunch-times when I came home from school. These were precisely the kind of books which made Angelica Deverell rich and famous, but I don't know who, in fact, their authors were. The covers were greasy and blackened, the stitching frayed, the edges of the pages were mustard in colour, but the content was, as Angelica would say, 'coruscating' and possibly 'iridescent'. They were about upper-class gals with soaring spirits and unorthodox beauty – red hair, or 'auburn locks' featured. They were pining after some lost or unsuitable man, and on a collision course with their families and convention. Their backdrop was the hunting field, where they were dauntless under an azure sky. At dusk the ballroom awaited; but this was not the ballroom of the whispering virginal debut. They were beyond first-night nerves, beyond condescending to the disapproving rustle of dowagers' fans. These heroines moved through the scene at midnight, through the melancholy ruins of the buffet, on to the dazzling expanse of moonlit terrace, and stood alone, listening to the cry of ancestral peafowl (if no nightingale was available), while the orchestra played a last poignant waltz. I expect the gals dwindled into matrimony, but I don't remember the end of these books; I only remember forever beginning them, senses filled with the frou-frou of silk petticoats and the perfume of gardenias. It was all a great change from Enid Blyton.

Angel is a book in which an accomplished, deft and somewhat underrated writer has a great deal of fun at the expense of a crass, graceless and wildy overpaid one. Taylor is a writer of impeccable taste, while Angelica Deverell is a high priestess of schlock. Taylor excelled at the short-story form, where Angel, with her almost demonic energy, seems made for the epic. Taylor is quietly and devastatingly amusing, while her creation never makes a joke, and is upset and suspicious if anyone makes one in her vicinity. Taylor is observant, while Angelica never notices the life that goes on about her; for her, the only true reality is inside her head.

Born in 1912, and producing her stylish books for three decades after the Second World War, Elizabeth Taylor was not the sort of writer who lives so as to excite prospective biographers. A clever, formal restraint is the hallmark of her fiction, and though the compass of her works is restricted she has a formidable technique. All the same, what Taylor knows – and it is the one odd fact that ties her to her creation, and drives her book – is that good writers and bad writers, when they are talking about their art, sound remarkably the same. Their early struggles are the same. Their inner triumphs feel the same. The only way in which they differ is that the bad writers, once they get the initial breakthrough, usually make more money.

The phenomenon of Angelica Deverell illustrates the axiom that nobody ever went broke underestimating public taste. Nobody told Angel of this fact; she just instinctively knew it. She writes the books she wants to read herself. Her mind is passionate and commonplace, quick and shallow, and so she fulfils a perennial demand that readers make, to be 'taken out of themselves', to be 'transported'. From book to book, Angel does not learn; nor could you learn from her books. She switches her settings when she is jaded, picking up her characters from an Edwardian house party and putting them down in a banqueting hall in ancient Athens, but she doesn't change her formula. When at last she does – when the demands of her ego override her instinctive knowledge of her market – then her royalties begin to dwindle. For any writer, good, bad or – as we mostly are – an ever-changing mixture of both, *Angel* provides a series of sharp lessons in humility.

The book begins in the last year of Queen Victoria's reign, in the red-brick terraces of the drab brewery town of Norley, where Angelica, the shopkeeper's daughter, having sulked and idled through fifteen years of existence, reveals to those about her that she is writing a book. Anyone who comes from an unbookish family, and who has made the same announcement, will vouch for what comes next. Her widowed mother and her aunt, a lady's maid, approach her with 'looks of bright resolve, as if they were visiting some relations in a lunatic asylum.' They feel amazed, exposed and betrayed: 'Story-writing!' her aunt exclaims. 'Where's she got that from?'

Angel feels herself the rightful heir of a world from which she is excluded. Her aunt works just outside Norley at Paradise House, and Angel is named after the daughter of the family who employs her. Angel has spent much of her life, in fantasy, strolling the lawns and warming herself before the marble hearths. Yet 'fantasy' seems too weak a word for her sense of entitlement, her driven desire to warp reality by visualising it as different. Angel has a tyrannical imagination that excludes experience, even excludes the spirit of enquiry; she has no idea in which direction from Norley the real Paradise House lies, and on the one occasion she is invited to visit she dismisses the idea in a way that seems pettish but which is actually protective of her inner vision. Angel believes she has the right to impose her imagination on others. She tells her teacher that she spends her leisure hours playing the harp: when the woman looks dubious, Angel is angry because her private world has been slighted. But she is grimly accepting of knock-backs because she knows she is only biding her time. Her triumph will be to turn her fantasies loose, in all their devouring power: and make them pay.

Angel spends only one evening scribbling in an exercise book before she decides – in fact, she knows – that she has found her vocation, the only thing that will make her happy, and the only possible route out of Norley. We admire her tenacity, her robust self-starter's confidence, and we know she has some ability, in her florid way – enough style to make her schoolmistress nervously 'scan Ruskin and Pater' before reluctantly concluding that Angel's homework is not plagiarised. But we fear for her when she bundles up her first torrid effort – *The Lady Irania* – and sends it to the only publisher she has heard of, the Oxford University Press. But Angel is not cowed by rejection, and a little later she strikes lucky. Her manuscript lands on the desk of Theo Gilbright of Gilbright & Brace. Fascinated and appalled, he asks to meet the author.

Angel, who has never been away from Norley, sets off alone to London, and off goes the reader with her, heart thumping, through the wretchedly hot and dirty streets, to an alien building where she is given a cup of tea in what she hopes is Dresden china. Despite the derision of his partner, Theo is inclined to take a risk on the manuscript. But there must be a few changes, he suggests. Perhaps they might tone down the more risqué passages – Angel, who is as ignorant of convention as she is scornful of it, has made Lady Irania's virtue the prize in a card game. Perhaps certain domestic details could be refined; for instance, one does not need a corkscrew to open champagne.

"'So will you take away your manuscript for a while and see what you can do for us?"

"No," said Angel.'

It is the book's central moment – perfectly judged, and almost too painful to be funny. Angel marches out into the hostile streets, and weeps in the ladies' lavatories at Paddington Station. She should have given in, she thinks, compromised, because now she has lost what she most wanted in life. 'Yet still she felt something obdurate in herself, even in her state of frailty and defeat. It was a hard, physical pain in her breast, which might have been indigestion, but was vanity.'

But even as she is making her way home to Norley, Theo Gilbright is thinking, 'so are we to risk Irania as it stands, card-scene and all?'

The critics are savage; the public is ecstatic. Angel thinks the public is right and the critics are jealous. One bestseller follows another, and Angel is able to take her bright brave little mother away from the corner grocery – which was her solace as well as her living – and transplant her to an opulent new house in the suburbs. The minor characters are beautifully observed. There is Theo, harassed but unfailingly kind. There is Aunt Lottie, who quarrels in the spitefully genteel language of a lady's maid, and Lord Norley, the local grandee, who comes calling one day; possessor of a brewery fortune, he has a hazy idea that by taking tea with Angel he is paying his debt to culture. With him is his niece Nora, a 'poetess,' who is enraptured by Angel – not just by her fame, but by her dramatic *jolie-laide* looks, her bony elegant body, the frailty that Angel has managed to conceal from everyone else. Lord Norley also brings his nephew Esme, the pretty, treacherous waster who will become Angel's husband.

Angel buys him; he agrees to be bought. Esme is Angel's opposite. He is a painter, his style observant and restrained, his taste advanced and original. But he works only sporadically, lacks tenacity, lacks courage, and he is easily diverted into days out at the racecourse, and expensive sexual adventures. A less subtle writer would have solicited our sympathy for Esme, as altogether more human than the increasingly demanding and eccentric Angel, but Taylor allows us to understand that Esme is not likable and has no friends. We understand that real life, real relationships, will always be second-best to Angel. She cannot engage; she gives too much to fiction and has nothing left over for life. We foresee that when she at last comes to own the ruin that is Paradise House, she will, in restoring it to its old grandeur, build a prison for herself.

The last chapters of the book are melancholy, as Angel's public deserts her and Paradise House crumbles again. A cussed old lady, she survives to see the Second World War. All her scenes of glory are vanished; the harps as silent as the peafowl, the ball dresses turned back to rags, the lady Irania just a bunch of old bones. But we feel that Elizabeth Taylor has allowed us a glimpse inside a peculiar but by no means unique psyche. Angel is self-deluded, at times almost deranged. She overrides the meek and the timid, she is callous in pursuit of the preservation of her glorified image of herself, and she is no admirer of 'human nature'. One could argue that the author is showing us Angel as an awful warning; that she is telling us 'this is how bad art is made.' But I don't think the book is as simple as that. It seems to me that what Elizabeth Taylor does is to de-romanticise the process of writing and show it to us close up, so that we are aware of that if ten per cent of the process is exhilaration, the rest is tedium, backache and the fear of failure; that, whatever the impulse to art, however little or great the gift, a cast-iron vanity and a will to power are needed to sustain it. Writers are monsters, she is telling us; how else would you be reading this book?

Hilary Mantel, 2005

PART 1

i

" 'into the vast vacuity of the empyrean,' " Miss Dawson read. "And can you tell me what 'empyrean' means?"

"It means," Angel said. Her tongue moistened her lips. She glanced out of the classroom window at the sky beyond the bare trees. "It means 'the highest heavens'."

"Yes, the sky," Miss Dawson said suspiciously. She handed the exercise-book to Angel, feeling baffled. The girl had a great reputation as a liar and when this strange essay had been handed in—"A Storm At Sea"—Miss Dawson had gone through it in a state of alarm, fearful lest she had read it before or ought to have read it before. She had spent an agitated evening scanning Pater and Ruskin and others. Though disdaining such ornamental prose, such crescendos and alliterations, before she would say that the piece was vulgarly over-written she hoped to find out who had written it.

She had confided in the headmistress, who also felt the need for caution. She thought it a remarkable piece of writing for a girl of fifteen; if, indeed, it was by a girl of fifteen.

"Has she ever done anything like it before?"

"Nothing. A line or two covered with blots."

" 'Lightning laced and veined the sky,' " the headmistress read. "Did you look through Oscar Wilde?"

"Yes, and Walter Pater."

"You will have to question her. If she is making fools of us, it isn't the first time."

Angel, when feeling dull, was liable to faint and had once told a story of being followed from school through the gas-lit streets on a winter's afternoon; though later, to a policeman, she confessed that she might have been mistaken.

She was questioned by Miss Dawson when the other girls had gone home. She doesn't believe I wrote it, she thought, glancing with contempt at the flustered little woman with the slipping pince-nez and bird's-nest hair. Who does she think wrote it if I didn't? Who does she think could? What a way to spend your life—fussing about with school-lessons, getting chalk all over your skirt, going home to lodgings at night to work out the next day's Shakespeare—cut to page this, line that, so that we don't have to read the word 'womb'.

She looked round the dreary, darkening classroom, at the rows of forms and long desks, and all the familiar maps and religious pictures. Once it had been a bedroom in a private house, The Four Cedars, which was now this school, run aimlessly as it was for the daughters of local tradesmen. Angel had often, during dull lessons, tried to imagine it as a bedroom again, with plush curtains drawn, a fire in the grate, a white satin gown over a chair and herself being laced into her stays by a maid.

"Well, I hope you will keep it up," Miss Dawson said dubiously. She dipped a pen into red ink and wrote 'Very Fair' at the end of the essay.

"Do you read a great deal, Angelica?"

"No, I never read."

"But why not?"

"I don't think it's interesting."

"Such a pity. Then what do you do in your spare time?"

"I play the harp mostly."

She doesn't believe that, either, thought Angel, seeing the suspicious look again tightening Miss Dawson's face. She was as resentful at not being believed about the harp—which was indeed untrue—as about the essay which she had certainly written herself, and with the greatest of ease and speed, just because she had suddenly been in a mind to do so.

When Miss Dawson dismissed her, she gave a little bobbing curtsy as she was expected to and ran downstairs to the cloakroom. The staircase was very dim. A light shone from an open door across the hall. The conservatory with its palms and eucalyptus trees was grey and ghostly. All of the girls had gone home.

The cloakroom had once been a large scullery. It was fitted with pegs from which only shoe-bags hung now and, in one corner, Angel's hooded cloak. Black-beetles often ran about the cracked stone floor and the walls were damp. There were bars across the window, and it was a frightening place at this time of day. The girls used the back door, where there were shoe-scrapers among the ferns, a row of dustbins, a heap of coke, and always a great many pale yellow slugs.

The lawns and carriage-drive, lighted windows and the four cedars themselves could be glimpsed from the side path and the tradesmen's entrance. Here, among the laurels, two girls, younger than Angel, were waiting. It was Angel's task to see them safely to and from school. Their parents were customers at her mother's grocery shop.

The two little girls, Gwen and Polly, had been apprehensive, waiting there in the dusk. The lamp-lighter had gone by long ago and the sky was now a deep blue. There was a smell of evening in the air, smoky and disturbing.

"I had to stay behind to hear my praises sung," said Angel. She was pulling on her woollen gloves as she hastened along the pavement. Gwen and Polly trotted beside her. They descended the hill, past crescents and terraces of Georgian houses and dark gardens full of whispering dead leaves.

"When you are at Paradise House," Polly asked, "do you ever go into the garden by yourself in the dark?"

"I take my dog with me—Trapper. We go all round the grounds. It's rather ghostly by the stables—just the sound of the horses blowing and stamping."

"Are they your very own horses?"

"They will be when I inherit."

"But who looks after them now?"

"Grooms and stable-boys. It is all kept in order and so is the house. There are dust-sheets over the drawing-room and drugget over the carpets, but the housekeeper sees that everything is polished and shining ready for the day when I can go there myself to live."

"It seems a pity," Polly said, "that you have to wait. Why can't you go there now?"

"My mother lost her inheritance because she married beneath her. She can never go back, so don't ever mention anything to anybody about Paradise House for that reason."

"No, of course not," they whispered quickly, as they always did. "But why mustn't we?" asked Gwen.

"It breaks my mother's heart to hear of it. If you breathed a word of it at home and it came back to her, I couldn't answer for the consequences."

"We wouldn't breathe a word," said Polly. "Will you go on telling us about the white peacocks?"

Every day they listened to the story of Paradise House. It was more vivid to them than the mean streets into which the crescents and terraces dwindled and which lay nearer to their own homes. Naked gas-jets burned in little corner shops, but the rows of yellow brick houses were dark: lights burned in those front parlours, behind the fern-tables and plant-pots, only on Sundays. Coal carts and brewers' drays clattered by, but there were no carriages. The sickly smell from the nearby brewery the girls had grown up with and did not notice.

"Will you tell us some more tomorrow?" Polly asked, stopping by the railings of their little front garden.

Angel often felt jolted when the girls stopped at their gate; partly, from having forgotten them; partly, from having to transfer herself too suddenly from Paradise House to this mean district with its warehouses and factories and great brooding gas-holder.

"I might," she said carelessly. They opened the gate and said goodbye to her; but she had gone on her way already, holding her cloak about her and hurrying along, full of her own strange thoughts again.

Halfway down Volunteer Street was a row of shops: a fish-and-chip shop from which children were running with hot, greasy parcels; a newsagent's; a chemist's where light from the interior glowed feebly through three glass bottles of red and green and violet liquid and coloured the bowls of senna pods and sulphur lying in the window. Next to the draper's and the last in the row was the grocery shop; there, Eddie Gilkes, the delivery boy, was packing up an order on the counter, weighing sugar into pink bags. The wedge of cheese beside him was covered with his dirty finger-prints. The saw-dust on the floor was scuffed about now at the end of the day.

Angel ignored Eddie's greeting and went through the door at the back of the shop. The dark lobby was stacked with boxes. There were jars of pickles and a cask of vinegar at the foot of the stairs. The smell of bacon and soap pervaded the upstairs rooms, Angel's cold, stuffy little bedroom and the bright living-room where Mrs Deverell was leaning towards the fire making toast.

A crochet-work cloth was spread over the green chenille one and the light shone down on the cups and saucers on the table. The room was overcrowded and it was difficult to push between the table and the other furniture, the horsehair sofa, the chiffonier, the treadle sewing-machine and the harmonium. Photographs covered every surface. The chimney-piece was draped with ball-fringed velvet and a bead fringe hid the incandescent gas-mantle.

Mrs Deverell shielded her face from the fire with one hand, but her cheeks were rosy. The room was very hot. "You're home late," she said.

"I wasn't in any hurry."

"You missed your Auntie Lottie. You know how she looks to find you here. I reminded you it was her Wednesday."

Angel parted the curtains and leant her forehead on the steamy window.

"Oh, it's hot in here. I don't know how you can bear it."

She longed to be walking in the country in the cold air and darkness. The reality of this room exasperated her; she turned her back on it and closed her eyes. She did not dare to stuff her fingers in her ears to shut out the sound of her mother's voice. She had forgotten her aunt's visit and was glad to find she had

11

escaped it. On such occasions she always felt herself brooded over, her mother's sister watching her so intently; too intently questioning her, about her friends and the school, particularly about the school, for which the aunt helped to pay the fees. The two sisters were tremendously impressed that Angel had escaped the board-school at the corner of the road. "Say something in French," they would urge her. Roughly and sulkily, Angel complied. They did not know that her accent was atrocious—as it would remain all her life.

> "Allons, enfants de la patrie!
> Le jour de gloire est arrivé.
> Contre nous de la tyrannie
> L'étendard sanglant est levé."

"It's amazing, isn't it?" they would say, marvelling that they had got their money's worth. Angel wondered why she felt ill-used and humiliated. She tried to ward off her aunt's curiosity; was vague and evasive; and when at last they left her in peace, she would kneel on the sofa and look down at the street, at children playing hop-scotch, skipping from ropes tied to a lamp-post; the milkman ladling milk into jugs; the organ-grinder with his monkey.

They would forget her at last, the two sisters, and Angel would listen to their conversation, to the stories of Paradise House, where Aunt Lottie was lady's maid. So often, as this evening, she did not see the street below because the great vision of Paradise House obscured other things. She discovered the rooms and galleries, paced the grassy paths between yew trees and statuary.

"She brought this lardy-cake from the cook," Mrs Deverell was saying. She took it, glistening and curranty, from the hearth. "It shows how much they think of her."

Angel let the curtains drop together and went to the table.

Her mother fetched the toast and the teapot. They stood behind their chairs. "For what we are about to receive, may the Lord make us truly thankful," said Mrs Deverell. "I could do you a boiled egg, if you like. Your Auntie brought me a few new-laids from the gardener."

"No, thank you, I'm not hungry," Angel said. She tipped the cat off her chair and sat down.

After tea, Mrs Deverell went down to serve in the shop. It was an unspoken assumption that there would be no advantage gained from sending Angel to a private school if she was to demean herself behind the counter when she returned. So she sat upstairs on her own. Her mother had given her a chemise to scallop, but she got no further with it from one week's end to another. When she made a stitch or two, she held the cambric up close to her eyes, but only if she were alone in the room. She was short-sighted and determined to hide it. She would be blamed for any mistake rather than give the reason for making it and run the risk of being forced to wear spectacles.

She was vain of her strange appearance, and in fact her colouring, her green eyes, dark hair and white skin, was remarkable and dramatic; but her features were already, at fifteen, forbiddingly aquiline; her teeth were prominent and her astigmatic eyes sometimes unfocused. Her hands she thought exceptionally beautiful and would look at them for minutes together, as she was this evening, spreading them before her, turning them, viewing them from every angle, imagining garnets clasped round her wrists.

"Madam's garnets would suit Angel," Aunt Lottie had once said, adding, "I'd rather garnets than rubies any day."

"I think emeralds are more Angel's stone," said Mrs Deverell. Angel went over this argument often afterwards. Some days she chose the emeralds, to match her eyes; this evening the garnets, to illuminate her skin.

At Paradise House there was another Angelica, Madam's daughter, whose name was never shortened. Aunt Lottie, in admiration of her mistress and all that she did, had had this name waiting for Angel when she was born. A boy's name was never contemplated, for Madam had no sons. Until Angel

13

went to school and learnt better, they always spelt the name with two 'l's.

The Angelica whose name had been copied was a month or two older than Angel; but not so tall, Aunt Lottie said. An opinionated little madam, she was described as plump; and pink-and-white. The garnets would be wasted on her. A string of seed-pearls was what *she* merited, with her insipid looks and her hands rough as boys': too much horse-riding and dog-washing, Aunt Lottie thought. Angel, resenting that other girl whom she had never seen but knew so well, turned her hands complacently, considering their shape, and their pallor.

She could hear the shop door-bell ringing below as customers came and went. So many women saved their shopping for the evening and a gossip while their husbands went to the Garibaldi or the Volunteer. In the cosy shop such confidences went on while Mrs Deverell weighed broken biscuits or drew the wire neatly through the cheese. "Not that I'd like it to go any further." Mrs Deverell had usually heard before. *She* had asked for it, she would say, or *he* had asked for it; who could expect other—in a world where marriages were not made by Mrs Deverell—than that they should turn out as they did, with wives pretending their bruised eyes were got from bumping into the wardrobe, or that they would pay a little off next week, then running to the pawn-shop with the flat-iron every Tuesday and fetching it under their cloaks the following Monday.

Mrs Deverell's own married life had been short and flawless in retrospect. Her husband had coughed his way through only a year and a half of married bliss. His photograph was all Angel knew of him. The memory of him had faded more than the photograph, which showed a wax-work of a man with a curly beard and ill-fitting clothes. Angel disowned him. Her brisk, brave, vivacious mother had long ago forgotten him. She had her sister and her neighbours and Angel to boast about to them. 'That Angel', the girl was called in consequence. She was solitary without knowing.

Lax and torpid, she dreamed through the lonely evenings,

closing her eyes to create the darkness where Paradise House could take shape, embellished and enlarged day after day—with colonnades and cupolas, archways and flights of steps—beyond anything her aunt had ever suggested. Acquisitively, from photographs and drawings in history-books, she added one detail after another. That will do for Paradise House, was an obsessive formula which became a daily habit. The white peacocks would do; and there were portraits in the Municipal Art Gallery which would do; as would the cedar trees at school. As the house spread, those in it grew more shadowy. Angel herself took over Madam's jewel-box and Madam's bed and husband. Only that other Angelica balked her imagination, a maddening obstacle, with her fair looks and all her dogs and horses. Again and again, as Angel wandered in the galleries and gardens, the vision of that girl, who had no place in her dreams, rose up and impeded her. The dream itself, which was no idle matter, but a severe strain on her powers of concentration, would dissolve. Then she would open her eyes and stare down at her hands, spreading her fingers, turning her wrists.

At other times she was menaced by intimations of the truth. Her heart would be alarmed, as if by a sudden roll of drums, and she would spring to her feet, beset by the reality of the room, her own face—not beautiful, she saw—in the looking-glass and the commonplace sounds in the shop below. She would know then that she was in her own setting and had no reason for ever finding herself elsewhere; know moreover that she was bereft of the power to rescue herself, the brains or the beauty by which other young women made their escape. Her panic-stricken face would be reflected back at her as she struggled to deny her identity, slowly cosseting herself away from the truth. She was learning to triumph over reality, and the truth was beginning to leave her in peace.

This evening passed without any sense of time going by. She was roaming through moonlit rose-gardens when she heard her mother shutting up the shop, rattling the chains across the door, then slowly climbing the stairs.

Angel was like a tableau of a girl fallen gracefully asleep over her sewing, the cat sleeping, too, at her feet. The fire had sunk low, just when Mrs Deverell was ready to hold up her skirts and warm her ankles for a moment or two.

"Oh, I dropped off," said Angel, yawning languorously.

"You always do. You'd do better to get off to bed." Mrs Deverell rattled the poker in the bars of the grate and took up the bellows.

"Miss Little came in for some soda. She was telling me that poor old Mrs Turner passed away last night with dropsy."

"How disgusting!" Angel said, yawning until tears fell. The first yawn had been affected. Now she could not stop.

Her mother put a little saucepan of milk on the hob and some cups and saucers on a tray. It did not occur to Angel to stir herself to help.

The next morning Gwen and Polly were not waiting at the gate as usual, and Angel, hesitating there, saw their mother watching her in the darkness beyond the lace curtains. As Angel looked towards her she stepped back from the window. The dark stuff of her dress merged with the shadowy room: only her colourless face could be discerned.

Angel gave a push to the iron gate. At the sound of it grating on its hinges, the woman came quickly to the window and rapped on it with her knuckles and shook her head. Her face looked pinched with suspicion and disdain, and Angel, going on down the road, wondered why she was feeling that she had been made despicable. She worried a little, hurrying lest she should be late, until she saw other girls dawdling in front of her.

She had never had any especial friends and most people seemed unreal to her. Her aloofness and her reputation for being vain made her unpopular, yet there were times when she longed desperately, because of some uneasiness, to establish herself; to make her mark; to talk, as she thought of it, on equal terms: but since she had never thought of herself as being on equal terms with anyone, she stumbled from con-descension to appeasement, making what the other girls called 'personal remarks' and offending with off-hand flattery.

Conversation would be dropped when she approached, as it was this morning between Ellie and Beattie, two girls of her own age. When she reached them, she came upon the sort of stubborn silence which meant that they hoped she would hurry on.

"Are we late?" she asked, with an affected breathlessness.

"We didn't think so," Ellie said.

"But if you fancy *you* are, do go on," said Beattie.

She slowed down to their pace and walked beside them. She began to talk about school, with no response from either of them. It was a less interesting subject than the one they had just dropped.

When Ellie stopped by the railings to tie a bootlace, Angel stood by and praised the smallness of her feet.

"They're no smaller than yours," Ellie said roughly.

Angel glanced down at her own, and seemed surprised to find that this was so.

"I suppose you mean you think they're small for *me*," said Ellie, and Beattie laughed suddenly.

After a long silence Beattie remarked thoughtfully: "So she decided on the cream merino, then?"

She implied that Angel's presence made no difference to the conversation she had interrupted, and they both continued it, with mysterious references, so that Angel could not join in. They had indeed been discussing Ellie's sister's wedding, but with more intimate conjectures than those concerned with her trousseau.

"You know I was telling you what Cyril said about the grey pelisse. . . ."

"Yes."

"Well . . ." She lowered her voice and both girls laughed. Angel tried to appear unaffected by the conversation. She despised their animation about such a home-made trousseau; could imagine the deplorably coy behaviour of the bride and

17

those around her; the wedding at the hideous Congregational Church, and the little house crowded with boorish relations afterwards. Although Ellie and Beattie were from better-off homes than her own, she had other standards to judge them by.

Ellie and Beattie had drifted pleasurably on to imagining their own wedding-dresses and to wondering whether they should go to Folkestone or to the Lake District for their honeymoons. To be married women as soon as possible seemed the sum of their ambition, to get what they wanted from life very early in it and then to ask nothing more, to remain in that state for the rest of their days.

"So exciting! Don't *you* think so, Angel?" Beattie asked slyly.

"What is exciting?"

"Why, getting married, of course."

"It depends who to," said Angel.

"You are always in trouble for ending sentences with prepositions," Beattie said.

"I shall begin and end my sentences as I please." She had stopped propitiating them. "And how can you or anyone be excited about getting married to someone you can't even give a name to?"

"Don't worry!" Ellie said crossly. "I don't suppose we shall have to wait long." To separate themselves from Angel, she and Beattie linked arms, which was against the school rules.

"If you fall in love," said Angel, "what do weddings matter? What have all these clothes and cakes and presents to do with that?"

She had begun this argument to belittle their enthusiasm and to revenge herself, but she was warming to it for its own sake. Until now she had thought of love with bleak distaste. She wanted to dominate the world, not one person.

"Oh, you're very clever," said Ellie. She almost gasped the words: her fury made her breathless. She pushed through the school gate in front of Angel. Her head was high and the colour bright in her cheeks. She had the contemptuous look Angel was often to meet in women, who, feeling their calm threatened by the unconventional, from fear of inadequacy fall back on rage; and Ellie's anger came suddenly in a great gust, so that she longed to spin round and hit Angel's pale face. "You would," she cried. "Of course, *you* would think such things. Who would expect *you* to believe in Holy Matrimony? Why, it would be very strange if you did."

She hurried on towards the school building and Beattie, looking rather frightened, hurried after her.

Angel could see Gwen and Polly scurrying ahead, too; like mice they darted into the cloakroom when they noticed her. She remembered the expression on their mother's face when she had come to the window that morning, and she felt menaced and bewildered. She pondered Ellie's words, turning them over and over in her mind, walking towards the cloak-room slowly, although the other girls had gone indoors. She was the last, and a bell began to ring for prayers.

The day went sluggishly by. An oil-stove was lit in the class-room, but the girls who sat by the window still shivered, chafing their chilblains. They stayed in their desks as one dull lesson followed another, except that sometimes they were told to stand and do a few feeble exercises, clapping their hands above their heads and swinging their arms. Hour after hour, they were made to learn lessons by heart, French vocabularies, psalms, history dates and the names of rivers, until their heads were so tightly crammed with facts that thoughts had no room to move in them. When the lists were learned they droned them in unison. For their drawing-lesson some tattered prints were handed round for them to copy. There were never any new ones and Angel had drawn the same windmill a dozen times. In needlework, they made chain-stitch patterns on pieces of unbleached linen which smelt of glue.

At midday, some of the girls remained. They stayed in the classroom and unpacked their sandwiches. No one spoke to Angel, who sat at her desk, unwrapped her lunch and ate it hungrily, staring out of the window.

By afternoon, a white fog began to blot out the great layered branches of the cedar trees; then the sky discoloured; by four o'clock it was the colour of snuff. The day had seemed endless.

Angel went dreamily home. Gwen and Polly were not waiting at the gate and she had no one to talk to, no one to take to Paradise House, so the only real part of her day was missing. She walked slowly through the foggy streets and when she reached home went straight upstairs to the living-room. Her mother was sitting by the fire, making toast, as usual, but she did not look round or speak when Angel came in. She waited until the bread was golden, turned it on the fork, and then said smartly, to conceal her trembling: "I want to talk to you, my lady."

"Well?" said Angel warily. She prepared to insulate herself against some shock. Although she could not guess what was going to happen, all day long she had felt threatened, felt that she was being drawn nearer each moment to some experience which might be utterly disastrous to her. She watched her mother taking the toast off the fork and spreading the butter carefully, frowning as if she were groping for a way to begin her complaint. Finding none, she pitched into the story somewhere past its beginning, so that at first she was unintelligible to Angel.

"You can picture what I felt like. . . . I never had a turn like that since your father died. 'I just don't know what to say, Mrs Watts,' I said. Stuffing her Gwen and Polly's head with such a conglomeration of lies I couldn't credit. Saying wicked things of your own mother. Married beneath me, did I? Just let me tell you this, my girl, if your father hadn't of built up this business like he did, we'd have been in the gutter by this time. So good he was, too, that I'm glad he was spared what I've been through today."

She began to cry, and by this time Angel had gathered something of what she was saying and was turned to ice. She faced blankness, despair, and longed for death, seeing no other end.

"You wicked, wicked girl!" Her mother cut off her sobbing and began to storm again. She was not nearly done. "To make up all those lies about a place you've never been to, nor ever likely to; but to go on as if you had some right there. And telling those innocent children; day after day, they said. Putting on such airs. Taking it on yourself. Oh, it was a treat for me, I'll tell you; hearing all about that. She's been a good customer, too. And friend. And now I just hope I never see her again, not so long as I live. How can I ever hold my head up, knowing all that she'll have to say among the neighbours? There never was a tongue wagged like hers. I know her. I remember when I was in the Chapel choir with her. I don't forget what she said about my own sister. But you!" Her grief suddenly gave way to vexation. She leaned towards Angel and hit her face. "I would rather have seen you dead at my feet than let you bring this disgrace on me." Then she stepped back, feeling ashamed, seeing the mark of her hand across the girl's cheek.

Angel had said nothing. She turned her back for a moment, waited for some strength to come to her legs, then managed to walk from the room.

Her mother ran after her and when Angel had locked herself in her bedroom, drummed her fists on the door; for she had not had what she wanted, an explanation. "Why did you? Why?" she sobbed.

There was no explanation, and Angel on the other side of the door in the dark cold room was silent. She felt strangely outraged; as if her mother had violated her.

She had no matches to light the gas and she began to undress in the dark, unlacing her boots and pulling off her black woollen stockings, leaving her clothes in a heap on the floor. She thought that her mother had gone downstairs to the shop, but she would not risk opening the door. "How dare she!" she whispered over and over again as she stumbled about the room, braiding her hair.

No light came into the bedroom. There were no street-lamps to shine in, for it was at the back of the building and the window was above a yard stacked with crates. Angel drew down the sash and let in some of the foggy air. Everything in the room, and the bedclothes when she lay down, felt clammy to touch. She lay in bed shivering, waiting for the evening, then the night, to pass. There was nowhere where her thoughts might turn, her escape was cut off, her retreat contaminated. "How dare she!" she whispered again.

After a long time, she heard her mother coming upstairs, pausing outside the bedroom and trying the door-handle. Then she rapped on the door and said: "Angel! You must answer me. You've had nothing to eat."

The girl had been thinking of food, as if it might comfort her to eat something, but she stared into the darkness and said nothing. She noticed a change in her mother's voice—anxiety muffling the anger—but she was indifferent to it.

Before she fell asleep an idea came to her that there was some comfort to be had—not food—if only she knew where to find it. Something, once, had made her happy, but she could not remember what it was.

She awoke in the night, aware of some change and strangeness; then the memory of what had taken place engulfed her. Her situation seemed as dreadful as before, and now she was nearer to—or already in—the next day and had no plans for dealing with it. She could not stay locked in the room for ever.

She got out of bed and crept along the landing to fetch a glass of water. Her mother was murmuring and turning in her bed in the room next to her own. Angel left her door unlocked and lay down again, pulling the bedclothes round her for warmth. I will never go to school again, she promised herself. Those sly little creatures, Gwen and Polly, watching me all day, knowing what would happen to me when I came home; and frightened because they had betrayed me.

She drew her cold feet up into her nightgown. In a panic she could discern some of the furniture now and the walls were paler. Soon there were footsteps in the street and factory sirens sounding and at the end of Volunteer Street a cart clattering across the cobbled Butts, as the old square was called.

It was when I wrote the essay, she suddenly thought. "The Storm at Sea." That was when I was happy.

She was glad to have remembered this, felt more at peace, and slept.

She was to be rescued from the next day's wounds by what looked like a miracle. Her mother wakened early and lay in bed wondering how she and Angel could take up their existence again, so shut in together and with the air so laden with embarrassment. It is how to get back to being ordinary again, she thought, as bereaved people do. Her anger had gone, but she felt she could never be easy with Angel now and would never succeed in hiding her uneasiness. Her spontaneity had overcome previous difficulties, such as discontent and sullenness; but she was sure that she could never be spontaneous again or use any words which were not weighed first; as now she was trying to weigh some for her meeting with Angel that morning.

She dressed when the time came and went into the parlour to rake out the fire and lay the breakfast. It was scarcely light yet, though people were going to work and soon she heard Eddie trying the shop door and went down to let him in. She cut a couple of slices of bacon for breakfast and went upstairs again. It was time to call Angel, and the confusion she felt made her cheeks flushed, so that she looked full of indignation still.

The girl was asleep. One arm flung over the honeycomb bed-cover, bare to the elbow, was a dark crimson, as were her neck and forehead. Mrs Deverell forgot her embarrassment and her rehearsed speeches and went to the bed to look more closely. In her sleep, Angel turned her arm on the cover, rubbing it up and down; then she opened her eyes and stared about her. Still half asleep, she began to scratch herself, first one arm, then the other, and frowned in a puzzled way.

"Oh, dear, what is it? What's wrong?" her mother asked,

laying her hand on the burning skin which was raised up in weals and blotches.

In a few seconds after waking, Angel had realised the situation. Her fears had dissolved and the day's behaviour was decided. She was ill and had escaped. As she rubbed and scratched, her skin grew more furiously inflamed and she was glad. If she were clever, she could make it impossible for anything to be said for days, except: "How do you feel?" or "What do you fancy?" She could easily be as clever as that, and began at once, with unintelligible mutterings and by staring at and beyond her mother as if she could not see her there.

Mrs Deverell filled a stone jar with hot water, wrapped it in an old pair of combinations and laid it at Angel's feet. Then she went to the living-room and took down one of the pile of books on the top of the harmonium and began to look up some diseases. After a while, hesitating between scarlet-fever and erysipelas, she panicked and took an extreme step, sending Eddie running off for Doctor Foskett.

In the medical book, erysipelas was given an alternative and more dramatic name, St Anthony's Fire, and, when the doctor arrived, Mrs Deverell, making haste to diagnose, used this term, having forgotten the other. Angel had not stirred, except to rub her arms and worsen the inflammation, since she had wakened. When her mother had asked her one anxious question after another, she had turned her face closer to the pillow; but now she felt awe and curiosity at such a strange-sounding, mystical disease. She opened her eyes and looked at the doctor and saw that he was trying not to laugh, as he bent down to take his stethoscope from the Gladstone-bag.

Angel lay silent while he listened to her chest. She was restoring herself, coating over her wounds as an oyster does. Falsehood could make her resilient, and the humiliation she had suffered was being tucked safely away. "When I was ill," she would refer to it in her own mind, expecting other people to behave in the same way. She had been brought up to fear the doctor. Tall, bearded, frock-coated, he seemed as frightening, as mysterious, as God. "You don't want me to have to fetch the doctor, do you?" her mother had often said when she had refused to eat food that was held to be good for her, gruel and hot milk with sugar and a nauseous egg-nog she was given at bedtime, "to fill her out". Now she saw that he was merely a busy and possibly irritable man, finding private amusement from the behaviour of his patients. She vowed that she would never contribute to his amusement, and she felt contempt for her mother for rattling on so absurdly and exposing herself to his observations.

"Well, I don't think it can be—what was it you suggested?—ah, St Anthony's Fire," said the doctor. "No, I think we can rule out that. What have you been eating?" he asked Angel.

"Nothing," she said listlessly.

"She didn't fancy anything," her mother said quickly.

"Have you had any shell-fish?"

"Oh, I wouldn't let her touch anything like that."

"Or potted meat?"

"No, doctor." Mrs Deverell sounded scandalised.

"Then it remains a mystery. Have you had your bowels opened?" he asked Angel and wondered if her disdainful closing of her eyes meant that she had or that she would not lower herself to answer him.

Mrs Deverell looked doubtful, her head on one side, suggested liquorice-powder and fell into vague murmurings while Dr Foskett packed his bag. He seemed disinclined to discuss Angel's menus for the day, sanctioned all that was mentioned and then said that to go without could do no harm. At this, Angel was in despair. She was painfully hungry. She comforted herself by thinking, it is better to be ill, than well. It is better to starve than have to talk to my mother, or go to school.

When the doctor had gone, leaving Mrs Deverell as mystified as ever, but relieved, Angel appeared to fall asleep again and the rash on her arms grew paler. Mrs Deverell went down to the shop, where she was sure that Eddie was helping himself to sugar-wafers.

Angel wondered how she could creep from bed and fetch

some food, but the peril of being discovered less ill than she had pretended, kept her lying there. She dozed, then woke and scratched the rash to make it worse, worried that it might vanish altogether. Mrs Deverell found time to steam a fillet of plaice, and when she brought it Angel sighed ungratefully and stared at the tray as if the very thought of eating defeated her. She was waiting for her mother to go. She wanted to be alone while she ate, and not only because she must hide her appetite. In a strange way, almost as if she were in love with food and drew comfort from it, she loved solitude while she ate. Talking at mealtimes irritated her.

"Don't you fancy it, then?" her mother asked. They were still wary with one another, but Angel's illness made conversation possible.

"I'll try."

The food was getting cold and Angel's exasperation made her hands tremble as she took up the knife and fork.

"Well, do your best. I must get back downstairs." Mrs Deverell drank a cup of Bovril behind the counter and whenever she was hungry took a biscuit from one of the tins, or a handful of sultanas.

Angel ate as slowly as she could, every morsel of fish and the two thin slices of bread and butter and drank some milk. When her mother came back the tray was on the floor and the plate was as clean as if it had been polished.

"So you finished it all? That's good."

"I'm afraid the cat did."

"The cat?"

"I couldn't manage it after all and the tray was heavy on my legs, so I put it on the floor and the cat ate it. I had a little."

"But I shut the cat out."

"You shut the cat *in*."

"Well, where is he now, then?"

"I got out of bed and put him outside."

"Oh, how vexatious! And the price the fish was! I did hope you would manage it. Isn't there anything that would tempt you for your tea?"

26

Angel could think of so many things, poached eggs, welsh rarebit, smoked haddock covered with butter; but she shook her head.

By the evening, she was painfully bored. Although she did not feel ill, she was suffering from a slackness of spirit, a heavy dullness in her heart. She longed for a different life: to be quite grown-up and beautiful and rich; to have power over many different kinds of men. To pass the time, she began to imagine herself living such a life, in one scene, sharply visual, after another. She did not bother with narrative or explanations. She simply, in her dreams, was at the centre of each scene, very much herself still, with her green eyes and her black hair but with a few things changed; she took a shade off the length of her nose, which seemed to her too long for romance.

She was at Osborne, wearing red velvet, when her mother brought in some bread and milk for her supper; and, as soon as she had eaten it, she made haste to return there. Bowing her head, she went down in a deep curtsy and her skirt spread out like a flower. Her garnets were a dark fire on her white skin. Then the old Queen did an unexpected, a gracious thing, which sent a murmur through those present. She leaned forward and kissed Angel's brow.

When Mrs Deverell had smoothed the bed, letting in all the draughts, making her comfortable for the night, as she called it, and left her in darkness, Angel went on with her pictures. She even attempted to set one of them at Paradise House, but her imagination had healed earlier than her heart and she winced at the pain she gave herself.

She was not tired and she lay for hours planning romantic triumphs for herself. The one obstacle to credulity was her mother. She could not bring herself to destroy her, was too superstitious to remove her, as she had removed half an inch from her own nose, and in all the scenes Mrs Deverell hovered tiresomely in the background. After a time, Angel thought of a solution. She could be my maid, she decided. As Aunt Lottie is Madam's.

27

By the next day, there were no visible symptoms of her illness. The rash had gone. She complained instead of nausea and headaches, and her mother persisted in bringing trays of the same meagre invalid food—a coddled egg at midday, one scallop for her supper—and took away the book she was reading.

Trapped, hungry, bored, she lay in bed all day. She had had a surfeit of day-dreaming and her mind was confused by too many pictures, which fell into fragments, into a bewildering muddle when she closed her eyes. She had imagined too much.

Her mother had taken the only book in the room, and Angel dared not go along the passage to look for it. Time unwound itself so slowly. As it was growing dark, she thought with panic of the long evening ahead with nothing to do but doze and dream and listen to the shop doorbell ringing below, to the far-away voices and the bubbling, warbling sound of the gas-jets. For a moment she thought of Gwen and Polly coming home from school without her. When she tried to wrench her mind quickly away from that, she realised how hemmed-in she was in all her everyday doings: there were wounds in all directions, and boredom was the enemy which brought her face to face with one misery after another.

Her mother brought in her tea and Angel saw with dismay the two small sponge fingers on the plate. She decided that whatever her complaint was going to be tomorrow, it should not be nausea or a headache, and she wondered if some trouble with her heart would leave her free to eat and read. She had never cared much for books, because they did not seem to be about her, and she thought that she would rather write a book herself, to a pattern of her own choosing and about a beautiful young girl with a startling white skin, heiress to great property, wearing white piqué at Osborne and tartan taffetas at Balmoral.

When she had finished her tea, and that was very soon, she got out of bed and fetched an old school exercise-book from a shelf, tore out some pages of map-drawings and began without hesitation on Chapter One. "In the year 1885," she wrote. It was the year of her own birth.

The words flowed without effort all the evening and she seemed to be in a trance. As soon as she heard her mother beginning to climb the stairs, she dropped the exercise-book under the bed and lay down and shut her eyes. "You look feverish again," her mother said despairingly. "Do you still feel sick?"

"Not now. Just faint."

"I don't know what to do, I'm sure. The doctor didn't seem to think there was any call for him to look in again. This bad weather doesn't help. You can't see a hand's measure in front of you for the fog tonight. A lot of throats about, customers tell me. They took Mrs Baker's Vera away with dip. this morning. Such a pretty little girl, too."

Angel was quite unmoved. She never cared about such things. As usual, she was just waiting for her mother to go away.

By bedtime, she was both excited and exhausted. Her right arm and shoulder were aching and her fingers were cramped. She had scarcely paused, either to consider what she should write or judge what she had written. Day-dreaming had paved the way. She knew what the rooms and grounds of Haven Castle looked like and could describe the Duchess's gowns and jewellery in detail. White peacocks wandered on the moonlit terrace the night Irania was born. The birth was prolonged for several pages. Then all of the blinds on the South front were drawn and the staff appeared, as if by magic, draped in black crape. Unencumbered by a mother, the heroine faced the future.

Angel, who had never grieved about human beings and could not be interested in Mrs Baker's Vera going to hospital with diphtheria of which she might die, now felt tears burning in her eyes for the woman in her story. At the funeral she mourned, not along with the tenants or even the family, but from a different plane: God's, perhaps.

When her mother had put out her light and said goodnight, she lay peacefully on her back, staring up into the darkness. She thought of the exercise-book hidden under her pillow, ready for the first of the daylight. It was the happiest evening of my life, she decided.

The next day was Sunday and because the shop was shut Mrs Deverell sat in Angel's bedroom by the little fire, doing her accounts. The bells of the old church in the Butts sounded muffled in the foggy air. It seemed a day sealed off from the rest of the week. In the early afternoon, it began to grow dark.

"What would you like for Christmas?" Mrs Deverell asked. Angel had scarcely spoken a word all day, was lying there, fuming, frustrated by this intrusion.

For once, she did not know what she would like. It was only a matter of time before she would have everything she wanted. As a famous novelist, she could buy herself both garnets and emeralds, a chinchilla wrap, a sable muff, her own carriage. All that separated her from such riches was the time it would take to transfer what was in her head to the pages of the exercise-book—time which her mother was now foolishly wasting.

Suddenly, she saw that she would have to be bold and ruthless if she were to succeed. She could not afford to be secretive any longer, or concerned with other people's opinions. Pulling the exercise-book from under her pillow she held it up for her mother to see. "I should like half-a-dozen of these," she said briskly. "With marbled covers just like this one, if you please. I am writing a novel and one is not enough." With a look of calm she opened the book, drew up her knees to make a rest for it and continued with her writing.

Her mother blushed and gave her a quick, suspicious look. Then she frowned and keeping her lips tight went on with her work. She had nothing to say. The silence in the room was so oppressive to her that when she had washed up after tea she came back to the bedroom wearing her little feathered hat and her black cape trimmed with silk fringe. She was carrying a hymn-book. "If you don't mind being left for a while, I thought I'd go to Chapel. It will be a breath of air," she said.

Angel nodded.

"Would you like to get up for a little while this afternoon?" her mother asked her next day.

Angel was afraid that this might be the first step towards sending her back to school and she decided that she was too ill. With extraordinary resilience, she had forgotten her original reason for not wanting to go to school. Now she was too busy. She would never again, she thought, be able to spare the time.

"My heart is no better," she complained. She kept to her heart trouble because the food had improved since she gave up having nausea. "I get a pain there and it seems to flutter and miss beats."

"I'll have to have the doctor again," said Mrs Deverell in a worried voice.

"Give it a day or two," Angel suggested. She hadn't time for the doctor, either.

"I'll send Eddie for him tomorrow if you're no better. No use going on like this if there's something wrong. I know your father had a tired heart and had to be careful. I think you ought to be lying down flat."

"All right," said Angel and lay flat. This saved time, as her mother then went away. As soon as she had gone, Angel sat up again and went on writing. Sometimes her back ached and she would stretch her arms and yawn. Her black hair was loose and spread over her shoulders, keeping her warm.

Her mother must have worried secretly and sent for the doctor, for the next morning he arrived unexpectedly. Mrs Deverell, looking rather guilty, brought him up to the bedroom, where Angel was hunched up over her writing. She raised her eyes when the door was opened, but did not smile or say good-morning.

"Here's Doctor Foskett," her mother said feebly. "I'll have to go down to the shop. Eddie's gone off with an order. Will you call me if you want me, doctor?"

He nodded and began to walk about the room, rubbing his hands. Angel watched him. When they were alone, he said: "So you've a tired heart, like your father?"

"I didn't say so." Angel looked suspicious.

He came closer to the bed and glanced down at the exercise-book, at a half page of florid handwriting. Lack of character, he thought, looking away at once. T's uncrossed, i's undotted, backward sloping capitals. Flourishes; curlicues.

"What do you say, then?" he asked.

"I said that my heart flutters and misses beats and that I have a pain."

He held his watch in one hand and her wrist in the other, checking her pulse, half turned away from her so that she was able to glare at his back.

"Your mother is worried," he said, putting the watch away in his pocket. His voice sounded rather accusing. Then he opened her nightgown and put the stethoscope to her chest. When he had done so, he took away her two pillows and made her lie flat upon the bed. "Now sit up," he told her. She obeyed him. "Now lie down. Sit. Lie. Sit." As his commands grew quicker, she became breathless, and indignant with him. When at last she was allowed to lie still, he sounded her chest again.

"You can have your pillow back. There is nothing in the least wrong with your heart, you know."

He is my enemy, thought Angel.

"Why don't you want to go to school?" he asked her, more gently. "Are you in some trouble with your lessons? Is this school work you are doing now?" He flicked the cover of the exercise-book.

"No." She shook her hair back from her shoulders, staring at him. "I am writing a novel." Under the bedclothes her fists were clenched and pressing against her thighs. She felt ferocity towards him, as if he had already laughed at her. "I am going to be a novelist," she said.

"A profession calling for a very strong heart," he replied.

"I *am* strong," she said proudly, forgetting for the moment that he was the doctor and why he was there.

"I think you are. So don't be cowardly and worry your mother for nothing. She's a brave woman. I admire her."

"You laugh at her."

"And I would laugh with her. She would understand."

"No one is to laugh at *me*." Her green eyes blazed at him.

"Who would dare?" he said lightly. "For you would never laugh at yourself. But perhaps a sense of humour is a drawback to a novelist," he mused.

"I shan't be writing funny books."

"No, of course not," he said gravely, and thought: I wonder. He paced about the room, then said: "As soon as I have gone, you must get up. No more trays and extra work for your mother. You could cook the dinner, in fact."

"I don't know how to cook and there's no point in my learning," she said.

He shrugged his shoulders and shut up his Gladstone bag with a snap. "If you want to leave school," he said, "you should tell your mother outright. No more of this heart nonsense."

"I *did* have the rash," she said angrily. "You saw it yourself. You speak as if I haven't been ill at all."

"Well, that's cleared up, hasn't it? Now don't forget. Up you get! You will have a much better light for your novel-writing if you are up. I will tell your mother there is no cause for alarm. Goodbye."

"Goodbye," Angel said dully.

He looked back through the door. "I hope I read your book in print one day."

"That will be up to you," Angel said coldly.

"You can start school again next week," Mrs Deverell said.

Angel had moved from her bed to the sofa in the living-room and was still writing.

"There would only be three days left to the end of the term," she said.

"Still, you might as well make the most of it, and you have to fetch your books and your shoe-bag."

"Eddie can get those. As a matter of fact, mother, I am never going back to school again. The doctor told me to tell you."

"Why should he do that? I'm sure he wouldn't say things to you that he wouldn't say to me. I don't understand what you mean."

"We talked it over together," Angel said calmly. "I told him I was wasting time at school and that I wanted to have a chance to write my novels. He agreed with me, but said that I must tell you myself. 'Outright,' he said."

"But we have to give a term's notice. And besides that, you can't hang about here all day and every day." Mrs Deverell's voice was full of dismay at the idea. "I was going to talk to your school-teachers and ask their advice about getting you a situation, but if I suddenly take you away, how can I do that?"

"There won't be any question of a situation," Angel said. "I am writing my novel and when I've finished it, I shall write another. I have thought of it already."

"Yes, but you must have a *situation*," her mother said, almost shouting from her exasperation. "You must have something to fall back on. Writing stories won't butter many parsnips, I can tell you."

"How can you tell me? You know nothing about it."

"And who's going to print them, I'd like to know. Who's going to pay for that?"

Angel, outraged by this insult, turned her head and looked out of the window. She knew that it was already settled that she should never return to school. Her mother was only putting up a pretence of battle.

"The neighbours will say you've been expelled, if you leave all of a sudden like that. If only your father was alive to advise me for the best. I know he'd say it was a wicked waste to give up your education. All that French thrown to the four winds, and the struggle it's been sending you to a private school all these years."

"Then it will be one struggle less for you from now on."

"I made the sacrifice on account of your future—so that you needn't just go and work in a shop like I had to. I imagined you in an office with good money and meeting nice people."

"An *office*!" Angel said faintly, closing her eyes.

"And I'd have thought you owed it to your Auntie Lottie to discuss it with her." Her vehemence was running down, Angel saw.

"Why Aunt Lottie?"

" 'Why Aunt Lottie?' indeed. You know full well she's helped to pay the fees. You have a lot to be thankful for, the way she's been like a second mother to you all these years."

But Angel thought one mother more than enough.

"She's a proper fire-spaniel, isn't she?" Aunt Lottie said with a wary cheeriness. Angel was sitting writing with her feet on the fender. Mrs Deverell had been talking to her sister in the shop, relating the week's problems, and they had both come upstairs wearing looks of bright resolve, as if they were visiting some relation in a lunatic-asylum.

"It does seem a pity, what I've just been hearing," Aunt Lottie said. She was rosy from the cold and she held her hands over the fire for a moment, then straightened herself and began to take the pins out of her sealskin cap. "I can't see anything against your going to school for just one more term. After all, we'll have to pay for it. Then if we could get you a nice job in an office, you'd have all your evenings for writing your stories. It's a shame not to make the most of your education, I think. All that French!" Now she had taken off her hat and was pushing the pins back into it, oblivious of the bitter feelings she was provoking.

Angel waited until her aunt had finished speaking, then, saying nothing herself, closed her book and went out of the room.

Aunt Lottie turned round in surprise and looked at her sister.

"So it's been all the week," said Mrs Deverell. "I don't know what's come over her." She sat down where Angel had been sitting and put her hand across her eyes. "If only Ernie were still with me! I never was so worried."

"It looks very much to me as if madam needs a good box

35

on the ears," Aunt Lottie said briskly. "You've spoilt her, Emmy. Story-writing! Where's she got that from?"

"When she comes back, don't say any more."

Mrs Deverell began to lay the table for tea. Twice Eddie called up the stairs that he was busy in the shop and she went down to help him.

The cook from Paradise House had sent some almond tarts, and Aunt Lottie arranged them on a plate.

"I'll call her," Mrs Deverell said uncertainly. She wondered if the girl would come, or even answer. Perhaps she had locked herself in her bedroom again.

"Tea's ready, Angel!" She tried to keep anxiety from her voice, but her sister could hear it and thought of the piece of her mind she was more than ready to give to her niece.

Angel came in, blinking at the brighter light. She seemed unconcerned, though vague. The three of them stood behind their chairs while Grace was said.

"It's kind of cook," said Mrs Deverell. She glanced at the almond tarts as she sat down. "They must think a lot of you."

"Well, it's eighteen years I've been in service there. I sometimes wonder what Madam would do without me," Aunt Lottie said complacently. "I don't think she could put on her own stockings, nor lay her hands on anything. 'Where's this? Where's that?' it is from morn till night. Only yesterday she said: 'We've been together since we were both eighteen.' I sometimes think we're more like sisters. I went on her honeymoon with her. We went to Paradise House together."

"Do you put her stockings on for her, then?" Angel asked. They were surprised at this unusual interest. The two sisters looked at one another.

"I do," Aunt Lottie said. "Is there anything so strange in that?"

"Well, it seems strange to *us*," Mrs Deverell said soothingly. "I don't think I should like to have someone do that for me."

"What happens on your half-day?" Angel asked. "How does she manage then?"

"She has to make do with ringing for one of the housemaids.

I always go in to tidy up when I get back. I take a pride in her clothes and she knows it. 'Look at this lovely new négligé we've got', she'll say, excited as a child." Aunt Lottie had turned to her sister, but Angel listened carefully. "I always feel proud of her when she goes down to dinner. Like on her wedding-day. She was a credit to me then. I've never seen gloves on any lady that fit like hers. When she goes to the Opera you'd think they'd grown on her: not a wrinkle anywhere. I glue the tops of them to her arms with a touch of spirit gum. I suppose it's a work of art, which sometimes she hasn't the patience for. Miss Angelica comes in and reads to her when she gets restless."

"What does she read?" asked Angel.

Aunt Lottie's glance back at her was full of suspicion. "Oh, some book," she said, wondering what was in the girl's mind.

It will do for Haven Castle, Angel was thinking. Irania, the heroine, lolled on a couch whilst someone like Aunt Lottie put on her stockings: with her gloves glued to her arms, she sat in a box at the Opera. Later, when as a bride she was brought to Haven Castle, her maid followed, carrying a jewel-case. Only death would part them.

ii

After Christmas, the days were of an enervating neutrality. The watery light stayed later each day, hung colourless above the railway-bridge and behind the grey and yellow brick terraces. The deep darkness of winter was over, the muffled cosiness of the foggy afternoons, and now there would be two months or more of biting winds raking the bare branches and this pale light stretching out a minute or two longer each tea-time—as if it were welcome, thought Angel. "Saving the gas," her mother said.

In the shop trade fell off, and during the long evenings the door-bell scarcely rang. Mrs Deverell removed the cotton-wool snowflakes from the window, wondering why she had bothered with them. Her spirits had risen before Christmas, with so much bonhomie about: now they sank rapidly. There were wholesalers' bills to be paid: left-over Christmas cakes, reduced in price, were stacked at the counter, but no one bought them. More than anything, above all her worries about money, she dreaded having to answer questions about Angel. Incoherently, to different people, she gave different reasons for Angel's having left school, among them—and the most foolish of all—that she needed her help at home. All of her neighbours knew that the girl never appeared in the shop, or made her mother a cup of tea or stirred out-of-doors to do the shopping. She remained consistently out of sight, and this began to give rise to gossip. "Wouldn't you just come to chapel with me?" Mrs Deverell asked.

"No, thank you."

"If you would only get out for a breath of air. You look so pale."

"I am always pale." For a moment, she looked up from her writing and stared in front of her: then smiled.

Perhaps she is going mad, Mrs Deverell thought in a panic. There was her Aunt Ethel who became so queer. To her, no malady was very likely unless there was some other instance of it in the family.

In the past, she and Lottie had been proud of Angel's superior airs: now she was afraid of them. Under their influence, her own strength of character was disintegrating into fussiness and timidity; she was full of feeble suggestions and propitiations; when the strain became too great, she made aggrieved speeches about sacrifices she had made, about the best years of her life and working her fingers to the bone. Angel ignored it all. She went on filling up her six exercise-books with a trance-like devotion. Sometimes, to stretch her limbs, she would walk about the room, stare in the looking-glass and rearrange her hair, which was drawn back from her forehead with a tortoise-shell comb, or go to the window and glance down, almost without seeing, at the unreal people walking on the pavement.

Her mother mentioned her writing only to Lottie. It

seemed to her such a strange indulgence, peculiar, suspect. There had never been any of it in the family before; not even on her husband's side where there had been one or two unhinged characters, including the queer Aunt Ethel.

On her sixteenth birthday, Aunt Lottie came to tea. She brought a painted silk handkerchief-sachet and an invitation to Paradise House. There were to be tableaux vivants in aid of charity, with Miss Angelica as a beggar-maid in a most bewitching gown of brown velvet all torn to shreds and patched with crimson satin. Madam had heard so much of Angel, and had said that she might sit with the maids and watch the dress rehearsal. "What a wonderful opportunity," said Mrs Deverell, looking flustered. She could tell from Angel's expression of disdain that she would not go.

"You could come in with the carrier and be there within the hour," Aunt Lottie said.

Angel was unsteady with anger and humiliation. To go to Paradise House in such a way! She imagined herself, dressed in her old serge school clothes, all that she had, sitting humbly among the maids, watching that other girl in her velvet rags. Being condescended to by those who thought themselves better, and treated as an equal by those who imagined themselves as good. I shall never go to Paradise House in that way, she thought.

"A wonderful opportunity," her mother repeated anxiously.

"I don't want to go." She was wounded and infuriated, almost too wounded to be able to let her thoughts dwell on what had been done to her.

"And why not?" Aunt Lottie asked menacingly.

"I am not interested in their private theatricals. Why should I be?"

"It strikes me you're an ungrateful little hussy."

"Now, Lottie, give her a chance to explain herself," Mrs Deverell said.

"There's nothing to explain," said Angel. "Nothing to explain that either of you could ever understand."

Will it be like this for ever? her mother wondered. Or

39

might it even go on getting worse, as it has done? Aunt Lottie seemed for the moment quite speechless.

"Well, if no one wants any more tea . . ." Mrs. Deverell said quickly and stood up. "For what we have received, may the Lord make us truly thankful," she added.

At Easter, Angel finished writing her novel. On the day after Easter Monday, she wrapped it up and addressed it to the Oxford University Press, whose address she found in one of her old school books. She waited until Eddie had gone out to collect orders, then, as soon as her mother left the shop for a moment, she ran downstairs with the parcel under her cloak. She took a florin from the till and set out for the post office. Her mother, hearing the door-bell jangling, came hurrying into the shop and saw Angel going down the street.

The air was like crystal, a shock to Angel after so much of being indoors. It was a brisk, blowy morning with some signs of spring. By the railings of the Board School two almond trees were covered with blossom.

An iron bridge went over the canal by the brewery and under it the water slipped by, brown, covered with bubbles, between the walls of warehouses. Angel saw it all with un-believing eyes, as if she had come back as a stranger after many years and felt amazed that it had altered so little.

In the churchyard by the Butts, the trees were hazed over with green buds, daffodils were almost in flower. The post office faced the churchyard, and when Angel had posted her parcel, she crossed the cobbled square and sat down on an iron seat among the graves.

The reality of the scene and of all she had noticed on her walk that morning had reduced the feverishness she had felt for the past months and had brought her to a state of convales-cence. She was afraid, and shrank from the coldness of the iron seat and the sight of the blades of green leaves stabbing the soft and mossy ground, and when the clock in the tower above her began to strike she flinched nervously.

People in deep mourning were coming into the churchyard. They paused outside the porch and whispered shocked words to one another before they entered. Some cabs drew up at the gateway and a woman was helped out of one of them. The wind blew her crêpe veil close against her face so that her white cheeks and the dark hollows of her eyes could be seen. There was a hearse drawn by plumed dark horses. It halted slowly, with a dreadful air of inevitability. It was what you waited for and it has come, the bearers seemed to imply, almost smug in their faultless reverence as they carried the coffin with its pale wreaths and black-edged cards towards the porch where a clergyman was waiting.

Angel stood up and followed it. No one glanced at her as she sat down by a pillar at the back of the church, which was still full of flowers from Easter Sunday, but smelt only of damp stone. For a moment, she wondered why she was there. Even if she had felt a need to renew contact with life, a funeral was a strange way of doing so: and she felt no such need: at sixteen, experience was an unnecessary and usually baffling obstacle to her imagination. This small, stunned congregation was less than life-size to her, and all of that morning she had felt the diminution of her surroundings. Nothing had been stored up for her return to the world: day by day, her environment had frittered itself away and now had a vitiated air.

A great deal of what she encountered irritated her, running contrary to her sensibilities. She had removed herself, romantically, from the evidence of her senses: the reality of what she could learn by touching, tasting, was banished as a trivial annoyance, scored out as irrelevant.

She unhooked a dusty hassock and knelt down as the others did. Her black woollen stockings were thin over her knees, and the hassock was cold. She cupped her face in her hands and closed her eyes, but was not listening to the prayer. I think I came in here because while I am waiting I have nothing to do, she decided. What she awaited was her miraculous deliverance. Her novel was an escape-thread spun out of herself, and so sudden and deep an alarm for its safety pierced her—just as she was rising from her knees—that she felt she must fly from the church and rescue it. What if some postman should guess its contents and from malignance throw it into the canal! Or if the train to Oxford collided with another in some tunnel and broke into flames!

At this moment, the coffin was hoisted from its trestle and carried down the church. Angel was the last to leave, and when she came out into the open, the hearse was gone; to the new cemetery on the outskirts of the town, she supposed. The slight disappointment allayed some of her agitation. She gave a threatening look at the post office and began to walk towards home. It might take two days, she supposed (but at *most*, she could not help adding), for the novel to reach Oxford; then she must allow another three days for the publisher to read it, which he could easily do, if he sat up late at night; and another two days (at most) for his reply to reach her. It would be a long week, with a long, long Sunday in it. She knew of only one escape from her boredom, and when she came to a stationery shop she went in and bought an exercise book with the last of her money.

"There's a parcel for you, Angel!" Mrs Deverell called up the stairs.

Her heart raced and she felt confused. It was a letter she had waited for, so why a parcel, she wondered in a panic? During the last week she had doubted postmen and publishers; now for the first time she felt a doubt about herself. Then life isn't endurable after all, she thought as she went halfway down the stairs and took the package from her mother. She opened it in her bedroom. A printed slip fluttered to the floor and she picked it up and stared at it. When at last she knew that there was no mistake, she was filled with anger. They had dared to give no reasons, omitted all excuses, had sent no letter. She loathed them, whoever they were, with the utmost ferocity; as maniacal as a vain woman jilted.

She re-wrapped the manuscript in the same piece of paper

with the publisher's label on the inside, and found another address from one of her school-books. She had no money for postage and could not get to the till while her mother was busy in the shop, so she gathered up all her school-books, which were all that she had to sell, and went out of the house by the back door. She made her way through the yard where there were stacked-up packing-cases, a clothes-line; a few ferns grew against one of the walls and one or two crocuses had forced their way through the trodden ground. A door led into a cinder path between high walls. Here were the back entrances of other houses; on dark nights a place of whisperings and rustlings, cats fighting, rats scavenging.

The bookshop was in the Butts, by the church, a musty, galleried building full of mildewed volumes that no one would ever read again. The young assistant seemed dubious about adding to them, and took the books from Angel, glanced at them and shrugged his shoulders. "I'll inquire," he said. When he came back, he was smiling with false pity. "No, I'm afraid we should have no use for them. We could offer one and sixpence."

"Two shillings," Angel said, burning with humiliation.

"Now, come," he said insolently. "You don't want to make me go all the way back and ask again for the sake of sixpence."

"Yes, I do."

He sighed extravagantly, but he went away and when he came back it was without the books. He handed her the florin with infuriating solemnity and, as she turned to leave the shop, called after her: "Don't spend it all at once, will you?"

"You ill-bred jackanapes!" Angel said loudly. He looked startled, but when she turned to close the door she could see him through the glass panel. He was bowed over the counter, as if weeping or in pain: for a moment she felt appeased, and then she saw that he was convulsed with laughter.

By the time the manuscript was next returned, the pain was blurred by her excitement over the new novel she had begun to write: the story of a great actress's triumph over a contemptuous world. (Those who had booed at first would, long before the last page, be taking the horses from the shafts of her carriage and drawing her exultantly through the crowded street.)

Almost methodically, Angel tied up the parcel again. Now that her school-books were all sold, she had no address to send it to, and when she had managed to steal some money from her mother's purse she set out for the Free Library. On one side of the municipal building was a museum full of stuffed animals and broken earthenware; on the other, across the draughty vestibule, was the library, dark with books all bound in greasy black leather. Angel could not get beyond the turnstile without a ticket.

"Complete the form and obtain a reference from a clergyman or suchlike," said the assistant.

"I want a book now, at this minute."

"I'm sorry," said the young man.

"I know that you are not," said Angel. "I will go through and *look* at the books without taking one away."

"I am afraid that until you have a ticket you are not allowed inside the library."

A woman waiting behind Angel laid her book impatiently on the counter, and at once Angel turned and picked up the book and opened it at the title-page. For a second, she memorised the publishers' address printed there; then, without speaking, she pushed past the woman and went out to the vestibule.

She hurried through the streets, her lips moving rapidly as if she were mad. At the post office she wrote the address on her parcel: Gilbright & Brace, Bloomsbury Square, London.

Going home, she felt tired, overcome by the lassitude of the spring evening; as if she had taken a rest after long exertion and found it difficult to rise up again. She shrank from the wind and the grittiness of the pavements. All that she saw and felt tired her, and she longed to shut out the world and be secure in the womb of her imagination. A boy bowling an iron hoop ran past her and she trembled at the noise he made with his hobnail boots on the pavement. One of the dreaded neighbourhood characters approached, a gaunt woman who walked stiffly, menacingly, her eyes glaring above a scarf which was drawn up to cover most of her face. Angel had heard that she had some sinister disease. Children stared at her, for there was a rumour that she had no nose. Sometimes as she hurried by they could hear her muttering: the scarf muffled her curses on the world or some reiterated plaint about the state of her existence. Today, as if she were sleep-walking, she stared ahead of her and climbed the steps of the Wesleyan Chapel. "At least she has religion," Angel thought, as if she had come upon a child playing with a broken toy.

When she reached home, she found Aunt Lottie there. She was still in deep mourning for Queen Victoria, and the black and braided dress was brightened only by a bunch of velvet parma violets which Madam had discarded. It wasn't the usual day for her weekly visit and she seemed excited and nervous.

"Where have *you* been?" she asked Angel. Mrs Deverell looked apprehensive.

"Out," said Angel, going over to the window and throwing her cloak on the sofa.

"Aunt Lottie's been waiting to see you, dear," said her mother.

"I had a message from Madam. . . ."

"Not more theatricals?" said Angel.

"Shall we have a cup of tea first?" Mrs Deverell suggested.

A silence fell as she began to lay the table. Aunt Lottie fidgeted with the parma violets and Angel looked out of the window. Rain had fallen earlier in the afternoon, and there were still places where the pigeon-coloured rooftops shone with silver. At the corner of the street, a child with shaved head and bare feet was skipping. Her thin arms kept crossing over her breast, the rope looped rhythmically above her head and her pinafore flew out as she bobbed up and down, and her lips moved as she counted.

"Aunt Lottie has a suggestion to make," said Mrs Deverell as the three of them came to the table.

But over this new offer from Paradise House even Aunt Lottie was dubious, and she hardly knew what reaction to hope for or which one would affect her less disagreeably.

"Madam wants a young maid to train under me ready for Miss Angelica. Up till now, she's managed with Nannie, with me to help on special occasions, but the time's coming when she'll need more than to scrape along like that."

"Poor thing!" said Angel scornfully.

"So Madam, having heard me talk of you, thinks it would be better for me to have someone I know to train into ways similar to my own, for she always is consideration itself to me. . . ."

"She is that," said Mrs Deverell.

"Madam, then, says for me to come this afternoon, hesitation is not in her make-up. 'You must go at once,' she said, 'and ask her mother.' So what do you think of taking the position? Do you feel that you have such a vocation?"

"I?" said Angel. The question came out on a deep gasp of astonishment.

"It would be nice for you to be with Auntie Lottie, and would comfort me to know you weren't with strangers," Mrs Deverell said.

"There's no life better," Aunt Lottie said smugly.

Angel stared at her. "Do you really dare to suggest that I should demean myself doing for a useless half-wit of a girl what she could perfectly well do for herself; that I should grovel and curtsy to someone of my own age; dance attendance on her; put on her stockings for her and sit up late at night, waiting for her to come back from enjoying herself? You must be utterly mad to breathe a single word of such a thing to me. Go back and tell your damned Madam what I think of her insult, ask her what she would say to someone who spoke of her own daughter so degradingly, and tell her that one day she will blush with shame to think of what she has done."

46

Her mother and her aunt sat quite still, as if they were waiting to be photographed, her mother with her head turned slightly aside and Aunt Lottie smiling down at her plate. When Angel had stopped speaking, there was silence. Her Aunt licked the tip of one finger and pressed it into some cake-crumbs on her plate. She had an air of preoccupation mingled with disdain. She licked the crumbs off her finger and brushed her lips with a lace handkerchief; then she lifted her head, looked up at the ceiling and seemed to be listening to her own thoughts. The silence nearly defeated Angel. It underlined her loud outburst. The temptation was to begin again, but she resisted it, knowing that Aunt Lottie was expecting, hoping for, her to become hysterical. She sat out the silence. Her mother, the most apprehensive of the three, broke it.

"I think you should apologise to your Aunt Lottie," she said quietly. "No matter how you may look at the matter, she was only passing on a message. She in no way merited such rudeness."

Now Aunt Lottie, still smiling faintly, raised her hand, shook her head quietly. "No apology, please, Emmie, I want no apology." She kept her voice much quieter than usual, to mark its contrast with Angel's. "I see that I have looked upon my work wrongly all these years. It never seemed to me to be dishonourable to be serving others. I never saw it in that light. We are all servants of God, I thought. I did my work humbly and as my conscience directed: and was glad to do it. Now I see that I was mistaken. I see that I was wrong not to vaunt myself more, be more puffed-up." As she warmed to her sarcasm, colour came into her cheeks and her composure began to break; she trembled as her temper rose: she fell into savage repetitions and bitter irony. "I see that humility and unselfishness and ungrudging work are not what are respected. Oh, quite the reverse. It's setting yourself up as high as you can; giving yourself superior airs, however unwarranted; being too grand to lift your hand to help another, not even your own mother, that's what's to be respected, it seems. . . .

47

No, please Emmie, may I continue? I have sat here week after week, biting back my words; I can't contain myself for ever. . . . No, pass on Madam's message I did, as I at least know what is due to my betters; but never for one moment think that I did anything but dread the consequences. I shall go back now and tell Madam what is true—that I could not be the instrument of bringing to her service what we have never had at Paradise House—vanity, selfishness, ingratitude. I am afraid you and I wasted our money, Emmie. There were times when we used to feel proud of all the learning she was getting, not knowing the seeds it was sowing. What use is French, I ask, if you are to spend your life sponging on your mother. . . . No, please, Emmie, may I . . .? trying to ape the lady? Lady! I will try not to laugh." She did not succeed; a curious snorting noise came from her. "I have spent my life with ladies and I think I may say that I know where the word applies. I shall be interested to see where all these grand ideas are leading to. Very interested. Very interested indeed."

She had gone on too long. She had made the mistake Angel did not make and now she could not stop. Triumphantly, Angel took a slice of bread-and-butter, folded it over and began to eat. She gave the impression that she was doing so only to pass the time; not because she was hungry. She had gained the ascendancy and all three knew it.

"I shall come to your house, Emmie," Aunt Lottie said. "For your sake, I shall come as usual; but I shall never address you again as long as I live, Angel Deverell, and if you choose to address me, be prepared to be ignored."

"Oh, dear! Oh, dear!" Mrs Deverell moaned.

"And what is more," Aunt Lottie went on, ignoring her previous threat, "don't expect to get another penny from me, not for any purpose whatsoever; not if you are starving in the gutter. And when I pass on, I hope that whoever I now decide to leave my little nest-egg and my few trinkets to won't feel themselves above accepting them." At the thought of her own death, she became even more unsteady and her eyes filled with tears.

"Now, Lottie, Lottie!" her sister said soothingly.

"Would you pass the jam, mother?" asked Angel, in a polite, indifferent voice.

After tea she went out. She walked through the streets, without wondering where she was going. I am quite alone and there is no hope, she thought. The argument between herself and her aunt went on in her head; sometimes, so intensely did she suffer what she thought, her lips moved and she muttered aloud.

The streets were grey and gritty. Lights were already shining through the bright, engraved and frosted windows of the public-houses, though darkness was an hour away. Outside the Music-Hall a long queue waited for the early doors of the pit to open. Angel passed the Prison, with its plumcoloured brick and dagger-like slits of windows. She felt very little curiosity about any of the lives that were lived inside these places where she had never been. She could perfectly, she thought, imagine what went on, in the public-house and the music-hall and gaol. Experience was a makeshift for imagination; would neither be, she felt sure, half as beautiful, or half so terrible.

At the back of the Prison were a little park and some public gardens. Children were bowling hoops around the boarded-up bandstand where the Temperance Brass Band played on summer Sunday evenings. A few people were walking briskly along the gravel paths, between wind-raked evergreens. These paths wound up towards a shrubbery on a small hill where there was a great cast-iron statue of a lion, a landmark for miles. Some boys were now walking round it, looking up at its huge testicles and sniggering.

This hateful town! thought Angel. She sat down on a seat and closed her eyes. The boys stared at her curiously, and one of them tapped his forehead and winked at the others as they went away.

She sat there alone, and the statue towering above her slowly darkened against the sky, became a menacing black shape, striding above the tops of the shrubbery trees. She faced and suffered her solitariness; braved out the agony of longing she now felt for someone to be sitting beside her to whom she could communicate her bitter loneliness. This desire for compassion was so overwhelming that her heart seemed to contract. She held her breath for seconds together and tightened her lips. When she heard someone coming towards her, she looked up and found the sky was dark. A park attendant came into the shrubbery, shouting. "All out, now! All out!" Angel stood up hurriedly and as she brushed past him, he said "Are you all right, Miss?" For she looked ill, he thought, or in some trouble; or both. But she did not answer him. She almost ran towards the Park gates, as if she could fly away from what she had suffered there, leave it up there, the pathos of her solitariness, with the lion and the dusty evergreens and the dark sky.

In the weeks that followed, her fortitude returned. Aunt Lottie came as usual and directed her remarks at Angel rather than to her. Angel continued with the writing in which nobody but herself believed.

In the early summer, a letter came from Gilbright & Brace. When she had read it, she had a delightful sensation of being lifted up, of rising towards the ceiling; her body seemed to have become as light as air; bliss flowed through her veins. She handed the letter to her mother, who read it through twice, looking suspicious at first, then bewildered.

"They want to print it?" she asked.

Angel nodded.

"What does it mean, thirty pounds?"

"What it says. That is what they will pay me in advance."

"Are you sure? Thirty pounds! Oh, I wish I had your Dad here to advise me. I wish there was somewhere to turn for advice. I could ask the doctor, I daresay, or Mr Phippin at the Chapel. Don't you go and sign anything, Angel; not till we've asked. Goodness knows what trickery they may be up to. I can't help thinking it's you that's meant to pay, and where do they think I'm to lay hands on thirty pounds?"

"*They* mean to pay," said Angel quite gently. "There's nothing to fuss about, mother."

She put the letter in her pocket, but kept her fingers on it. She stood looking out of the window. The ugly street below was golden with sunshine and full of gay sounds.

"It's a beautiful name for any book—'The Lady Irania,'" said Mrs Deverell. "Oh, I don't know what to think. I feel quite flustered and put out. How can I explain it to people? What are they all going to think? And if you go to London, like he says, how am I to leave the shop to go with you?"

"You won't," said Angel. "I shall go alone."

iii

Gilbright & Brace had been divided, as their readers' reports had been. Willie Brace had worn his guts thin with laughing, he said. *The Lady Irania* was his favourite party-piece and he mocked at his partner's defence of it in his own version of Angel's language.

"Kindly raise your coruscating beard from those iridescent pages of shimmering tosh and permit your mordant thoughts to dwell for one mordant moment on us perishing in the coruscating workhouse, which is where we shall without a doubt find ourselves, among the so-called denizens of deep-fraught penury. Ask yourself—nay, go so far as to enquire of yourself—how do we stand by such brilliant balderdash and *live*, nay, not only live, but exist too. . . ."

"You overdo these 'nays'," said Theo Gilbright. "*She* does not."

"There's a 'nay' on every page. M'wife counted them. She took the even pages, I the odd. We were to pay a shilling to the other for each of our pages where there wasn't one, and not a piece of silver changed hands from first to last."

"So Elspeth read it, too?"

"Read it? She devoured and gobbled every iridescent word."

"So will other women."

"I should hope more reverently."

"Perhaps that too. I feel an extraordinary power behind it

all, so that I wonder if it is genius or lunacy. I was quite fascinated."

"And so was I. Especially at the way they treated the champagne."

"She isn't the first writer to have it opened with a cork-screw and she may not be the last. What does that matter?"

"All those butlers, too! Well, you back your fancy, Theo. Also deal with her when she comes. Elspeth and I imagine an auburn transformation and a moleskin cape smelling of camphor, a neat little moustache and a Gladstone bag stuffed full of translucent manuscripts. More and more Lady Iranias. The Irania Class we can call them, like ocean liners. All I ask you to do is to have her tone it down. The card-playing scene may well land us in trouble. Some of these old ladies don't know how inflammatory their writing is. It is too much to hope that she will be inflammatory herself. Angelica Deverell is too good a name to be true."

"The address is puzzling—Volunteer Street; and Norley is a dreary old town."

"Some old lady, as I say, romanticising behind lace-curtains."

"It even sounds rather sordid."

"She may be an old man. It would be an amusing variation. You are expecting to meet Mary Ann Evans and in walks George Eliot twirling his moustache."

Yet nothing Willie Brace could guess or invent was half as astonishing to them as Angel herself when she was shown in one afternoon. The partners were sitting waiting for her in Theo's office, but Willie went out as soon as he had shaken hands. He dared not glance at Theo, and outside on the landing he steadied himself for a moment, clutching the rail of the banisters in an agonising spasm of stifled laughter.

Theo was glad to be left alone with Angel as she sat down on the edge of her chair and glanced severely about the room. She was late for her appointment, for she had been lost in London. Paddington Station had been complete confusion to her, and when she had reached Bloomsbury, with so many pauses to study the street-map she had bought, she seemed to have hurried from one square to another, like someone in a nightmare, and then all round this last square looking for the right number.

Theo saw her pale face glistening, guessed that she had been late and anxious, imagined her walking too quickly through the hot streets. Her boots were dusty and her hair untidy. He often noticed that people visiting London invariably got themselves covered with smuts which Londoners managed to escape.

He rang for some tea, giving her time to get back her breath and look about her. Then he said: "Don't think me impertinent, but I really expected someone a good deal older."

"Do you mean that now you won't publish my story?"

"No, of course, my remark had nothing to do with that."

"What *had* it to do with?" Angel asked suspiciously.

"A publisher is bound to make conjectures about an unknown writer's age. It may seem irrelevant to you, but we should be less willing to risk ourselves over a first novel by someone of seventy than we should if it were by someone with years of writing ahead of them. 'Under or over?' we ask ourselves. That means 'forty'."

"Did you think I was over forty, then?"

"We gave up guessing. You might have been a bald-headed old man for all we knew."

He saw her stiffen. She lifted her chin. He realised that she had great pride and not a trace of humour in her. " 'Man'?" she repeated. "You knew my name. I shouldn't have deceived you."

I must never be facetious, he thought. He poured out the tea and gave it to her.

"Do you think you will write another novel?"

"Oh, yes. I can let you have another one in a few months."

"So soon? You must be careful not to tire yourself too quickly, or write yourself out."

"I should never do that," she said simply and drank her tea.

"What is the theme of the new book?"

"It is about an actress."

"Are you interested in the theatre, Miss Deverell?"

"I have never been to one."

"Then you are a great reader, perhaps?"

"No, I don't read much. I haven't got any books, and nowadays I am always writing."

"But even so, most authors take some interest in the works of others. Is there no Public Library you could join?"

A little colour came into her cheeks and she said, "I don't think I should want to."

"Then if I send you some novels, will you read them?"

"What will they be about?" she asked cautiously.

"I can't make a hazard at your tastes, unless you can tell me something you have read and liked."

"I quite liked Shakespeare," she admitted. "Except when he is trying to be funny."

Mr Gilbright got up hastily and walked to the window. He appeared to be deep in meditation as he looked out over the square. "And?" he asked gravely, after a while.

"I liked *The Three Musketeers*, although I have only read bits of it in French when I was at school. And a book about a German baron who kept his wife shut up in a tower, but would never allow her to be seen by any other person. He took her meals to her himself and spent hours brushing her hair."

"How did it turn out?"

"The book was taken away from me before I reached the end. I had to make up the rest for myself."

He realised the hunger she had suffered; the deprivations of her wilful, ranging imagination, and said, "I should like to know what you invented."

"That she died and he lost his reason. He told no one and would not let her be buried. He kept her body locked up in the tower and every day he sat there, brushing her hair. One day a servant followed him there and saw him putting jewels on the corpse's hair and singing a lullaby. When he was made to bury her he leapt blubbering into the grave and stabbed himself."

"I am thinking how unwise it is to take books away from young people before they have finished reading them," Mr Gilbright said. "I shall be hard put to it to find you anything as powerful as that when I am looking for a book to send to you. You have an unusual vocabulary for one who reads so little."

"I never forget a word," she said simply.

"And the longer they are the better you like them?" he suggested.

"They all have their uses," she said in a more reserved voice.

He sat down at his desk again, aware that his questions were arousing her suspicion, and shuffled in a business-like way through a folder of papers. "Miss Deverell," he began, "we should like to publish your book, as I have said, and I hope we shall make a success of it. In a capricious world, no one can be sure. Obviously, there are some suggestions to put forward and some alterations we hope you will make." He smiled, but felt authority ebbing from him. "That is usual," he said quickly. "For instance, we cannot have a character called the Duchess of Devonshire as there is one in . . . in everyday life; if a duchess's life could ever be so described. But that can soon be changed. We can easily find a way out of that. Perhaps you have erred on the lavish side. I don't know much about grandeur, and great establishments, but I thought we might cut down and manage with one butler, eh?" His jocularity was coldly received. "May I give you some more tea?"

"No, thank you."

He studied the papers on the desk, and then taking, as he told himself, the cue from her writing, said robustly, "The game of cards in Chapter Nineteen—the wager that if he, Lord Blane, wins he shall sleep with Irania. . . ."

"I didn't say 'sleep', I said 'lie with'."

"Ah, yes, quite right. I don't know that we shall keep out of trouble with that. It may offend certain sections of the public. We have to be more than careful. There are some risks we cannot take, you know, and a great deal of your writing is more powerful than is generally permitted. I think your description of childbirth might be toned down. It is extremely harrowing. And this," he glanced at the manuscript lying before him, "this about biting her lips until the blood ran down her throat. Do you think that is possible?"

"Oh, yes," said Angel.

"Did you mean 'outside' her throat, or 'inside'?" he asked nervously.

"Inside."

"Oh, good! Yes. Well, I expect you see what I mean. I daresay I know more about the reading public than you, and you will take my word that I have an idea as to what will pass among the weakest of them. We publish for them, alas, 'the bread-and-milk brigade' my partner calls them. They decide. They bring the storms about our ears. For them we veil what is stark and tone down what is colourful and discard a lot that—for ourselves—we would rather keep. So will you take away your manuscript for a while and see what you can do for us?"

"No," said Angel.

She made her way back to Paddington Station, feeling exhausted and depressed. She would not take a cab as Mr Gilbright had suggested, but pretended that she preferred to walk and enjoy the air. She was worried about money and feeling hungry, and when she came to a dingy little tea-shop she studied the price-list, whitewashed on the window, and went in. The tiled tops of the tables were steamy from cooking that was going on in a back room, and there were alarming sounds of food being thrown into boiling fat. Angel ordered a glass of sarsaparilla and a piece of pastry covered with long shavings of coconut. Two men were sitting at the next table eating faggots and peas. They were wearing bowler hats, though one man took his off for a moment to scratch his head.

When Angel, in her usual penetrating voice, asked the waitress if there was a w.c., they laughed aloud. "Certainly not," said the waitress. She looked prim and indignant, but as Angel left she could be heard joining in the laughter.

Angel was wishing that she had not bought the drink, and felt almost faint with the pain in her bladder. Each step was difficult. The streets became an imprisoning maze; her serge dress smelled of sweat. I have accomplished nothing, she thought. Her manuscript was still in the office, but even now, perhaps, Mr Gilbright was making a parcel of it, so that it would reach her home almost as soon as she would. She was sure that his excuse that he must consult his partner was simply his way of delaying awkwardness.

She stepped aside as a man in a baize apron carried some gilt baskets of flowers into a house. There was a white awning above the entrance and a red carpet waiting to be unrolled from the top of the steps. These London streets, early on this summer evening, had a peace she had never known in Norley; but the quiet was menacing and nightmarish to her. I might die, she thought. She remembered an old story of her mother's and Aunt Lottie's, of one of their girlhood's friends who had been taken to the Crystal Palace by her fiancé. Such was her sense of delicacy that she would not excuse herself from his company for one moment all day long. Reaching home too late, she had collapsed and died. "Her bladder broke," said Mrs Deverell. "What about *his*?" Angel had asked, and was told to behave herself. When at last she came to the station she walked more hurriedly. Each jolting step was misery to her. In the Ladies' Waiting Room, she glimpsed herself in a looking-glass. She was an absurd figure: her straw hat was crooked above her pale and glistening face, her hair untidy, and her dress creased. It was not at all her own idea of Angel Deverell.

She bolted herself into the lavatory and began to weep, covering her face with her gloved hands. I wish that I had given in, she thought. I had everything to lose and I have lost it.

Yet she still felt something obdurate in herself, even in her state of frailty and defeat. It was a hard, physical pain in her breast, which might have been indigestion, but was vanity.

"We should not have let her go alone. Someone should have seen her to the station," said Theo Gilbright. "Is she safe to be wandering about London?"

"Is *London* safe," asked Willie Brace, "with her wandering about in it? She is surely mad?"

"I don't know. Under that passionate inventiveness and romanticism and ignorance, I thought I sometimes noticed shrewdness and suspicion. She does not find things amusing herself, and she is on the lookout to prevent anyone else doing so—particularly if it is to be at her expense."

"Which it is bound to be. So we are to risk 'Irania' as it stands, card-scene and all?"

"It will be nice strong meat for the unsophisticated, and delicious stuff and nonsense for some connoisseurs." After a moment Theo said: "When I think of her, I dislike myself for saying that. I hope . . ."

"And what do you hope?"

"I hope she is not to be too much laughed at."

"*I* am hoping that *we* are not."

Theo picked up one of the tea-cups. "Just as she was going— and I must say she looked at the end of her tether, but still as obstinate as a mule—she took up this cup and examined it carefully and then said 'Is this Dresden china?' "

"Good God!" said Willie. "What did you say?"

"I just said 'no'. I couldn't tell her that Miss Hooper bought them for us in Berwick Street. Perhaps it wouldn't have made any difference if I had. She didn't listen to me. I am sure she had decided that they *were* Dresden and that was that. I hope she gets safely home. I think someone should have come to London with her."

"From what I saw, I think she ought to be locked up. I sat

58

in my office on my own and laughed for half-an-hour. And there is Elspeth at home dying to hear all about her. I am to get back as fast as I can."

He was halfway down the stairs when Theo came out on to the landing and called to him.

"What is it?"

"Of course, tell Elspeth," Theo said. "She will know that she must be discreet. . . . But, no one else."

"A nice little story about her girlhood will be our only hope, as I see it—released a day or two before publication, as only I can arrange it."

"No," said Theo. "No little stories."

"The waif has played on your heartstrings," said Willie. His expression was puzzled as he looked up the stairs.

"No stories," Theo repeated. "I beg of you, Willie." And he turned back towards his office door.

"It is the first time I have tasted wine," said Angel.

"Does it come up to your expectations?" Theo asked.

"I never had any expectations about it." She drank it steadily as if she were parched with thirst. Then she said: "I suppose it is very much as one would have imagined it."

Mrs Gilbright suffered a moment's dismay about her husband's beloved claret, then noticed that Theo himself was smiling.

"My mother would be shocked," said Angel calmly. "She belongs to a Temperance Society and wears one of those badges in the shape of a bow of ribbon to show that she would never take a drink, not even brandy if she were dying. Of course by temperance they all mean the opposite—total abstinence."

"I am worried if we have given you anything your mother would disapprove of," Mrs Gilbright said.

"I am going to live my own life."

"Yes, I am sure that you are." Mrs Gilbright managed to give Theo a warning glance as his hand touched the decanter, and he left Angel's glass empty. He said: "You describe the sensations of drunkenness well for one who has never tasted wine."

"Thank you."

Before this visit, he had tried to prepare his wife for Angel's abrupt manner, which was so much in contrast to her involved and ornamental style of writing. The evening had been dreaded in consequence. Angel had been asked to stay overnight and Theo had fetched her from Paddington Station in a cab. No other guests were to be invited, and the three of them, Mrs Gilbright thought grimly, must sit out this appalling dinner-party on their own.

Until now, she had sided with Willie Brace, laughing at the passages he had read to her from *The Lady Irania*, and, teasing Theo about his 'Angel ever bright and fair', had wondered why he should dream of publishing such vulgar nonsense or put himself out to please an unattractive and precocious girl.

"She may become a gold-mine to us," he had said, but knew that it was with a protective insincerity.

"Shall we wait and ask her to dinner when she *is* a gold-mine," his wife had asked. "And if she *must* come, may not Willie and Elspeth be invited, too; to help us through the ordeal?"

"No, Willie and Elspeth would laugh at her. They would be tempted to draw her out."

"So might I be tempted."

"I should be hurt for her sake if you teased her."

"I think you are being very tiresome about her. And it is very tiresome for me, to have to have her sleep here."

"We could not let her go back in the train late in the evening."

"She could come to luncheon."

"Please, Hermione!"

It was an autumn evening and leaves were in the air and all over the pavements and gardens, when Theo brought Angel to his house in St John's Wood.

I am not nervous of a girl of sixteen, Hermione thought, as she rose to greet her. But she was nervous of her own behaviour to the girl, with Theo watching. She resented his air of vigilance and protectiveness, and knew that she would be wise to hide the resentment. She was ready to offer kindness to the girl for his sake, but Angel ignored her; she treated her as if she were of no account, and rudely kept her head turned towards Theo.

I am not laughing at her any more, Hermione decided. In fact, I am a little frightened of her. And why is she so suspicious about everything she eats? Does she think that I am trying to poison her?

Angel found the food tasteless and unidentifiable: the fish in aspic, the chicken buried in a sauce among a confusion of mushrooms and pieces of hard-boiled egg. She felt disdainful and looked it. She was wearing a crumpled dress of sea-green muslin and her black hair hung down to her waist. Hermione could imagine her sitting under the sea, casting spells, counting the corpses of the drowned. She asked a maid to light more candles, for the room seemed suddenly cheerless: gaiety was quite lacking and she felt chilled.

Angel was disappointed in the house and despised the modern furnishings, the lack of sumptuousness. Instead of gilt and marble there were plain oak and pottery tiles. Branches of copper-beech in an earthenware jar seemed a bleak economy to her when one could see from the drawing-room window the tree from which they had been picked. The dullest etchings framed in ebony were suspended on long cords from the picture-rail, and on the dining-room walls where, in her opinion, family portraits should have hung, was an arrangement of willow-pattern plates and Japanese fans.

After dinner, Theo asked his wife to play the piano, and she was glad to shelter behind the music for a moment and not to have to stumble on with attempts at conversation. She could not blandly sit out the silences as Theo did, and all of her efforts at ending them were like throwing damp twigs on a dying fire. Her remarks were never taken up and her questions—which became almost hysterically impertinent—were answered as abruptly as perhaps they deserved.

She played some Mendelssohn, and Angel began to fidget; dropping her coffee-spoon, she went down on her knees to fetch it from under the sofa. Theo begged her to leave it, and when she would not, he, too, went down on all fours. Their heads bumped together. Hermione peered round the side of the piano and saw them crawling on the floor. Shaking with laughter, she longed for Willie Brace to share this delightful picture.

As soon as she had settled down again, Angel began to look about the room, and Hermione was conscious of her head turning from one object to another. She was plainly not listening to the music and suddenly asked in a loud voice: "Are those real pearls your wife is wearing, Mr Gilbright?"

Hermione, who had been leading up to a crescendo, played the next chord very softly and heard Theo say in a vague, amused voice: "Yes. Yes, I think so."

Of course, *I* am not *here*, thought Hermione and some of her temper came out in the next few bars. Theo thought it an unusual interpretation, with crescendo becoming diminuendo and forte changing to piano according to Angel's behaviour and his wife's reaction to it. Hermione's tortoiseshell cat was lying on its cushion by the fire, and Angel now put her coffee-cup on the tray, filled the saucer with cream and took it across to the cat, which blinked in surprise before she began to drink.

Hermione stopped playing. "I am afraid she will be sick if she has that," she said in a clear, high voice of vexation. "She has been fed already. In the kitchen."

"Oh, it will do him good," said Angel. "I love cats."

Hermione dropped her hands in her lap and began to turn the rings on her fingers: a danger-sign, Theo knew. "Do play some more," he coaxed her. Angel, kneeling by the cat, said: "He loves it, you see. He has nearly finished it."

"She," said Hermione distantly.

"Just one more little thing," urged Theo. "Some Scarlatti."

"No," said Hermione. She closed the music-book and stood up. "If Miss Deverell will excuse me for a moment, I must just go and feed my canaries."

"I don't care for birds," Angel said.

Just as well, thought Hermione, for there wasn't a canary in the house. She went to the morning-room and sat there in the cold for five minutes. She would tell Elspeth and Willie later that she escaped to stifle her laughter, but really, as Theo knew, she had come away to control her anger.

"There! All gone!" said Angel, taking the saucer away from the cat. "He was hungry, poor old thing. Was your wife ever presented at Court, Mr Gilbright?"

"No, I don't think so."

She sat down on the sofa again. The cat got up from its cushion, stretched and yawned, then sauntered across the room and sprang on to her lap. It was the first time Theo had seen Angel smile, and it was a prim and unwilling smile, which saddened him. He wondered what Hermione could be doing, but was glad that she had gone. He watched Angel fondling the cat, then he took a deep breath and said in what he hoped was an off-hand voice: "I wish you would tell me about your home. I went through Norley once, but only in a train."

She stroked the cat until sparks flew from the fur: there was agitation and electricity in the air. She hesitated, then she said: "It is a hideous place. There are miles of ugly streets of poor houses. And the people are all mean and stupid. My mother has a little grocery shop and we live above it. There are three rooms." She lifted her head and looked up at him defiantly, until she saw his expression of concern and sympathy and her eyes filled with tears. Her first impulse had been to tell some imaginary story, make some mystery about her address, but that reaction, so natural to her, was followed by what she regarded as a temptation to tell the truth. Having succumbed to it she felt exhausted. "I don't want anyone to know anything about me," she said anxiously. "None of what I told you seems true to me and I know that one day I shall stop believing it."

"You are a strange girl," he said. "I think you are brave. I admire you."

"And why should you admire her?" Hermione asked. "For I am sure that is what I heard you say as I opened the door."

"I was saying that I think she is brave."

"Oh, and won't she *have* to be!"

Hermione usually enjoyed this last part of the day when, alone at last, getting ready for bed, they could make unguarded judgments on people they had met or entertained. She had a lively observation, a sharp tongue and enjoyed slashing to shreds a whole roomful of guests, for Theo's amusement. This evening, nothing amused him: his usual tolerance had ebbed away; yet she could not be quiet, as she knew she ought.

"That terrible meal! The silences! You didn't help much, truly, Theo. And when I rushed in with silly, harmless questions, I was simply rebuffed. Did she think I really cared if she were ever in Italy or liked Browning? I was made to feel that I had been impertinent. Had I?"

She was sitting at her dressing-table, beginning to take her hair down. He came and stood behind her and took the pins out for her. She dropped her hands into her lap and sat looking at him reflected in the looking-glass, his grave, kind face, the untidy red beard and hair: he was a broad, clumsily-built man and she waited patiently while he fumbled with the hair-pins: when he stooped to pick up those he dropped he breathed heavily, for he was getting enormously fat in middle-age. She teased him and he smiled. Her hair came down coil by coil, and when it was all unpinned he began to brush it.

"Are there any?" she asked.

"Any what?" But he knew, for she asked the same question every night.

"Grey hairs."

"None." There were a few, but she could not have seen them herself.

"*Did* I ask questions at dinner that I shouldn't have?"

"I don't think so. She is abnormally touchy."

"Tremendous offence taken at almost everything I said. And yet it is all right for her to ask you if my pearls are real. While I am sitting in the room and supposed to be playing the piano for her entertainment."

"Don't be cross. It did no harm."

"But why does she think that she may behave in that way? No wonder that she writes like a servant-girl! What can her background be? Where does she come from? From what conceivable kind of home?"

"I don't know."

He kissed the top of her head and moved away. She could no longer see him in the looking-glass.

"Are you protecting her from me?" she asked suspiciously and, when he did not reply, she lost her temper again. "Oh, Willie is right," she cried. "You will make a laughing-stock of yourself. How can you have such blindness in you, such delusions? A gold-mine, indeed! A rude, unpromising, grotesque gold-mine, if ever there was one."

From the shadows he said gently: "Please hush, my dear! Don't let yourself be angry over such a pathetic young person. I shall send you off to feed your canaries again."

Her indignation would not give way to amusement. She said: "You know I never try to interfere in your business affairs, but I can't help regretting your name being associated with such freakish nonsense and knowing that people will laugh at you."

She had braided one side of her hair and now began on the other. To her astonishment, she found that her hands were trembling. In her thoughts about Angel she knew that 'distaste for' had become 'dislike of'. She wanted the book to fail.

iv

"In all my life," Aunt Lottie told her sister, "I was never so disgraced. Nor ever saw Madam so angry. When I looked out of one of the windows and saw that book lying on a seat down on the terrace, my heart turned right over." She pressed her hand to her breast in case the same thing should happen again. Her sister poured out some more tea for her. This story was being told for the second time, and although in its repetition it lacked suspense it was filled in more richly with detail. The first version had been a stark explosion, beginning with "That girl of yours!"

Sometimes, when she was alone with her sister, her manners lost some of their Paradise House daintiness, and now she had both elbows on the table and both hands to her cup of tea which she was blowing to cool. "Last Monday—no, I'm telling a lie: it was Tuesday, of course, because the dressmaker was there. Miss Angelica had come up from the garden for a fitting of the crushed-strawberry nun's-veiling and had left the book on one of the seats. That's silly, I remember thinking, because it was clouding over for rain. Then I thought the book seemed familiar and I realised what it was. Oh, dear, my legs might have been jelly. Well, after that, I suppose Madam must have come along the terrace and picked it up. I didn't see, because the dressmaker called for me to talk about altering the bronze silk. The sewing-room is in a lobby off the landing, and there I was standing by Madam's dummy, handing pins to Miss Toogood, with the door ajar, when I saw Madam herself coming up the stairs holding the book between finger and thumb as if it was poison-ivy." Aunt Lottie demonstrated this, with a slice of bread-and-butter. "She went into Miss Angelica's room, and I excused myself from Miss Toogood and went quietly along the landing. I heard Miss Angelica say: 'But, Mamma, all of my friends are reading it.' Then Madam said: 'I shall ask Palmer to put it on the kitchen-range. I hope I have said enough and can trust your good taste in the future.' I thought she was coming out of the room then, so I went back to Miss Toogood. 'You look queer,' she said. 'I have these giddy spells,' I told her and she let it go at that, barring advising some iron pills. I don't know how I got through that day, but nothing was mentioned until Madam was dressing for dinner, then she put on one of her funny little smiles. 'Oh,' she said, 'what an odd coincidence it is,' she said, 'that this new authoress who has caused such a sensation has the very same name as your niece.' My face flamed up. I could see it in the mirror. 'Perhaps you've heard of her,' she said; then she said: '*Have* you heard of her?' I couldn't answer, only to say: 'Oh dear, oh dear, madam.' 'So there *is* a connection?' she asked. 'I would rather have seen her dead at my feet,' I said. I couldn't help the tears falling."

Mrs Deverell looked uneasy, but sympathetic. "What did she say to that?"

"She asked our Angel's age, and when I said 'seventeen' she just shook her head. Then she laughed, but not a nice laugh, and she said: 'And to think that I once considered her as a maid for Miss Angelica! Well, I can't lay blame on you for your relations and I shan't do so. It is an unsavoury book and we will just forget it. There will be no need for you to mention it, or your niece, in this house.'"

"Whatever would Ernie say to all this?" Mrs Deverell moaned.

"*His* side has something to answer for," said Aunt Lottie. "No one can point to anything on *our* side, that's one thing."

"But Ernie would have been just as upset as us. He was such a good, quiet man and never caused any trouble to anyone."

"There was his sister Ethel. Have you forgotten how she used to carry on? Burning incense and flying into tantrums and wearing those outlandish clothes."

"We just used to put it down to her never marrying," said Mrs Deverell tactlessly. "And *she* was religious right up to the time when they had to take her away; but wild horses wouldn't drag Angel inside the Chapel nowadays. I don't see any likeness."

"Too much; or too little; both are as bad where religion is concerned."

"Perhaps Angel's a real clever girl, after all, and we don't understand," her mother said wistfully.

"You could be excused for thinking so, in your position, I

daresay; but there's no doubt, Emmy, she has brought us all down, and stopped she must be from dragging us still farther."

"She's at it now. In her bedroom, writing."

"It makes me shudder to think what's coming from her pen. You must tell her you won't have it—that it's got to be put a stop to."

"I can't," said Mrs Deverell hopelessly.

"Emmy!" Aunt Lottie lowered her voice and her cheeks flushed. "Tell me, where did she find out all that . . . you know . . . the facts of life."

"Certainly not from me," said Mrs Deverell proudly.

Angel came in and sat down at the table, ignoring her aunt.

"The tea isn't very fresh," Mrs Deverell said anxiously.

"It was quite fresh when you called her," said Aunt Lottie.

"Yes, you shouldn't neglect your meals, Angel. I think you've been at it long enough for one day."

Angel looked tired. There were dark shadows under her eyes, as if she had smudged them with her ink-stained fingers.

"*I* think she's been long enough at it for ever," said Aunt Lottie. "I can see that much more of it and my life won't be worth living. It's all round the servants' hall as it is, because of course Palmer *didn't* put the book on the kitchen-range. Cook took charge of it. She keeps it under one of the big dish-covers and lends it round. The sniggering that goes on, and the insinuations I am exposed to, Emmy, you can imagine for yourself. 'What about a nice game of cards?' the footman dared to say to me. They all know what he meant by that. I could have slapped his face. And with Madam upset and the under-servants tittering, it will be lucky if I can keep my position."

"Give it up, then," Angel said casually. "Tell them to go to the devil. Retire."

"Retire! I like that!" Aunt Lottie gave an imitation of one of Madam's nasty little laughs. "And what, pray, should I use for money if I did?"

"I would give you enough."

"Oh, you *would*! That's very generous of you, I'm sure."

"No, it isn't. I shall have plenty."

"And what makes you think that?"

"My book is a success and so will all the others be that I am going to write."

Her calm infuriated her aunt. "I don't know what you mean by a 'success'," she said loudly. "I should have thought it was more of a disgrace. Madam's word for it was 'unsavoury' and cook was only too glad to be able to point out a piece from the newspaper, saying it was gibberish." She pronounced the word with a hard 'g' and made it sound vicious.

"The people who are right are those who buy it," Angel said. "And they will go on buying it. Mr Gilbright says so. So I shall always have plenty of money, and if you want any of it, you're welcome."

Before they could answer, she left them and went back to her bedroom. Here, she leaned against the closed door and shut her eyes, struggling to control her anger. She hated the word 'gibberish', however it was pronounced: it bit into her like acid. There were other words, equally hurtful, which reviewers had used and which she would never be able to hear without feeling pain.

Her vanity had been stunned by the way in which her book had been received. No trumpets had come thrusting out from behind clouds, proclaiming 'genius' and 'masterpiece'. For a long time nothing at all had happened, and then, slowly, the abuse and sarcasm had begun. The very passages of which she had been most proud, had been printed as if they were richly humorous; her dialogue, her syntax, her view of life, her descriptions of society were all seen to be part of some new and quite delicious joke. No one had wept, it seemed, when reading the funeral scene—unless it was with laughter.

She had destroyed the cuttings as soon as she had read them, but they had been photographed upon her mind. She could remember every word of mockery they contained. Some were unsigned, but the worst, the one with the word 'gibberish', was above the name Rowland Pearce. Him she hated with unswerving ferocity and tried to find solace in imagining scenes in which she was able to express her contempt for him and to humiliate him in public. She had sent off a long letter to the newspaper: it was full of sarcasm and indignation, and this morning she had seen it printed with a gleeful footnote by the reviewer, as if it were a continuation of the joke. At the same time—too late—a letter had come from Theo Gilbright. "Be calm: resist reading the reviews, if you can: above all, never answer back."

The book was selling well, but she had expected fame and praise as well as money. She was baffled and alarmed and worn out by the violence of her fury. She longed for some way of healing herself and wished that she might finish the novel she was working on and start another. She would call it "The Charlatan' and it should deal with a literary hack, an impoverished scribbler, a novelist manqué, a twisted and embittered man, making a despicable living by reviling the work of better writers than himself, assuaging his jealousy and impotence by destroying what he could not himself create. She imagined him with the utmost vividness: a misshapen figure of a man, with a stained waistcoat and a sneering voice. He had repulsive personal habits, no friend in the world, and a name as much like Rowland Pearce as she could manage.

PART 2

i

TO the older people in Norley, Alderhurst had once been a remote upland village where the children went in wagonettes on Sunday School treats. Its water-tower was a landmark for miles and its bluebell woods and silver birches were famous. As time went on, industry made Norley an impossible place for industrialists to live in; the Georgian residential streets were too involved in areas of working-class houses and had fallen into desuetude. By the end of the century the houses being built all over old estates, old farmlands, had reached Alderhurst. Laburnums and other suburban trees mingled with the silver birches, and hedges of spotted laurel and golden privet hid the lawns and the gravelled sweeps in front of the new houses where it was now fashionable to live.

By the time Angel and her mother went there to live, the roads had been made smooth and pavements laid. The water-tower rose above the thinned-out woods. Very few of the inhabitants felt the sadness of the place; but Mrs Deverell was one of them. In the days of the Sunday School treats she had thought it an enchanted country; she had plundered sheaves of bluebells from its woods and had loved to run shouting between the trees, with snapping twigs underfoot and brambles catching at her skirt. Her memories were all of happiness; even of the year when it had rained. She had sheltered with her coat over her head, and listened to the drops beating down from leaf to leaf. When it had stopped, a rainbow had come out behind the water-tower and the earth and air had smelled poignantly sweet.

"I never thought I would live here," she had told Angel.

But nowadays she often suffered from the lowering pain of believing herself happy when she was not. "Who *could* be miserable in such a place?" she asked; yet, on misty October evenings or on Sundays, when the church bells began, sensations she had never known before came over her.

"It's your age," Lottie told her. "Madam's been the same. Pecks at her food, they say, and keeps sighing, and the tears always ready for the turning on."

"Yes, that's how it is," she agreed.

She sometimes felt better when she went back to see her friends in Volunteer Street; but it was a long way to go, Angel discouraged the visits, and her friends seemed to have changed. Either they put out their best china and thought twice before they said anything, or they were defiantly informal—"You'll have to take us as you find us"—and would persist in making remarks like "I don't suppose you ever have bloaters up at Alderhurst" or "Pardon the apron, but there's no servants here to polish the grate." In each case, they were watching her for signs of grandeur or condescension. She fell into little traps they laid and then they were able to report to the neighbours. "It hasn't taken *her* long to start putting on side." She had to be especially careful to recognise everyone she met, and walked up the street with an expression of anxiety which was misinterpreted as disdain.

The name 'Deverell Family Grocer' stayed for a long time over the shop, and she was pleased that it should, although Angel frowned with annoyance when she heard of it. Then one day the faded name was scraped and burnt away, and on her next visit to Volunteer Street, she saw that "Cubbage's Stores" was painted there instead. She felt an unaccountable panic and dismay at the sight of this and at the strange idea of other people and furniture in those familiar rooms. "Very nice folk," she was told. "*She's* so friendly. Always the same. And such lovely kiddies." Mrs Deverell felt slighted and wounded; going home she was so preoccupied that she passed the wife of the landlord of The Volunteer without seeing her. "I wouldn't expect Alderhurst people to speak to a publican's wife," the woman told everyone in the saloon bar. "Even though it was our Gran who laid her husband out when he died." All of their kindnesses were remembered and brooded over; any past kindness Mrs Deverell had done—and they were many—only served to underline the change which had come over her.

At a time of her life when she needed the security of familiar things, these were put beyond her reach. It seemed to her that she had wasted her years acquiring a skill which in the end was to be of no use to her; her weather-eye for a good drying day; her careful ear for judging the gentle singing sound of meat roasting in the oven; her touch for the freshness of bacon; and how, by smelling a cake, she could tell if it were baked: arts, which had taken so long to perfect, fell now into disuse. She would never again, she grieved, gather up a great fragrant line of washing in her arms to carry indoors. One day when they had first come to Alderhurst, she had passed through the courtyard where sheets were hanging out: she had taken them in her hands and, finding them just at the right stage of drying, had begun to unpeg them. They were looped all about her shoulders when Angel caught her. "Please leave work to the people who should do it," she had said. "You will only give offence." She tried hard not to give offence; but it was difficult. The smell of ironing being done or the sound of eggs being whisked set up a restlessness which she could scarcely control.

The relationship of mother and daughter seemed to have been reversed, and Angel, now in her early twenties, was the authoritative one; since girlhood she had been taking on one responsibility after another, until she had left her mother with nothing to perplex her but how to while away the hours when the servants were busy and her daughter was at work. Fretfully, she would wander about the house, bored, but afraid to interrupt; she was like an intimidated child.

Angel worked incessantly, locked in the room she had chosen for a study. When she had finished a book, she would pause with exhaustion and wonder if she could not rest for a while, travel, spend some of the vast amount of money she had earned. For a day or two, she would relapse into the indolence of her childhood and sit inert in her chair with the cat on her lap, for hour after hour. The idea of the holiday faded: there was no one to go with her, except her mother whose chatter vexed her; and she was afraid that while she rested she might be forgotten. The publication of some other woman's novel would send her scurrying back to her study: men writers did not affect her so strongly.

In the study, she had suffered hours of great bitterness and anger. Her morbid resentment of the faintest criticism was unfortunate in one so subjected to printed derision and abuse. The pain seemed worse as it became more familiar. Rowland Pearce, who, as Ronald Price, had come, cringing, to a bad end in her third novel, was only a symbol to her of the throng of mockers, the 'jostling jackanapes' as she had called them, "those who would sneer at Shakespeare because they could not write *Hamlet* themselves." When Theo Gilchrist told her—and no one else would have dared—that Rowland Pearce was also a novelist of great distinction, she had said that she could very well visualise the anaemic tosh that he would write, a man who knew nothing of literature, or of good behaviour, either.

"It is glandular," Willie Brace told his partner, when he heard of this reply. "That inordinate vanity, the insufferable touchiness. She is all for you, Theo, your very own Guardian Angel, and may you never be bludgeoned to death for having to oppose her."

Theo had long ago invented a senior partner, a Mr Delbanco, who was too aged to travel to London, although he maintained an unreasonable interest in the firm. To his caprices Theo was bound to defer. It was he who put forward suggestions and advised alterations (chiefly to avoid litigation) in Angel's manuscripts. "For myself, I am satisfied, but Mr Delbanco is a little uneasy," was a recurring strain in Theo's letters, and when Angel swept Mr Delbanco's suggestions scornfully to one side, or wrote one of her staggeringly vitriolic letters, Theo felt relieved, as if he had just managed to dodge a furious blow.

The harmless and not very successful fiction of Mr Delbanco made a unique relationship in Angel's life, for with Theo Gilbright she was spontaneously honest: as far as her self-delusions would allow her, she spoke the truth to him and the only deception between them was his. The gold-mine had prospered and some of his feelings towards her were bound to be self-congratulatory. The more the critics laughed, the longer were the queues for her novels at the libraries; the power of her romanticism captivated simple people; her preposterous situations delighted the sophisticated; her burning indignation when some passing fury turned her aside from her plot into denunciations and irrelevancies, swayed some readers into solemn agreement and others into paroxysms of laughter. Many were shocked by what, in those days, was called 'outspokenness' and by her agnosticism—for in her books only fools and hypocrites were made to believe in God —and to be spoken against once or twice from pulpits had been of some assistance to her. Her distaste for religion had begun when she was taken as a small child to chapel and was a rationalisation of what had been in the first place simply a hatred of the building itself and its yellow, varnished pews and sea-green window. Her dislike spread to all that went on there, the women's tremulous voices in the choir, the banality of the hymns, the unctuousness of the Minister. Her loathing had spread and intensified as she sat there: it took in the dull faces, old ladies' beaded bonnets, bedraggled feather boas and all the camphorous Sunday clothes and the stifling small-talk on the pavement outside when the service was over. "I wanted something beautiful," she told Theo Gilchrist. "Nothing to do with God. I think that if someone offered me a hundred pounds to go to that chapel again, or one like it, my legs would become paralysed. I should never be able to drag them towards it or force myself to go inside."

She spoke to him of her childhood as to no one else and almost as if, by doing so, she might be rid of it. He listened with compassion. Sometimes he wished that in her writing she might be half as direct and simple as she was when she talked to him; but he knew that she never would be and that they both might profit less if she were. She would never write about the kind of life she had known when she was younger. She escaped from it to her dukes and duchesses, her foreign counts, her castles and moonlit terraces. There were dungeons and crypts and family vaults in her stories, but not cemeteries; the only poor were penniless beggars; and the seaside always was abroad. She wrote with ignorance and imagination, and Mr Delbanco had constantly to be on the watch to guard her from her own solecisms, from wrong modes of address and strange phrases of Italian or French. Theo had never had to busy himself so much with rules of precedence and protocol and he longed to take a rest with the happenings in some ordinary middle-class family.

He sometimes longed, too, to take a rest from the hazards of her correspondence. Two or three times a week, her letters, carelessly scrawled in violet ink, arrived at the office with her complaints about the insufficiency of his advertising, his lack of chivalry in not challenging her critics, the shortcomings of Mudie's, the negligence of compositors. She accused him of cheese-paring; her advances, she said, were so niggardly as to be insulting. She mentioned great sums which had been paid by other publishers to other women novelists—to Miss Corelli and Miss Broughton—and suggested that from the fortune her books had provided him he was subsidising the bungled efforts of all the other writers on his list. "As it is by *my* industry that these poor little books are published at all," she wrote, "it would be merely civil of you to acquaint me with your future plans for spreading this charity about."

"Success hasn't gone to her head," Theo argued with his wife. "I remember the first time she came to the office. It was a hot day and she was tired and dusty and bewildered; but, all the same, vain and indomitable. She was born like it, I swear. I can see her howling herself rigid in her cradle. They are never happy, these sports which ordinary, humble people throw off: they belong nowhere and are insatiable."

Once he saw a large cactus-plant in a flower-shop window. From one unpromising, barbed shoot had sprung a huge, glowering bloom. It looked solitary and incongruous, a freakish accident; and he was reminded of Angel.

The Birches at Alderhurst was a red brick house with a great deal of coloured glass let into the panels of the front door and round the edges of the downstairs windows, so that lozenges of red and blue slanted across the tiles in the hall and over the rich wallpapers of the rooms. In the white and gold and crimson drawing-room a parrot and a marmoset spent uneasy hours together, with bouts of nervous hostility and long wary silences. Parrot-seed was scattered over the Turkey carpet; encouraging mice, the servants said, but they said it only to one another. They cleared up after the marmoset with murmurings of disgust and said that the house smelt like the Zoological Gardens.

Almost as soon as the house was bought and the rooms so richly furnished, Angel began to doubt if it was the best setting for her. It lacked romance and atmosphere. She remembered her school, the grey walls and the cedar trees, and the pictures she had in her mind of Paradise House, and she knew that her own house expressed nothing but the fact that she had made money.

Her discontent began with the Gilbrights' weekend visit. Hermione Gilbright's detestation of her had not lessened because, as a gold-mine, Angel had surpassed Theo's dreams. To spend from Friday to Monday under her roof was the dreariest duty to her, and she complained for a fortnight that her husband had not the power to keep business affairs and social life in separate compartments.

They drove from London on Friday evening in Theo's new De Dion Bouton. At her first glimpse of them as they turned in between the laurels, Angel could guess that Hermione's face was sulky behind her veil. She reminded herself of the shabby house in St John's Wood from which they had come, that the sales of her last book had far exceeded the others and that she was a very famous novelist indeed. She smoothed her crimson satin dress and glanced at her white hands for reassurance. Then she sat down at the piano and began to improvise dreamily, with the soft pedal down to blur mistakes and so that she could hear approaching footsteps.

The piano was on a daïs, and when the tired and dusty Gilbrights were shown in and she let her hands fall into her lap with what was supposed to be a start of surprise and rose to welcome them, Hermione was obliged to tilt back her head and look up at her.

"And I was listening for the car," Angel told her. "I had hoped to run out and welcome you."

Theo sensed his wife's irritation, and knew that Angel would not have lied in such a way if he had been alone.

Mrs Deverell, dressed like a rather grand housekeeper, took them to their room.

"*Her* life is one I shouldn't care to live," said Hermione, when she and Theo were alone. "Did you notice the photograph of Angel garbed as one of the muses, sitting on a marble seat in a trance, with her mother standing up behind her at a respectful distance? It was among the conglomeration of stuff on the piano. I always notice photographs first when I go into rooms. I am sorry there are none in here. I would rather have them than that mooney girl with the pitcher. Or this goitrous peasant maiden with the tambourine. Dinner will be dreadful, and only the first of three. Now, if I put on the amber satin I shall clash furiously with her. Or was that a tea-gown she was wearing? I have read of tea-gowns. Oh dear, and there are no canaries for me to feed if things get bad. I shall have to take refuge with that evil-looking parrot. Wasn't it impressive, that first glimpse of her with her hands straying over the keys: I see now what the phrase means. Are you thinking that all I say is in execrable taste? Because that is what you look as if you were thinking? *Are* you thinking that?" she repeated more sharply when he did not answer her. "Thoughts, for instance, about the sanctity of hospitality, about being under her roof, and breaking bread with her?"

"No. I was simply thinking how vulnerable she is."

"If she could hear, she would dislike that remark more than anything I have said."

"Perhaps."

"And perhaps she *can* hear. Oh, what made me choose yellow for a dress? I forget that I have gone so grey. I shall be a pathetic sight, which is worse than being macabre, so she will have the best of it. And of what use are topazes to me now, at my age? It is I who am vulnerable. The only ascendancy worth being in is to have more years to live. She is young and famous and rich and has fine hands. And I am ageing and grey and getting fat and burdened with a sulky husband who forces me into situations of the most intolerable tedium and shows no gratitude for my forbearance."

"Forbearance! You are a spiteful little chatterbox." He put his hands on her shoulders and kissed her as she sat at the dressing-table. "If you go through this with flying colours— but not so flying as to invite suspicion—I will buy you a nice present, a souvenir. I *am* grateful, for I know you will really try in spite of all you say. And you aren't *really* grey, you know. I can still see a lot of brown hairs."

She began to shake with laughter, and love for him brought sudden tears to her eyes, and she turned aside to hide them.

Hermione's colours were not flying throughout dinner: they were dipped, less in submission than wonderment. She soon became convinced that Angel was mad, that her own high spirits could never counter such insanity and were not called upon to do so. She fell back into a state of relaxed fascination while Angel attacked Theo on business matters and questioned him closely upon details which he could not have been expected, by anyone but Angel, to carry in his head.

From time to time, Hermione made a flurried, murmured attempt at conversation with Mrs Deverell, who kept her eyes on her daughter, with the look of bewilderment which had become her everyday expression.

Theo listened patiently, as he had often to do, even with authors less tiresome than Angel, to stories of his own inadequacy.

"My mother was in the biggest bookshop in Norley and found that they had not a single copy of *An Eastern Tragedy* left. That was a week ago. This morning she called again to look round—as you often do, don't you, mother?"

Mrs Deverell nodded. She was, in fact, sent there regularly, to pry and ask questions, and was well-known from these appearances.

"Again, not one copy! In a locality where—heaven forbid that I should boast—but there is, *must* be, if only among inquisitive and gossipy people and not in literary circles at all, a constant call for my books. Imagine the turning away of dissatisfied customers that goes on, day after day!"

"They could order more," said Theo. He was rather enjoying his food, and Angel, who chose wine in haphazard ways, according to its expensiveness and the attraction of its name, had struck lucky with the Nuits St Georges.

"But I think there must be your part of it, your business of seeing him supplied. I know that, if he were in the least encouraged, he would put in a whole windowful of my books from *The Lady Irania* onwards."

"'Irania' is out-of-print," Theo said foolishly.

"And isn't it high time it was *in* print again?"

"That is rather Delbanco's side, you know."

"Who? . . ." began Hermione.

"Mr Delbanco," Theo said, turning to Mrs Deverell, "is the power behind the scenes."

After dinner, they walked round the garden. The evening air was still, scented with pinks and syringa. Two more whole days! Hermione thought restlessly. She pinched at the leaves of lemon balm and held her scented hand to her face. "What is this called?" she asked.

Angel bent down and examined it, suspicious, as if it had

no right to be there. She was always too busy writing about what she thought of as 'nature' to go out of doors to look at things. "Mother, do you know the name of this plant?"

Mrs Deverell, who had been trailing them down the winding asphalt path, rather, Theo thought, like a wardress guarding prisoners at exercise, came up to investigate.

I wish I hadn't asked, thought Hermione.

Mrs Deverell, no longer used to having her opinions asked, looked doubtfully at her daughter. "I think that's what your Auntie Lottie calls Lad's Fancy," she said.

At the mention of her aunt, Angel turned and walked on. They followed her, encircling potting-sheds and a shrubbery. On either side of them, the young fruit-trees were an intense green in the fading light. Against this acid, lucid greenness, Angel's crimson dress, which had turned out *not* to be a tea-gown, was as bright as running blood; and Theo slackened his pace for the pleasure of watching the red upon the green as she walked ahead of him along the petal-covered path.

She seemed not to notice that he had fallen back. Without any warning, she was smothered with a choking feeling of unhappiness and disappointment. The warmth of the darkening, perfumed air would, on any other evening, have driven her indoors to her desk. It was an hour when not to be in love sets up a painful agitation: to be in love may be more painful, but is appropriate and can be borne, perhaps, with more composure.

Why is there no one? she wondered, facing the house as she walked on, hastening away from the others without knowing what she did. She drew her silk scarf more tightly round her shoulders, clutching it to her with her hands crossed on her breast. She had looked forward to this evening, to the pleasure of punishing and impressing Hermione and having Theo to talk to. But he had said nothing. She herself had gone relentlessly on about sales, royalties, shopkeepers, unable to control her tongue: as her mistake grew, she had wilfully added to it. He will be under my roof, she thought, glancing up at the eaves, where birds—martins, if she had known—had built.

It isn't as I thought it would be; and he is the only friend I have. She was rarely so truthful with herself.

As she came close to the house, the walls threw warmth out towards her: the brick still held the day's sun. She turned at the door to wait for the others. Theo came first. He was holding a flower in his hand. "A present from your own garden," he said and slotted it through the large brooch on her bosom. He had sensed her agitation and seen her clasp her arms about her as if she were shuddering. And now, at this gesture of tenderness with which, from some half-formed wish to comfort her, he had surprised her, tears filled and magnified her eyes.

"You are cold," he said hastily, and he re-arranged her scarf on her shoulders and urged her on into the hall before her mother and Hermione could see.

"You miss nothing, Hermione," he told her when she re-marked upon this scene later—"most affecting," she called it.

"I am only warning you. Don't trifle with *her* feelings."

"For heaven's sake, I gave her a flower—from her own garden."

"She would think it was the *thought*. . . ."

"The thing had snapped off. I didn't even pick it, just picked it *up*. I was going to put it in my own buttonhole, then the other seemed more polite."

"It was the thought," Hermione repeated. "She isn't like other women. She embroiders everything to suit her own vanity. Once roused, she could be a tigress."

"A broken-off flower can hardly be expected to rouse anyone."

"I am only warning you. The flower itself is neither here nor there. I *know* what she is like. I feel it in my bones. Nothing would be trivial to her, because she is so hungry for love. That gesture, that flower would mean what a whole basketful of orchids and a sonnet would mean to other women. Or why did she have tears in her eyes? She has poured all that passion into her novels, but there is plenty more to come. She dare not suspect it in herself, for there is nothing in her everyday life to meet it, and that she would never admit. I am sure she believes that she is beautiful and wonderfully attractive to men besides being famous; but her self-protectiveness would forbid her to ponder why so little comes of it. How sensible she is! Let her *be* sensible. There is no kindness done by denting her armour or even reminding her that she wears any."

"Madame Heger!" he said. "That's who you are. It is a delightful situation. My rôle of the Professor I like very much."

She was fussed and nettled—just at that point, he knew, where she would suddenly see that she had gone too far in absurdity and would begin to laugh at her exaggerations.

"Poor little flower!" he said. "What risks I ran with it."

"I expect that at this moment she is pressing it in some vast, heavy book."

When Angel had pressed her flower and put the book away in a drawer, she sat by the empty fireplace with her white cat on her lap. She thought of Theo and Hermione alone in their room. They would be undressing, going over their day, discussing, comparing; quite different, she imagined, from their everyday selves.

Mrs Deverell came in, to say goodnight, she explained; but really to fuss about the next day's meals, the tea-party especially. She had ordered this, that and the other, quantities of everything; but would it be enough—for titled people, she wondered?

"I wish he wasn't coming," she kept saying. "When I woke up this morning, it came on me with a rush. It's really true! I thought. It's really going to happen. Such wicked ideas came into my head, how I wished he'd fall off his horse and break his leg or that his carriage would overturn, anything rather than him come here. I don't know what they'd say to this in Volunteer Street. I don't know what I'd have said myself if anyone had told me five years ago that I'd be pouring out tea for a lord."

"I'll pour out the tea," said Angel.

"Well, perhaps he won't come. That's all we can hope."

"He'll come," said Angel.

"I wish tomorrow was over. I'm so glad Lottie can manage to come and give me a hand. She can always tell me how things ought to be."

"Lottie?" Angel said sharply.

"Yes, she promised she would come over soon after dinner, I mean lunch. She will have to stay the night, I suppose."

"How dare she invite herself here?"

"*I* invited her. I felt I would never manage on my own. I never looked more to Lottie than I do now. She knows what people like that expect."

"Why did you try to hide this from me? I had to know it in the end."

"I didn't try to hide anything—why should I try to hide my own sister? It's just that I've had so much to think about with these visitors and so on, I never thought to say beforehand. . . ."

"I will *not* have Aunt Lottie here. It isn't her day. How can I ask Lord Norley to meet her—for all I know, one of his friends' maids? We may all be equal in the sight of God, as you are always telling me, but we are not all equal in *my* eyes, and it is *my* house and there are some embarrassments I won't inflict on visitors who come here."

"It was only just to put me wise as to the arrangements. She will be quite happy to keep behind the scenes."

"And what do you suppose the servants will make of that? Isn't it possible for us to give someone a cup of tea without your running to your relations for advice as to how to pour it out?"

"I can't stop her now," Mrs Deverell said, simply and humbly. Her meekness brushed Angel with a moment's shame, and she could not prevent the thought rising: Once she was my mother and told me what to do and I did it, and now she is nothing—unless she is a child who has done wrong and cannot get forgiveness, can only hope that the punishment will pass. To be moved and shamed angered her further, and she tried to cover the wound with another show of vexation. "It is too bad," she began. Then the scene petered out into unreality. She felt exhausted, yawned and yawned, and then could not pick up the threads of what had gone before. "Oh, I'm tired," she moaned, thrusting her hands into her hair and lying back in her chair.

"I'm ever so sorry," Mrs Deverell said softly.

"In the morning," said Angel. "I can't think now."

"Well, goodnight, then. Shall I take the cat?"

"No, leave him."

Mrs Deverell went unhappily to bed.

Lord Norley brought two of his week-end guests with him. Their presence irritated him and he would far rather have packed them off to tea with Angel on their own and had an hour's peace, and he was sorry that there was no way of doing this.

"Oh, dear, there are two people in the carriage with him," Mrs Deverell said. She had been listening for the sound of the wheels on the gravel and darted away from the dining-room window to hiss at Lottie.

"Madam always has extra cups on the tray," said Lottie, who had never been so full of advice.

"Our china won't disgrace us, that's one thing," Mrs Deverell said, clutching at small comforts.

"Madam's, of course, is priceless."

"We had better get out of this room before we are trapped."

"I, for one, am staying here."

"That you can't, Lottie. Angel won't hear of it."

"Then I'm afraid Miss Angel can do the other thing. You may have slackened *your* principles, Emmy, since your way of life has changed, and I sometimes wonder if you don't have any recollections at all of how we were brought up, chapel three times Sundays and the wonderful example of Dad and Mother. You may be glad to shake hands with Lord Norley and have him under your roof, but I never could. What is there to him, after all? Brewery money and a brewery title, and all the wicked harm his trade's done to the town. . . ."

"Oh, Lord, she *does* look fierce and clever," Mrs Deverell said, with her eyes on the gravelled sweep, where the carriage had now stopped. "I must be in with Angel before the door is opened to them."

"There's a lot Lord Norley's got to answer for—he can give away his parks and his art galleries and try to salve his conscience any way he pleases; but I've seen them Saturday nights, you've seen them, too, the men fighting outside the Garibaldi and the Volunteer and their children standing by with bare feet in the rain. That's where his money came from. Human frailty, I say to myself, when I pass his father's statue in the Butts. Human weakness lined *your* pockets, I say. I notice you're not wearing your Temperance badge today, Emmy."

"They're coming! They're coming to the door. Oh, ring, Lottie, for the extra cups." Mrs Deverell sped across the hall into the drawing-room where Angel and Hermione were sitting in silence with albums of engravings open on their laps and Theo was struggling, as he had struggled since luncheon, not to fall asleep.

As the door was opened, Hermione raised her head from her album with a look of pleased expectancy; for anyone different was welcome, might make time pass more quickly. Then it will be time to dress for dinner, she promised herself. And when *that* is over, there will be only four more meals left. She was ready for a little diversion, but quite unprepared for the scene which suddenly broke up the introductions. The young woman who had at first seemed to shrink back at the sound of her own name, blushed, hovered, trembled, then almost ran across the room, flung herself down on her knees at the hem of Angel's dress, took Angel's hand and kissed it. ("It was a lovely moment," Hermione said afterwards to Elspeth and Willie Brace. "I wouldn't have missed it for the world. Angel so blissfully took it in her stride, as if it were as usual as anything could be. If she had had a sword and could have knighted her it would have been even more magnificent.")

The two participants in the tableau seemed unaware of any other people in the room, and held their pose for what seemed to Theo to be an agonisingly long time.

"So that's how it was," Lord Norley was saying to no one in particular. "As soon as she knew where I was coming, there was nothing for it but that *she* must come, too. All right, Nora, that's enough, my dear. Forgive her, Miss Deverell. Homage from one authoress to another, you know."

"No, Uncle," the young woman said firmly as she stood up. "I would rather you didn't mention my feeble scribblings in *this* house."

"You are a writer, too?" Theo asked, feeling that someone should.

"I write a little verse," she admitted.

"Under what name?" Hermione asked carelessly.

"Under my own name." She appeared disappointed that her own name had meant nothing to them, and that her feeble scribblings were taken at her spoken valuation. No one made soothing sounds of recognition or approval, and she longed to tell them that Queen Alexandra had accepted one of her poems entitled "La Princesse Lointaine."

"I'm afraid that in the . . . excitement, I didn't hear your name," said Hermione.

"Miss Nora Howe-Nevinson," Lord Norley said loudly. It was not an easy name to say and sometimes he made the most embarrassing mistakes. "My niece. And may I present my nephew, Mr Esmé Howe-Nevinson?"

Brother and sister were alike, too much alike to do either any good; for Nora's jaw was as square as her brother's and her upper lip as downy, while Esmé's skin was fine, as delicately coloured as hers was, his eyelashes were long and sweeping like a girl's and his brown, waving hair full of pretty golden lights.

87

Quite delicious! thought Hermione, as she took his hand.

"It was Miss Deverell, you know, Esmé," said Lord Norley, "who gave us the Watts."

"Most generous," his nephew murmured.

"Presented a very fine Watts to the Norley Art Gallery," Lord Norley explained to Theo. "You ought to make a point of seeing it. One of the Town's treasures. Miss Deverell herself is another."

Angel was dreamy with so much adulation. It was a perfect afternoon that could offer such riches and offer them in front of Theo and Hermione. Hermione thought that she looked indecently sated: as if her self-infatuation demanded no more for a while: she was exquisitely at peace.

Then—so very soon—she was jolted from her trance. Esmé Howe-Nevinson handed round sandwiches, put a whole one in his mouth and settled down to a long study of Angel: he seemed to be regarding her with fascinated curiosity, with a lively, dancing look, unlike his sister's spaniel gaze. Angel was conscious of it and felt uneasy. As she poured out a cup of tea, her hands were clumsy; the smallest action she was obliged to make became an ordeal.

"Why Watts?" Esmé suddenly asked, still looking intently at her.

"I don't understand," she said suspiciously.

"I meant, why did you choose Watts, of all painters? Or *didn't* you choose him? Perhaps it was the Town Council or some such set of ignorant old duffers."

"I won't allow that," said Lord Norley. "They're a fine body of men and not one of them a ha'p'orth better off for all their trouble."

"You don't approve of Watts?" Angel asked Esmé. "I will take full responsibility. *My* choice, *my* money, *my* ignorance."

"And I asked *why?*"

"Watts is too famous a painter to need an ignorant writer to justify him."

"I consider you rather discourteous, Esmé," said Lord Norley.

"And so do I," said Nora passionately.

"I don't mean to be. I had often wondered how those appalling pictures get into the provincial art galleries and here was my chance to find out. Forgive me, Miss Deverell, if I seemed to you to be rude. It must have been such a very expensive picture and so soon will be worth nothing. I regretted the waste of money."

"Esmé!" said Nora. Her voice sounded automatically shocked, as if he had scandalised her many times in the past and now her reactions were only formal.

"I must ask your advice in future," Angel said. She turned away from Esmé and fidgeted with the china on the tray in front of her.

"Yes, do," he said seriously. "It would give me great pleasure."

"Esmé is a painter himself, you know," said Lord Norley, glad that the awkwardness was passing off so well.

"I *see*," Angel said softly.

"Such horrible pictures! Barmaids and jockeys, barges in the fog, back-streets in the pouring rain, slag heaps . . . the seamy side of life. . . ."

"And allotments," Nora said spitefully. "Don't forget the allotments, Uncle, with all the horrid little tool-sheds and rubbish-heaps."

"And cemeteries," Esmé said cheerfully. "I am particularly fond of my cemeteries."

This imperviousness to criticism—even about painting which sounded to her as unpromising as could be—astonished Angel. Mischievousness made Hermione lean forward and say: "May I tell you that I know and admire your work, Mr. Howe-Nevinson? It is a great privilege to meet you." She smiled engagingly and let her eyes rest on him.

"Good God," Theo prayed. "Don't let *her* go down on her knees."

"Thank you," Esmé murmured faintly. "So kind!"

He knew that Hermione was lying, and why; and was amused for her sake that his sister and Angel reacted with indignation, as she had obviously intended. He was sorry that her satisfaction had to be so private. He would have been glad to share it and to find out why even such a little triumph was necessary to her.

"Well, there now," said Lord Norley, in a comfortable voice. He was full of such vague phrases. Chairman of so many committees, he carried everywhere with him the conviction that conflict hindered, even in private life. Lack of agreement held back the agenda. Any dissent, in a drawing-room as elsewhere, filled him with the anguished thought that he would not be able to leave on time, to hurry back to his hobbies. Acquisitiveness he had inherited; his father had simply acquired money and had handed on so much of it that the urge to collect could run, in his son, into more varied channels, to the tracking-down of lustre jugs, Greek coins, old prints and maps of Norley, butterflies, birds' eggs, Oriental Spode. When he turned from the sunlight of these pleasures, people seemed only insubstantial; his niece and nephew, for instance. He was always kind to human beings, in the manner of a man who does not like dogs but would not countenance any cruelty to one. He gave them his time and some of his attention. Restless shadows, they moved before him. He handed them prizes, counted their votes, raised his hat to them in the street, dined with them, attended their funerals. He thought it right that they should claim some of his time, as on this afternoon, so that he should not spend the whole of his life indulging in his own pleasures; but they meant very little to him; he understood the smallest part of what they said, and all the finer shades of meaning in their conversation eluded him.

"*When* have you seen any of Esmé's pictures?" Nora asked Hermione.

"Oh, I never can remember dates."

"I really meant 'where'?"

"Well, he *did* have that exhibition I arranged for him in Bond Street," said Lord Norley, telling Hermione, although, he did not realise it, exactly what she wanted to know.

"It was delightful," she murmured.

"As far as I could see, no one ever went to it," Nora said,

90

leaning back in her chair again, defeated.

"How kind of you to arrange it for him, Lord Norley," Angel said.

"No, no, the least I could do. Always pleased to help. His own parents—my poor sister Carrie—passed on, you know."

He turned to have a little chat about widowhood with Mrs Deverell, who lost her head and began to describe her own long struggle to make ends meet and pay for her daughter's school fees.

"Mother, will you have some more tea?" Angel said in a clear, loud voice. The words seemed to freeze in crossing the room and broke with a brittle commotion in Mrs Deverell's head. She started and stared and shook her head. Theo came to her with a dish of sponge-cakes and stood by her, smilingly, soothingly, as she ducked down her head and snatched at a cake she did not want, but she was glad to have him there, screening her.

"Would you ever come to see my paintings?" Esmé asked Angel as they were leaving. "Although, of course, you would not like them. I expect you would say that when there is so much ugliness in the world, why add more to it, wilfully. But I have forestalled you and said it first, so now you will have to think of something else."

"If I come," she reminded him.

"If you come."

He left it at that and turned away to speak to her mother.

"*When* shall I come?" Angel asked him, just as he was going—it seemed to her that it might be for ever.

"Nora shall write to you," he said. He followed his sister out of the house, humming a little tune.

At dinner, Hermione suggested that Theo should take Angel for a drive in the De Dion Bouton. "Mrs Deverell and I will be quite happy here chatting. I will lend you my dust-coat and veil and goggles, and if you go as soon as dinner is over you will have plenty of time before dark."

Angel had never been in a motor-car before. She was dressed up and helped to her seat, and Hermione and Mrs

Deverell came out to the gravelled sweep and waved goodbye. There was an air of gaiety about the occasion. Hermione looked forward to an interesting tête-à-tête with Mrs Deverell and Mrs Deverell felt suddenly free of constraint.

Perched up as high as the dusty hedges, Angel felt giddy and nervous. The landscape looked bilious through the green mica goggles; the breeze flapped the veil against her mouth. Theo had put on a cape and a cap with ear-flaps and was unrecognisable except for his beard. By the water-tower, where there were some old cottages, children in pinafores stopped their play, leant on their hoops and stared as the car went by.

The hedgerows were creamy-green with cow-parsley, buzzing with flies which rose up from horse-droppings. The sky looked quite thundery and the elm-trees heavy with darkness until Angel lifted her goggles for a moment's reassurance and saw the cloudless blue and the fields of buttercups bright in the sunset.

"I don't know where we are going," Theo shouted. "We will let the motor take us where she will."

Angel had no idea where she was. Although they were near to her home, she had no sense of location: her walks were always aimless and left no impression on her, except to remind her vaguely of mud in one direction and a bull to beware of in another.

"Are you enjoying this, or disliking it very much?" Theo asked.

"I feel very happy."

There was a strange ring of enthusiasm in her voice, and he would have turned to look at her if he had dared to take his eyes from the narrow, twisting road. The drive exactly suited something in her mood; she liked the sensation of being borne along, relaxed, secure behind her veil and isolated by the noise and, because of it, freed from the difficulties of conversation, left to her own thoughts.

"It was a dramatic compliment Miss Howe-Nevinson paid you," Theo said after a while. "I am glad when writers have such compensations for all their pains and setbacks." For himself, he could not imagine a worse punishment than to have someone pay such embarrassing homage; but he knew that Angel had taken it differently and as it was meant. "He—the brother—was handsome," he added.

"In a girlish way," Angel said pettishly.

He let her drift back into her day-dreaming. He guessed where her thoughts were, for he had overheard her desperate words: "*When* shall I come?" as Esmé had turned to go, and knew that she must have been hard-pressed to bring herself to say them. She was bound to fall in love some time or other, he thought. But I hope no harm comes of it. He could not imagine any brightness or ease ahead of her. Her sternness, the rigorousness of her working days, her pursuit of fame, had made her inflexible: she was eccentric, implacable, self-absorbed. Love, which calls for compliance, resilience, lavishness, would be a shock to her spirit, an upset to the rhythm of her days. She would never achieve it, he was sure. For all the love in her books, it would be beyond her in her life. He said: "If we go off to the left, we shall find our way back to the main road. It will be in the homewards direction and we can be back before the light goes."

She would have liked to drive on for ever, peacefully, jolting along in the warm air until it grew dark. The great brass lamps would be lit, drawing pale moths out of the blackness, bringing one tree forward after another, shining on closed flowers, on owls sitting on posts and cats' eyes among the tall grasses.

On their right, mist was gathering over a wooded valley. A chalky, rutted lane went off at a sharp angle to the road, descended steeply through the interlacing branches. A signpost, tilted a little downhill, was painted with the words "To Paradise House Only." Angel turned her head sharply, looked over Theo's shoulder, steadying herself with a hand on the door as she raised herself to see farther—but there was nothing to be seen except the tops of trees; not a glinting window or a chimney-stack. It was all submerged, embowered, like the castle of the Sleeping Beauty. She swayed against Theo and clutched at his arm to save herself falling forward from her seat.

"A lovely view," he said, turning his head briefly. "Paradise House," he read. "An enchanting name."

She said nothing. It was a strange moment for her: the shock of recognition, finding that the house was real, had some location. Before, it had seemed to her like heaven—situated nowhere. She had only half believed in her Aunt's stories of being taken by the carrier the seven miles to Norley: whether the house lay south or north of the town she had never wondered. She would—if she had known—have avoided going in its direction; yet this evening's discovery had done no harm; the evening itself seemed outside time and on the fringe of magic; the house, smothered in leaves, unseen, was safe in her imagination, as it had been since her childhood.

She took off the goggles, loosened her veil and let the cooling air blow softly about her. When they reached home, it was still light, but candles were burning in the drawing-room. They could see the flames all wavering one way in the draught from the open window. Hermione was playing the piano. Aunt Lottie, who had seen claret being decanted for dinner, and had gone off in a huff to her sister's bedroom, where she had spent the evening mending some lace and eating her dinner from a tray, had now come downstairs. Angel—and she was too exhausted from emotion to be annoyed—could see her sitting by the window, nodding her head in time to the music. At the sound of their arrival she had turned to glance at them and then, as if to imply that they, and all motor cars, too, were insignificant, she turned back again to her enjoyment of Schumann.

Theo went round to open Angel's door and hand her down. She swayed a little, as if she had stepped out of a boat and felt the ground unsteady. She smiled, untied the veil and took off her hat, loth to go indoors; then she said again what she had said earlier in the evening: "I feel very happy."

He thought that at that moment, in this unusual mood of

94

gentleness, she looked lovely; but he remembered Hermione's warnings and was careful not to say so.

"Oh, such an evening!" Hermione whispered when they went to bed. "All day, apparently, the aunt has been concealed here, but as soon as you'd gone, she came out. She is a lady's-maid. I could tell that at once—her lace collar was so good, though darned, so obviously one of her perquisites. Now, Angel is no Angel to *her*. She disapproved of the novels and has a very proper sense of shame about them. The girl has turned out badly and that is all there is to it. And they had such hopes for her, thought how proud of her they would be, she and her sister. 'I *am* proud of her, Lottie,' Mrs D. said, but in such a trembling and defiant voice. Well, Lottie wouldn't take a penny from her, from Angel. She told me this when Mrs Deverell had gone out of the room to fetch some candles she was too afraid to ring for. I should doubt if a penny had ever been offered, shouldn't you? One of these days she *may* have to take one, because things have gone from bad to worse with her employer—though she can still, it seems, give away her old lace. The poor lady is recently widowed and cannot keep up the place—the glories of its past! You should have heard. There is talk of her going to live with her married daughter at—where was it? Somewhere like Leamington Spa. Yes, I am sure it was Leamington Spa. The question is Will Aunt Lottie be asked to go too? She's been with her Madam since they were both eighteen, she said. She even went on her honeymoon with her, if you please. Madam would never manage to face Leamington Spa without *her* in attendance. But do they realise that? Ah, we've had it all the time you were away, and I have entered into a state of anxiety about it myself. I long to know what happens. As soon as she heard you coming into the drive, she altered. She said: 'Don't mention any of this to my niece, if you please'." Suddenly, waspish: "You will never guess the name of Madam's daughter."

"No?"

"Angelica. As Madam does everything right, naturally the name she chose for her daughter was the best there could be, so it was all settled when Mrs Deverell had a daughter, too. And guess the name of Madam's house! It is so fairy-tale, so unlikely, that Leamington Spa will be a terrible come-down."

"Camelot Towers," he suggested, yawning.

"No. Paradise House."

"How very strange," he said.

The summer went by and Angel heard nothing of Esmé. Lord Norley was in Scotland, she was told when she telephoned his house, trying to establish some contact, however indirect. Her mood of gentleness ebbed away and she grew morose with frustration. She felt that she dared not hope that she would ever meet him again, and yet there was not a single hour of the day when such hopes did not disturb her. She strove to recreate him for herself, and cursed her memory for keeping no more of their meeting than a few sentences. She went over and over the catalogue of his features, trying, without success, to reassemble them into his likeness. He was rude to me, she would tell herself: I never want to see him again: and then would be filled with cold and bitter longing. If she could have back her moments with him, she thought, she could do better with them; not waste so many, as she had, in looking at other people and listening to them.

Her work failed her. She had reached a desperate, claustrophobic stage of being imprisoned halfway in a novel: there was too much behind her for her to retreat and not a glimmer of light ahead. She sat for hours without writing, staring at the last few words on the page, seeing no significance in them. Her characters fell into frozen poses, speech died on their lips: they had sat at a banquet for weeks and she had not the power to bring them to their feet again.

She made an excuse to go to see Theo simply because she needed to communicate with someone and there was no one else. He was surprised when he read her letter asking if she could come to him for advice about her writing. To make such a request was not in her nature, and he was apprehensive. Advice had always been the last thing she had wanted and the last thing a sensible person would have offered her. Willie Brace had predicted that her fire would burn out as suddenly as it had blazed. "Then we shall have her on our hands; we shall have the trying business of watching her refusing to admit the magic's gone, blaming everybody but herself that she can't any longer cast the spell." Theo wondered if he was about to be proved right.

Angel got ready for her visit to London in better spirits. There was something vehement about her clothes and her bearing as she climbed the stairs to Theo's office. She was in a more positive frame of mind than she had been for months; the journey and the change of scene had turned her thoughts outwards, away from the frenzied impotency she had suffered so long. But in spite of this, Theo thought that she looked strained, and he remembered his partner's premonition.

At first, she was so pleased to be with him again that she began her usual badgering about her sales and his inadequacy in promoting them. She made him have figures turned up and analysed, and was amazed and indignant that he did not carry them in his head. Then, as he turned to put away some papers, she saw him glance at his watch and at once her hectoring ceased. I cannot go back home without any help from him, she thought. In a panic, she foresaw the end of her journey, her return to the same dreaded state as before. She had not visualised anything beyond her visit to Theo, and now she realised that it must soon come to an end. When he enquired about her new novel, she shook her head despairingly.

"It only drags along," she said, as if it were some despicable thing whose progress was not her responsibility. A bad attitude, Theo thought gloomily. "The ending seems to have nothing to do with the beginning and there is such dullness in between."

"Perhaps you need a holiday. You've worked very hard— a novel a year is something formidable to keep up."

97

"A holiday wouldn't do any good, or make any difference. I should have to take myself with me."

"And what is so very wrong in that?" He tried to sound robust, but the change in her disconcerted him.

"It is myself I need a holiday from," she said.

"Writers often feel that their work is stale, but the mood passes."

To hear from him what she had perhaps come all the way to London to say herself, alarmed her. The sound of the word "stale" plucked at her nerves; from superstition she denied it.

"No, I am only dissatisfied with myself for doing the same thing over and over again. I want this novel to be very great and quite different from all I have done before, so I feel an extra anxiety, perhaps. I think I shall rewrite it, move it right out of its present-day setting and have it all take place in ancient Greece."

Theo was startled and horrified at the idea of such a transference; he wondered what she would do without her lords and ladies, could imagine the state of her scholarship and also the fiendish gloating of the critics.

"That is what I came to ask your advice about," she said. She leaned back in her chair and rearranged her marabout stole about her shoulders.

"Present day society is so much your forte," Theo said carefully. Heaven knew she made enough mistakes with that. "And can any characters which fit so well into that, be lifted bodily from it and planted down two or three thousand years back?"

"Human nature never changes."

"In some essentials it may not, but there must be a great deal other than essentials in a novel—customs, fashion, manners, the fabric of day-to-day existence. . . ."

"I can read up what I don't know," she said. "From other books."

"It will take a great deal of reading to give you more than a superficial feeling for the times."

"Then I will do a great deal of reading," she said calmly.

"But to what purpose?" he asked in dismay. "For what advantage?"

"I see you are quite set against the idea."

"You asked for my advice and I can only give it. What I say is, take a holiday. Go away somewhere exciting. Forget all about your novel. When you come back, you will feel quite different about it, the staleness will have gone. . . ."

"There *is* no staleness. . . ."

"Well, the dissatisfactions will have dissolved. You will see that it is a very good novel after all."

She shook her head.

"You were determined about it before you came."

This was not true. In the train, the vague idea had settled in her mind. She had closed her eyes and imagined a sunlit world of dazzling marble and diaphanous draperies: it was like a picture by Lord Leighton, one of her favourite painters. She saw the Edwardian banquet at which her characters had all gone drowsy with dullness, changed suddenly into a Greek frieze: it became busy again, with slaves pouring out wine, bearing in great baskets of figs, playing lutes. Lord Rawley could be given some such name as Demetrios or Telemachos, and the heroine changed from Emmelina into Persephone. The plot could remain the same, or be improved. Emmelina's scandalous liaison with her father's bailiff made a less powerful situation to her now: to fall in love with a slave would be quite a startling way of losing her reputation. The conifers of Surrey began to change into silvery olive-groves.

The whole idea had been little more than a game she had played in the train and she had quite forgotten it until the moment when she had to try to capture Theo's attention, give him some reason for her visit, and drag him away from the attractions of that word "stale"; for say it and it will become so, she felt, as lonely people do.

"I must warn you that your public won't like the change," Theo said. He knew that she liked such phrases as 'your public' and he used them often. "They always want 'the mixture as before'."

99

"They won't know," said Angel. "I mean to publish the book under another name. Then we shall see what the critics have to say. It will be amusing—when they have finished praising it—to say that it was I who wrote it, the ignoramus they have so long despised, the writer of gibberish and balder-dash and all the other complimentary words they have used."

"I beg of you . . ." Theo began.

"No, I am quite determined on it."

"I know . . . I have so often seen . . . that tricks are not for-given. The people who believe in you will lose their confidence and feel themselves fooled. You must be straightforward."

"I shan't be the first author to have changed her name."

"I most strongly advise . . ."

She shook her head, smiled in an exasperating way, blew gently on her marabout stole, watching it flutter.

"You are teasing me," he suggested helplessly.

"I never tease people."

They sat in silence for a moment or two, then Theo pushed aside a pile of papers with a gesture of impatience. "Do you always have your own way?" he asked her.

She lifted her head and looked at him. Her eyes were full of sadness. "Nearly always," she said.

"If I can help you . . ." he began desperately.

She stood up and was smoothing her gloves. She frowned.

"About your holiday . . ." he said.

"I shan't have a holiday." She thought: Esmé might write to me; his sister might ask me to go to see his paintings and I should not be there.

He followed her downstairs, glancing dejectedly at his partner's office-door. "How is your mother?" he asked as he took her hand to say goodbye.

"My Aunt says that she seems unwell and is losing weight. But there is no earthly reason why she should not be in the best of health," Angel said indignantly. "She has everything she wants and nothing to do all day. Goodbye, and thank you for giving me your time and advice."

"It was a great privilege," said Theo.

Angel continued to ignore her mother's condition, her lack of appetite and her listlessness. That autumn, Aunt Lottie went to live at Leamington Spa, and all of her pleasure and relief at being chosen to accompany Madam was spoiled by her anxiety at leaving her sister.

Still restlessly discontented, Angel began to take long walks in the afternoons—to turn over in her mind, she believed, the next few pages to be written: but in that she deluded herself; for in the damp autumn woods nothing of Ancient Greece came to her. Novels were no longer games that she made up in her head as a part of day-dreaming. Her day-dreaming lay in a different direction now, and it was of Esmé she thought on those long walks; the idea of Esmé, rather; for she was forgetting fast, against her will, what he had looked like and how his voice had sounded.

She bought a great dog to keep her company on these walks. He—Sultan, she called him—would crash on ahead of her through the undergrowth, nosing the ground, as clumsy as Caliban, missing all of the wild life about him, yet bewildered by intimations of living creatures near him too quick for him to see; of a feinting, teasing proximity; a camouflaged watchfulness; derisive scamperings. Sometimes he came back to Angel for reassurance, his tongue flapping as he panted towards her. She was all of his life: when she was not with him, he slept. He was docile and cowardly and sycophantic.

Then one afternoon his bewilderment and lack of self-respect and fearfulness broke in a frenzy of destruction. Goaded for so long, despised by swift, shifting creatures in the grass, by pheasants going up in a clamour under his very nose, unnerved as he was and disconcerted, he rounded suddenly on his environment, decided to try his strength once and for all. A Yorkshire terrier ran yapping from a gateway and Sultan pulled up, hesitating and trembling, before he leapt upon the terrier and set his great jaws at its throat.

Angel was afraid. At first she could do nothing; then, like her dog, she smothered her fear in fury, ran forward and began to lash his back with the lead she was carrying. At this, Sultan lost all control; he shook the terrier until its yelping stopped: then he backed away from his victim, puzzled that its resistance was over. As its mistress came running to the gate, she cried out in horror at the violence of the scene—the great slavering dog and the demented-looking woman with the leash in her hand. Sultan turned aside, slinking close to the hedgerow, his bloodshot eyes wary, slobber dropping from the corners of his mouth. He started and cringed at every sound and was ready to snarl again if it would help him. Dusty and bloody, the terrier lay dead.

"You should keep your dog indoors if you cannot control him," Angel said coldly.

For a moment, she thought that the distracted woman was going to run forward and strike her and she stepped back a pace. Grief at the sight of the dead animal overcame violent anger; tears incapacitated the woman. "I can't touch him," she sobbed. "I know he's dead. The great brute has killed him and I can't pick him up."

"Can't you call a gardener?"

"Yes, and I can call the police as well."

"Your dog attacked mine, you know."

"Attacked! This poor little thing? And you were hitting them, urging the beast on, the worst thing you could do. I saw you as I came down the drive. I called to you and you wouldn't listen."

Sultan browsed warily in a ditch full of fallen leaves.

"If I can reimburse you in any way, you must let me know," said Angel. She glanced down at the watch that was pinned to her breast and looked as if she were going to hurry away.

"I know who you are," the woman said quickly. "I know perfectly well, and you are as insolent and ungracious as I have always heard. My husband shall speak to the police."

"Then I will discuss it with them. I dislike conversations with hysterical women."

She called to Sultan and he crept towards her. She could feel the woman's outraged indignation, the silence in which one abusive threat after another was rejected as unworthy until it seemed that there *were* no words for the occasion: she half-expected physical violence—a stone thrown after her, perhaps—and she trembled as she walked on, trying not to quicken her pace.

In her agitation, she took a wrong turning, and she was exhausted when she at last reached home. A bicycle was propped against the front wall of the house, and she remembered that she had promised to see a reporter from the Norley newspaper and was an hour late for the interview.

When she opened the drawing-room door, she was astonished to see her mother sitting there with a blotchy-faced young man who was studying a photograph of Angel at the age of six months, a photograph Angel herself had for long meant to destroy. The baby was sitting upon a lumpy fur rug, the wrinkled soles of her bare feet enormous and out-of-focus.

"Her eyes weren't really crossed like that," Mrs Deverell was saying. "She must have had the wind."

She was flushed and chatty and did not seem in the least dismayed when Angel asked for the photograph and tore it in two and only then turned to the young man to apologise— in the manner of one doing him a great favour—for being late.

He had scrambled to his feet in a frightened way and now said that something or other had been a pleasure. He is dreadfully unpresentable, Angel thought, and in the middle of what he was saying she went to the fireplace, and pulled the bell-rope.

Sultan ranged about the room as if it were all different now or he thought it should be: yet he had not established his status after all, for Angel had not spoken to him on the walk home and he was unsure of what his act of ferocity had meant or what it boded for him. He ignored Mrs Deverell and began to sniff at the young man's boots, then to lick his hands. The young man put his hands in his pockets.

"Twining," he said in a startled way, answering Angel's request for his name. "Desmond Twining."

"Sultan has scratched his leg," said Mrs Deverell.

"Yes. Mr Twining, before you go, I will give you a report for your newspaper of an incident that took place this afternoon. You can print it with a few comments I will add for you on dog-owners who let their vicious pets loose to roam the roads and savage other dogs."

"Oh, dear," he murmured timidly, wiping slobber off his trousers with his handkerchief, apologetically, as if it were his fault it was there. "I don't think it would be in my department." He looked gloomily at the notebook which lay on the sofa beside his bicycle-clips. There was not a stroke of shorthand in it yet; more than an hour was wasted, except for the facts about her early life that he had gathered from her mother's conversation. These he was fast forgetting, and he longed to open his notebook and jot them down before it was too late; but all the paraphernalia of tea were brought in and he had as much as he could do to manage his tea-cup and get rid of the fringe of cress between his lips as he ate a sandwich. Mrs Deverell, who suddenly looked ill and extinguished, sipped a little of her tea and hurried from the room.

"Anything my mother said to you before I came," Angel told him, "must be forgotten or ignored. She is unwell, you know, and falls into strange inaccuracies." She had never before acknowledged her mother's ill-health and did so now only to suit herself. "What you want for your purpose, I can tell you. I think that I know by now what the public expects of me. Will you have another sandwich?"

He pushed the last of the cress between his lips and leant forward. One without any greenery would be easier, he thought, choosing another sandwich. Then he took up his notebook and opened it discreetly, leaving it on the sofa beside him so that he could jot things down though hardly seeming to.

"You were born in Norley," he began. "Of course, that we all know."

"But do we?" Angel asked with false sweetness. "If you know that, it is more than I have been able to establish myself. My infancy seems to have been wrapped in mystery. Brought

104

to Norley at a very young age I certainly was; but from where, I cannot discover. My mother's reticence hides some old grief and I would not, for that reason, question her, or ask about my father, whom I never saw."

She leaned back in her chair, turning her hands one way and another, to display them to herself, catching the firelight in her rings. The young man was quite flabbergasted, as he afterwards told his editor. Was she confessing, almost boasting, of her own illegitimacy? His uncle had gone to the Volunteer Road Schools with her father, Ernie Deverell, and there was a faded photograph of him, knicker-bockered and waxen-faced, in a group taken in the asphalt playground. Mr Twining had intended to mention this connection, and it was on account of it that he had been chosen for the assignment. "A little common ground may set the ball rolling," the Editor had said, and his phrase, which had sounded vague enough at the time, now seemed a preposterous assumption. Clutching at a sunnier interpretation of her words, Mr Twining asked: "He died, then, when you were a child?"

"Perhaps," said Angel. "Or perhaps later: or not at all."

While he was trying to sort this out, he took a bite from his sandwich. It was crab, he thought, or some sort of paste made with crab: whatever it was, it was quite bad.

"There was someone in those early days," said Angel, safely eating chocolate cake, "who was spoken of as my father; a timid, harmless little man, I have gathered. I am sure I should have found him an excellent person, though of little account. Indeed, I owe him my name. But it is all so fraught with mystery, as I have said, and I think that in your little piece about me you may hint at mystery; but, for my mother's sake, leave it at hints. For myself, I feel beyond such pettifogging conventions."

Nauseated and alarmed, he at last managed, by not breathing, to wrench down what was in his mouth. Then he drank some tea and felt waves of heat spreading over him; his heart thumped; he was so flurried that tears pricked his eyes. And all this time had passed and there was nothing in his notebook and not a thing in his head, either, but hints of mystery which could never be of any use.

"I sometimes wonder if I have foreign blood," she was saying. He agreed that this might be so, for her black hair and her white skin were just what he always imagined when he heard the words "foreign woman." She looked magnificent in her dress of peacock blue, with her long hands lying in her lap; the dog, now mercifully sleeping, at her feet.

"You began writing . . . when?" he asked, poising his pencil above the notebook and trying to forget the potted crab.

"I was fifteen." She suddenly remembered the appalling circumstances in which she had begun her first novel—the mingled shame and indignation from which she had fled to writing; the pretence of illness and the boredom and loneliness she had endured. It seemed long, long ago. I could not live it again, she thought. All is changed for the better and I have escaped.

He had something to write down at last, and she then gave him a list of her novels and their dates, which he could have looked up for himself in the Public Library.

"Won't you have a piece of this chocolate cake, Mr Tinsel? It *is* Tinsel, isn't it?"

"No, Twining, I'm afraid. I haven't quite finished my sandwich," he said, glancing at it.

"You mustn't let our discussion put you off your tea."

"No." He stopped breathing, took another bite, swallowed desperately and prayed, Oh, please God, let it stay down. Make it stay down.

Sultan stirred, stretched himself and passed wind. Angel reached out and took a bunch of peacock's feathers from a vase and began to fan the air.

"Have you any message?" Mr Twining asked earnestly. "A summing-up, perhaps, of what you strove to express in your novels, a word, a piece of philosophy for our readers?" He had rehearsed this question as he toiled up to Alderhurst on his bicycle and was glad to bring it out now to cover his embarrassment.

"I should like to call for a wider understanding of spirit, a tolerance and breadth, a deeper response to life," Angel said placidly, still fanning.

Sultan now lumbered over to Mr Twining and began to sniff at his plate. "May I? Is it allowed?" Mr Twining held up the sandwich, coyly questioning, his face quite radiantly hopeful.

"Oh, he is so spoilt," said Angel, and leant forward and took a sandwich from the dish and dropped it in front of Sultan. "Let him have one to himself: not steal bits of yours."

Sultan pushed it with his nose, sniffed at it and turned away.

"Quite spoilt," Angel said again and, as she bent down to pick up the sandwich, Mr Twining put the rest of his into his jacket pocket.

"Oh, but it isn't . . ." Angel began. She opened the sandwich and examined it. "I don't think it is good, not fresh: no, it is *poisonous*. How *dare* they?" She threw it on the fire in disgust. "*You* had one," she said accusingly, turning to stare at Mr Twining.

"*Mine* was all right."

"It couldn't have been. They were all made from the same nauseous stuff." She went to the bell and rang it.

"I didn't notice anything—"

"You must have done. You just sat there and let me offer one to Sultan, knowing that it might poison him. I think that is abusing my hospitality, Mr Twining. I could never have forgiven you if anything had happened to poor Sultan. He has had enough to try him for one day. Bessie!" she said to the maid when she came in, "are you trying to poison me?"

"No, madam."

"The sandwiches are bad."

"I'm sure I didn't know, Madam."

"Please take them away before any more harm is done. It is a lucky thing that I felt too tired to eat. Now, Mr Twining, if you have anything more to ask me, will you do so."

He had thought of one or two questions and read these out to her. She listed her hobbies haphazardly: playing the harp

107

and learning Hebrew, astrology, painting on silk, needlework. "These I made," she said, patting one of the black satin cushions embroidered with sequined peacocks. She had bought them at a bazaar she had opened.

"And what future plans have you—for writing, I mean?"

"Many; but I shall not divulge them. The literary world is ever watchful: there are many who would rather steal a march than follow an example."

"May I quote that?" he asked, not quite certain of her implication.

"As you please," she said indifferently.

"And your favourite authors?" he asked, coming to his last question rather abruptly, for he was afraid that he was going to be sick.

She considered other writers aloofly. "Shakespeare," she said reluctantly. "Perhaps Goethe," she added, using a pronunciation of her own.

"And of modern authors?" he asked, unaware of the danger in which he placed himself.

Her face had a strange quality of darkening in anger, the blood gathering under the white skin made her look as if a shadow had fallen over her: then the sun suddenly came out.

"Only one comes to my mind," she said. "One of my own sex."

"Marie Corelli?" he suggested confidently.

"Marie Corelli? I am afraid that in my opinion Miss Corelli writes like a Sunday-school teacher. I meant Miss Nora Howe-Nevinson, Lord Norley's niece. A very great poetess who can proudly take her place with Tennyson and Shelley."

Mr Twining jotted this down in haste; then he took up his bicycle clips; apologised for his visit and bade her goodbye. As soon as he had turned the bend in the drive and was out of sight of the house he dismounted and was sick in the laurel bushes.

When Mrs Deverell had crept away at tea-time, she went to

bed, and was not to get up from it again. Angel visited her before dinner and paced about the bedroom in annoyance, full of curt inquiries and the resentment that the idea of other people's illnesses bred in her.

"Is there nothing you want, then?"

"Nothing, thank you, dear."

"There are idle hands downstairs if you do. You need only ring."

"No, nothing, thank you."

"In what *way* do you feel ill."

"Just the pain I've had lately—in my chest, you know."

"You must have eaten something." In Angel's mind all illnesses were the fault of those who suffered them—some negligence or over-indulgence. "By the way, those crab paste sandwiches at tea were quite bad. How they could have made them without vomiting, I don't know."

"Oh dear, not now," Mrs Deverell implored.

"Sultan might have been poisoned. Do you think you ought to see a doctor?"

"No, I shall be better in the morning. I think it is only indigestion—but such a pain in my chest."

"Probably wind."

"I daresay."

"You ought to take more care of what you eat."

"I get so hungry and then after a few mouthfuls I can't manage any more."

"It sounds like a clear case of wind to me," said Angel. "I'll get back to work, if you are sure there is nothing you want."

"I just wish Lottie would come," Mrs Deverell whispered, and two tears ran out of the corners of her eyes on to the pillow.

"Well, she'll be here for two days after Christmas."

Christmas seemed far away, and Mrs Deverell thought that she would never have the strength to reach it. When Angel left her, she gave herself up to the tears and they flowed away from her face until her cheeks were sore. She was crying for her sister and for the safety of the old days amongst her neighbours. She had no feeling of security in her daughter's home, and in the night she dreamed that she was running all the way to Leamington Spa: time was short and she kept losing her way. The next day she suffered an internal haemorrhage. A telegram was sent to her sister; but the journey from Leamington took too long, and Mrs Deverell died without seeing her.

"There is a Miss Howe-Nevinson," said Bessie.

Six months after her mother's death, Angel was still in black from throat to toes. She had a purple suède-covered book of poems in her hand when Nora entered.

"Oh, my dearest Miss Deverell. Only yesterday, on my return from Italy, did I hear of your tragic loss. I could not keep myself away from you, not even to write to you first. My impulsiveness is a by-word among my friends. Oh, it seems such a short time that we were all happy together in this room. Say that I didn't do wrong in coming to you."

She had put forward her cheek to be kissed and a tear sat prettily on her veil. Then she drew back and looked with anxiety at Angel. So much black accentuated her thinness and her pallor. She had discovered this accidentally, standing before her long looking-glass on the funeral afternoon, and, pleased with what she saw, decided to prolong her mourning, a convention she would otherwise despise. One of the Volunteer Street practices, she would have called it, contemptuously.

"You are ill," Nora announced. "And tired. And, for all my inquiries since I came back, I hear nothing of that overdue novel, and, to be quite frank, we are all exasperated by the delay."

"I am beset by servant-troubles," said Angel. "At the moment, there is only Bessie, whom you saw, and some mumbling old crone who does the rough, as she calls it, and leaves pails of dirty water about in dark corners and dusters on the stairs. If I complain, she tosses her head and threatens to go."

"Our greatest novelist bothered with buckets of water and having to lower her eyes from far horizons to dusters left on staircases!"

"My mother managed the servants," Angel said. Managed them badly, she had often told her, but the truth was that after her death, no one but Bessie would stay. Mrs Deverell's timidity with them had aroused their protectiveness, not their scorn: now that she was dead they saw no reason for enduring Angel's tantrums and her exacting ways. Only Bessie stayed on. She had gone into service from an orphanage. She knew nothing of any other world and was afraid to make changes; to live in the shadow of tyranny she thought an inevitable pattern of life.

"You shall talk to me of your mother," Nora insisted. "I am not one of those selfish people who avoid such conversations. I know what it is to be bereaved, and how much one suffers from having one's lost loved ones banished, their names unspoken. It is a conspiracy among people who hope to avoid the trouble of giving comfort; and I will not be part of it. You shall talk and talk as long as you please and I shall listen."

"But there is nothing to say."

"Ah, there must not be reserve between *us*. You yourself have made us seem kindred spirits. Moreover, undeservedly, you have elevated me almost to your own sphere. I think you know what I am speaking of." She opened her bead-work bag and took out a strip of newspaper. "When I returned from Florence, there was a note from my uncle and this cutting from the *Norley Advertiser*. I read it at first unbelievingly. It did not seem possible to me that you could have read and praised my poor verse; that you should place it where you did was incomprehensible. When I could grasp that it was true, I felt as if the gates of heaven had opened wide."

So my flattery brought her, Angel thought. Not my mother's death or anything else but the charm of being over-praised. She had cast out her silken thread and months later had drawn back her prey.

111

This was unjust to Nora, who had a great capacity for worship—especially adoration of her own sex—and would have returned to Angel whatever had happened.

"I am staying with my uncle," she said. "Tomorrow, I shall come over again. . . . I am sure that you will not deny me that pleasure . . . and I shall settle down to make myself useful to you. How better can I serve literature than to banish you from the domestic sphere? I shall shoo you off to your study and turn the key, too, if you are intransigent. Then, with Bessie's help—not to say the old crone's—I shall find plenty of ways of being busy. I can mend gloves and iron veils and make cakes and preserve gooseberries. Don't look round, wondering where you can find gooseberries in April—they are only metaphorical. I might even rise to great heights and engage a cook for you, some wonderful treasure, who will be a constant memorial to me."

Angel gave one of her rare smiles. So much coming my way, she thought. She bided her time, then asked after Esmé. What was he in her mind now, she often wondered? Little more than a beautiful face haunting her, a memory of elegance and vivacity. The memory was an obsession, though: she was staked on it, she felt.

Nora bent her head and looked vexed. With her head at that angle, her moustache showed dark on her lip. She had a censorious air.

"Perhaps I *can* speak to you of him," she said. "To my uncle I may not any more. His name must not be mentioned under that roof. There was trouble in Italy and I will not try to hide it from you—you have such a wide acceptance of life. Esmé was always unstable. He was expelled from school for laying wagers. We have no money of our own, you know, or none worth speaking of, and *shall* have nothing but what comes to us from my uncle. Yet knowing that, knowing how sternly self-disciplined my uncle is, how ruthless in denying himself worldly pleasure when his duty is to be done—in the face of that puritanism, my brother deliberately flaunts his waywardness. Useless for me to warn him that he was putting our futures in jeopardy, and useless for me to try to hide his misdemeanours—there have been so many."

Angel was silent. Nora's words cascaded over her so fast that she could not snatch any meaning from them. She tried to compose her expression into one of polite, impersonal concern. Nora saw her moisten her lips before at last she asked: "What kind of misdemeanours?"

"His adventures with his unsuitable friends, gambling, extravagance. When our parents died, I kept house for him. There were parties in his studio which woke the neighbourhood. I would lie in bed, shrinking from the thought of the morning when I must face the servants. I stayed at home, rather than meet people who might complain or think that I was party to it all, or tradesmen who might be offensive in speech as they often were in their letters—about money, usually. My brother is attractive to women, but quite heedless and forgetful. Perhaps he did not realise what hopes he encouraged, but while he was being charming—and he often contrives to be both rude and charming at the same time—I would watch with a feeling of doom. I knew that I should be asked to pick up the fragments when whichever poor girl it was at the moment found herself cast aside. It was I who would endure the scenes and tears and the protestations. They would come to me and beg me to intercede or arrange meetings; so few had any pride or modesty where he was concerned. And they would never believe that there was nothing I could do to help. I was often blamed for the collapse of their romantic hopes: they saw me as a possessive sister who would not give up her place in his home. They could not bring themselves to find any inadequacy in themselves, and thought that I had taken away from them what in fact they had never had."

"And your brother remained free?"

"Until Italy," said Nora. She felt a sense of drama as she said these two words. A curtain should have fallen here, with an interval of conjecture and anticipation before Act Three began. Instead, she marked the pause by standing up and going over to the window. She sighed and seemed full of impatience and anxiety. "Oh, the narcissi!" she exclaimed. "Drifts of them, like the milky way. You should always have white flowers around you."

Angel did not quite like the sound of this: she was suspicious and exasperated by the interruption. She ignored the narcissi and wondered how she could return to Esmé. After seeing Nora's contempt for the lack of pride in her brother's "poor girls", she was careful not to betray herself. Both astutely waited. Then Nora gave in and said: "Italy was my uncle's Christmas gift to us—to Esmé and me. He is a kindly old man, you know, and so dogged in trying to see the best in all of us. He has always been dogged about Esmé's wretched painting—unless he thought that it was something to keep him out of mischief . . . and if he thought that, he was sadly wrong—so Esmé must go to Florence to see the paintings there, and I should go with him—a part of the project which didn't suit him at all. It was a ludicrous situation. *I* went to all the Art Galleries and the Churches and Esmé was never to be found. I shall never forget those months—the loneliness, the premonitions of disaster, the sense of evil and betrayal. He came back to England before me: without a word to me, he simply disappeared. I was left to manage the journey alone; but, before I could set out on it, I had to face the hideous squalor he had left behind."

Staking a great deal, but shrewd as to the risk she ran, Angel said: "I am sure this is painful for you to speak of, and you may regret having told me. Would you not rather banish it altogether from your mind?"

She was right in thinking that Nora was too far gone in histrionics to pull herself up, and rather cynically watched her come back to the sofa and sink down on it, quite given over to the horror of her recollections.

"He had most of our money and took it with him, or had to give it up before he went. I was searching his room for some clue to his disappearance when the storm broke over me. The padrone was banging on the door, requesting a word with me. A word! Thousands of words, rather. I had discovered the letter Esmé had left for me, but I had no chance to read it: the words—Italian I could not keep up with—overwhelmed me. I must pay money, I began to understand—very much money; not just money for our rooms, but money for his daughter. I could hear her wailing somewhere along the corridor—one of those pretty Italian girls, but she would grow fat in middle age, like her mother. I had been nervous for some time about her provocative ways, with Esmé: she waited on us at meal-times and managed somehow to be both servile and challenging. It was quite disgusting. I said 'Si, si', over and over again, but the dreadful man went on ranting, waving his arms above his head, clasping his hands on his heart, letting his eyes fill up with tears—oh, I never want to go to the Opera again. In the end, he went away, but I knew that at any moment he might come back. I had promised the money, without any idea of how to get it. Then I opened Esmé's letter and realised that I must. It was the feeblest note, just to say that he had been obliged to go, that he could not wait to warn me; the girl had made accusations against him, which were true—more or less true, he wrote; but that is too difficult to understand—and she had spoken of the gravity of her condition and his responsibility for it, which he could not disprove. Oh, I felt soiled and cheapened—I was forced to haggle with shopkeepers over my mother's jewellery and take much less for it than I could ever have believed. I was virtually held prisoner; wherever I went, trying to raise money, I could see the girl's young brother following me at a distance. Their family honour was set at a certain price and Esmé had not paid it. When I was at last able to, they were quite gay again and chirruped about me like birds as I packed my trunk to come away. They had the audacity to send their kind regards to my brother.''

Angel admired such insolence and laughed with delight. "And he?" she asked. "Esmé?"

"He was not at home when I arrived. He had gone to my uncle's, the servant said. So I packed again and I, too, came to my uncle's. Esmé has not been there. After my account of Italy, I think he will never go there."

"You told your uncle?" Angel asked in astonishment.

"Yes. He is the head of our family, I suppose—the only responsible person I can turn to."

"But will not that ruin Esmé's chances with him?"

"I have no doubt that it will."

Angel stared at her. "I have no brother; but if I had, I could never behave to him in such a way."

"My dear Miss Deverell, we cannot all be as saintly as you, or so blessed with family-feeling." Angel's glance became suspicious. "I have lost a great deal by championing Esmé and I cannot afford to lose any more. I am also disgusted and ashamed. I want no reminders of him in my life. I should be content to settle down without him from now on."

"It is a very lonely thing, to have a house to oneself," Angel said.

"I must try to make something of it, and when it becomes what you say it will, I shall beg of your company for an hour or two."

"You may come when you wish," said Angel, and she went to the garden door to let in Sultan who was barking there. "I ask one thing of you: do not cut yourself off entirely from your brother, who may one day need you desperately."

"It is he who has cut himself off from me."

"Yes, at the moment that is true. Sit, Sultan! I am afraid his paws are dirty."

Nora thought that he had been rolling in cow-dung, for he stank abominably. "The darling!" she said, patting his head quickly.

"Yes, he is so affectionate. Your brother, you know, is only like so many other high-spirited young men, a little spoilt by women, because of his romantic looks." She was sure that she sounded detached and analytical, but there was no one to hear except Nora, who was not deceived.

"Your Lord Chalfont in *The Butterflies* reminds me of Esmé," she said.

116

"I think that I can understand such men although I am a woman."

Nora tried to push Sultan's muddy paw from her knee and he snarled and put back his ears.

"Are you nervous with dogs?" Angel asked coldly. "Come here, Sultan. You are not appreciated." She seemed not to notice that the dog ignored her. "You should never let an animal know if you are afraid. It is asking for them to be unfriendly. They smell your fear, you know."

"He is such a beauty, but I didn't want to force my attentions on him. Some dogs hate to be fussed."

"He loves it."

Nora decided that it was time to go. "I will remember what you said about Esmé. You are so wise and I—at the moment—so full of indignations and precipitate judgments. Perhaps I shall come to your way of thinking, in time. And, meanwhile, may I come again tomorrow? I want to make myself useful to you, to relieve you of some of your burdens, to serve literature in my humble way."

"I shall look forward to it." Angel thought that Nora had expressed herself very properly. They kissed and said goodbye.

The next day Nora returned. She was to stay for more than thirty years and to make herself useful untiringly, relieving Angel of many burdens. Her service to literature was more difficult to assess. She gave up writing her own poetry to devote herself to her friend. The sacrifice helped to lengthen the list of Angel's books. The poetry was lost and the novels were gained, and posterity was as indifferent as it could be about both.

117

PART 3

i

"GILBRIGHT & BRACE, Estate Agents," Willie Brace said, giving the letter back to his partner. "Now what is she up to?"

But Theo could not say. He had borne much from Angel in fourteen years and had lost his capacity for wonderment.

"Why us?" asked Willie. "Why not ask Mr Fortnum or Mr Mason who dispatch the caviare, or Monsieur Worth who gives in to her about her hideous clothes? They must make just as much money from her as we do."

"Why come to London at all?" Theo said unhappily. "I prefer her safely in the country."

"Who wouldn't? Unless the people who live in the country?"

"Where do we begin?" Theo looked at the letter again.

"Take your hat and go out this instant—she says we are to answer by return of post. Somewhere central. You don't want her near St John's Wood and I don't want her anywhere near Chelsea. I like the idea of Kensington Gore. You should be able to find something commodious and inexpensive. Inexpensive!! I am sure her last half-yearly cheque from us was three thousand pounds."

"Oh, dear, commodious and inexpensive!"

"Once she gets to London, she may like it and stay for ever. Then she will come and *say* her complaints instead of writing them. I expect she is going to start a 'salon'. I visualise pilgrims winding across the Park. No, perhaps something more Sibylline—consultations with the oracle of Kensington Gore."

"She says that she is coming to sit for her portrait," said Theo, looking at the letter again. Willie did not seem convinced. He went off humming 'Angels ever bright and fair'. He had been doing so for fourteen years and Theo had never thought it amusing.

In one thing Nora had failed Angel: she had not managed to conjure up her brother. She had been housekeeper, secretary, lady-in-waiting, and had delighted in the daily immolation and her place in the background. Her capacity to serve and adore was deeply exploited: the maternal feelings which sometimes unsettled her were useful in calming Angel's tantrums.

The obsession with Esmé—with someone whom Angel had seen only for an hour—she found difficult to understand. She knew that he was unusually handsome, more attractive to women than was good for him, and that Angel seemed to meet only elderly men and certainly no one who was worthy of her, but the perplexity remained. The long conversations they had about Esmé were tinged with the resentment and jealousy Nora had suffered since they were children and he was the more fussed-over one. The blacker the picture she painted, the more infatuated Angel became, and sometimes, like a child, she would ask for a particular story again.

Esmé, since Italy, remained elusive. The house that he and Nora had shared, their parents' house, was sold. He was abroad at the time, had been in France, his bank-manager could tell Nora, but had moved on again, perhaps to Italy.

"Italy has fatal attractions for him," Nora was rather pleased to tell Angel. She wished that she would give up the steady concentration on Esmé and face his true and ineradicable nature once and for all. They had continued for years in the absurd pretence that Angel only inquired about him from politeness to his sister and listened to the reminiscences for Nora's part in them. "He won't have me to rescue him this time," Nora said.

I wish that I could rescue him, thought Angel. I would go to the ends of the earth. I would take the vile girl by her shoulders and shake her till she cried for mercy. The word 'Italy' had violent associations for her: she thought only of scheming, predatory women—their brief beauty soon to be overlaid by grossness—lying in wait to ensnare such men as Esmé, to captivate then corrupt, to bleed heartlessly and reject.

At last, word came from Lord Norley that Esmé was in London. He had rented a studio in Chelsea; or would do so as soon as his uncle could advance some money. He seemed to take it for granted that his escapade in Italy was forgotten. Whether or not Lord Norley complied Nora could not discover. "He will never ask *me* for money," she said. "With Mamma's jewellery—all I had to remind me of her—lying there in that shop-window in Florence."

"It may be sold by now," Angel said absent-mindedly. She was beginning to fret. She had worked hard and needed a holiday, she said, and she even conceded that Nora had worked hard as well. A card inviting her to a garden-party at Buckingham Palace came at a useful time, and she wrote immediately to her publishers, as she had written to them over the years for all the commissions she could not trouble herself to place elsewhere—reference-books, silks for their wives to run about the shops matching with braid, or pots of Hymettus honey from Soho—to find, for the summer months, commodious, airy and inexpensive furnished apartments, with a park nearby where Sultan might be exercised.

Hermione found the apartments, as she had always found the matching braid. "It is part of my homage," she told Theo, then added: "I know that they will not do, as the braid never did, even when it matched to the most exact degree. The rooms won't be lofty enough; Lulworth Gardens not a good enough address and the grass plot in the middle too shady for Sultan, or too exposed. She will say that Number Seven is unlucky and will notice at once, as I did, that the caretaker smells of drink and damp is coming through the wallpaper at the top of the stairs."

But Angel, in her tremulous excitement to move in, noticed nothing. Nora was alarmed to see how hopeful she was, how childishly excited as she went from room to room, examining the furniture and making plans.

"We are so lucky to find anything at all at this time of the year," she said.

Nora would not have dreamt of saying that it was Hermione who had found the apartments for them. Her astonishment at hearing Angel call herself lucky only added to her apprehensions.

The plane-trees at the edges of the pavement and in the Gardens in the middle of the Square were dark with their summer leaves. From the windows of the first-floor drawing-room their branches were all that could be seen; they kept out the sun and tinged all the gilt furniture with green. Angel loved the shabbiness of the room, its pale colours and faded wallpaper. The yellow satin on the chair-backs had split and frayed, looking-glasses needed to be re-silvered, portraits were blackened and often indistinguishable and she adopted them all as ancestors. The worn elegance was what she had been unable to achieve at Alderhurst, where everything, though costly and comfortable, was new. "I always feel," Hermione had once told Theo, "that things will still have the prices marked on them. I imagine I am in Harrods, looking rather incuriously about me and wondering all the time 'How much?'"

Since her mother's death, Angel's fanciful inventions about the past had grown daily more outrageous. There was no one to inhibit her or to remind her of the truth. On the day of Mrs Deverell's funeral she had had her last-but-one glimpse of Aunt Lottie, who returned to the house after the service for long enough to accuse Angel of neglecting her mother and keeping Lottie herself in ignorance of her illness: she added a few frank comments on her niece's disposition and then left.

At first, Nora had believed Angel's stories about her origin, her early days, the mystery surrounding her birth, the hints of foreign, even noble blood; old splendours, romantic depriva-tions. Then even grander notions followed and contradicted the first, and Nora, with her heart full of love and understanding, saw the lies as a pathetic necessity, an ingredient of genius, a part of the make-believe world from which the novels came. She could not afford to be disillusioned about Angel and she managed not to be. She had given up her home for her, her way of life, her verse-writing; she was staked upon her: the only threat was her own self-criticism. She learnt to sense the outrageous lies before they were spoken, and became tensed ready to deflect them, quickly leaving the room or becoming deaf; or else absorbing them, with compassion and her poet's vision.

Lulworth Gardens was full of new hazards, and some of Angel's stories about her lately-acquired portrait-ancestors were disastrously comic; her sense of period was so vague and her notions of country-life wonderfully sensational. A handsome young man among dogs was going off to shoot his rival in a duel, not pheasants among the autumn foliage; a lady in an Empire gown had been a mistress of Charles the Second. No one dared to question any of it. It isn't untruthful, Nora told herself. Or, if it is untruthful, then so are 'Romeo & Juliet' and 'Hamlet'. She was sure that Shakespeare had not confined his inventiveness to his plays. To spread it over everyday life was a sign of an exuberant genius. Exuberant Angel really was, that summer. She went to the Royal Garden Party in violet satin and ostrich-feathers with purple-dyed chinchilla on her shoulders; amethysts encrusted her corsage and mauve orchids were sewn all over her skirt where they quickly wilted. Glances of astonishment she interpreted as admiration.

As soon as the Garden Party was over, she turned to the real business which had brought her to London, and when she had discovered Esmé's whereabouts from Lord Norley, she set out to find him. It was one of the few excursions on which Nora was not asked to accompany her. She was going, she said, to inquire about an evening-wrap at Reville's; she made coy references to Nora's approaching birthday and there were hints of secrets and surprises. To everyone but Nora, Angel was at her most embarrassing when she was trying to be arch;

her smile became monstrously roguish; she was altogether too
tall and bony for such behaviour.

Nora was not surprised to see her set off on foot with Sultan.
She liked walking in London, and often on sunny evenings
made Nora accompany her, sometimes to the Albert Memorial,
which she admired very much, or for a stroll along the
embankment. Sultan went everywhere with her, even to the
dressmaker's where he had once lifted his leg over a roll
of silk which was propped against the wall and quite ruined
it.

It was a long walk to Chelsea. When, after an hour, Angel
came to the street where Esmé was living, she was much
stared at. Children dancing round a barrel-organ backed away
at the sight of Sultan, who ambled along beside her, panting
and dribbling. It was a hot, sunless afternoon: the pavements
were gritty and dust swirled down from the end of the road
where the river ran by. The street was busy, noisy with
children, the din of the barrel-organ and a rag-and-bone man
shouting. Barges hooted on the river. A boy shovelled horse-
droppings into a hand-cart, and when he moved on the
pigeons came back and settled in the middle of the road. As
Angel walked away from the embankment, the long street
became quieter; the houses were now sometimes semi-
detached, with flights of steps leading into heavy porches, and
they stood back in small gardens with a few trees. When she
came towards this end of the street it was quiet; there were no
children playing there until suddenly they came running down
the road at the sight of a watering-cart. They leapt into the
edges of the arching spray and jumped over the water which
began to criss-cross down the gutters, trickling dust-coated to
the drains.

The sudden noise of the children brought Esmé to a window,
one of the two highest at the front of the house. He pushed
down the sash as far as it would go, and at the sound Angel
looked up. He saw her standing at the open gate with a slip
of paper in her hand. Her dog had already entered the garden
and was roaming about among some clumps of ferns. Esmé

123

knew that he had been seen and that it was too late to step back from the window as he instinctively wanted to: they made signs of recognition, she with a regal movement of her large hat and he by raising his hand in a tentative and even half-placating way. Then he turned from the window and looked at the untidy room. There was no time to put it to rights; his landlady was already directing Angel up the stairs and he went out to the landing to receive her. He could hear her harsh voice with its ugly accent, and remembered it so well from their one meeting. Sultan came first, scratching on the linoleum-covered stairs; then Angel appeared on the half-landing and smiled up at him—a remarkable smile, he thought: he could not know that it was compounded of relief after long waiting, and triumph, and love.

Her first impression of the room dismayed her, for she had never seen such squalor. No one in Volunteer Street would have left a greasy newspaper lying on the table. There were even a few dried-up chips left in it. That the nephew of a Lord—as she thought of Esmé—should do so, troubled her. He gave her a chair near the window and pulled on a velvet jacket over his shirt; then, as an additional gesture of hospitality and courtesy, he screwed up the crumpled newspaper and threw it under the table.

"I remembered you at once," he said.

This seemed to her an extraordinarily superfluous remark, and she ignored it and called to Sultan to come away from sniffing at the newspaper on the floor. "Remains of my luncheon," said Esmé without shame. It was years since Angel had eaten fish-and-chips from a shop, and she had sometimes secretly longed to do so again, but she gave a vague look of not understanding what he had said.

"Some days I have faggots for a change," he added, trying to enlighten her. "Do tell me, how is my sister?"

"Nora is very happy and well," said Angel, implying that she took the credit for this. "We are in London for the season."

"Oh, me, too," said Esmé.

"You once told me that you would show me your paintings. I have heard so much about them since then, from Nora and from my publisher's wife, that I am interested to see them for myself. You rebuked me for giving that Watts to the Norley Art Gallery, and I wonder if I could make amends by having them put one of yours alongside it."

"They wouldn't," said Esmé.

Her smile was enough to tell him that they would do as she bade them.

"You wouldn't like my sort of painting."

She glanced round the room. Canvases were stacked facing the wall, some cobwebbed *to* the wall; the easel was empty; there were some brushes in a jar, and a dinner-plate which had been used as a palette was now heaped with cigarette-ends.

In one of her novels she had described an artist's studio, a room with a great north light, a daïs, a divan draped with brocades and velvets; there were lay figures and costly properties, exotic furnishings, leopard-skin rugs, burning incense, a profound silence. Esmé's room, with its two dusty windows, the street-voices coming through them, the torn linoleum on the floor, was a shock to her which she was finding difficult to overcome.

He went to the canvases and stooped over them secretly; a large spider ran out as he disturbed them. One or two he pulled out and studied intently with surprise or slow recognition. He muttered and pottered about for a while as if he had forgotten her.

"Well, it is all *your* idea," he said at last, and he turned the easel towards her and set up a canvas on it. It was the picture of a level-crossing in a blurring, rainy dusk in winter. He saw her look of consternation, then her wary glance at him. Her reaction was masked until she could be sure that he was not fooling her. At first, she could think of no other reason for his having shown her the picture, so utterly unlovely it seemed to her. It depressed her as if she were really waiting there for those gates to open, one drizzling late-November afternoon. Then she saw that Esmé himself was looking at the painting without any signs of malice or disgust, and she wondered what she could say to him. Without waiting for her comments, he exchanged the level-crossing for some allotments. After some others, he put up a canvas brilliant with blue sea and sky, violet-shadowed white walls, red flowers. Just as, at last, she felt able to exclaim with pleasure, he took the canvas from the easel and said impatiently: "Italy. I can't paint in Italy. Too much colour."

At the hated name, she said shakily: "Too banal a subject for *your* gift. I prefer you in England."

"Oh, I am so glad. I couldn't imagine you liking all my dull colours, as Nora used to call them. So few people do."

"I do," she said firmly. "The level-crossing is my favourite."

"And so it is mine. I showed it to you first to create a good impression."

"I should like to buy it, if it is for sale."

Esmé appeared to be considering this suggestion, which had never come up before. She watched him, going over his features as if she were learning them by heart, putting right what her memory had failed her in, dwelling in triumph on what she had remembered. He looked older; his face, beneath the eyes and about the mouth, was puffier than it had been— the marks of suffering, she thought, not of debauchery, as Nora would have had it. His delicacy and ease of movement, the frail look his too-long hair gave to him, touched her heart as desperately as at her first meeting with him.

He considered the picture. "Yes, I should think it is for sale," he said doubtfully. He was not ready for her to ask its price, and was deeply worried that when she did he might say too much or too little.

"Would you consider three hundred pounds?" she asked, with thoughts of the Watts in her mind.

He had been wondering if he dared mention twenty pounds, and could not hide his stupefaction.

"Framed, of course," she said smoothly, seeing his expression.

He was suspicious of the situation. At his first sight of her, he had known that he must keep his head and make no commitments; he had determined to be agreeable while she was there, get rid of her as soon as he could and then find some other lodgings. Her visit boded no good for him, he was sure, and if she was not acting as a spy for his uncle, she had come as an emissary from Nora, with tedious reminders of money owing. Her offer disrupted his smoothness of manner and upset his plans; he admired her for her strategy, but he mistrusted her even more deeply. He was not to be bought or caught.

"You can have it for two-fifty for all your kindness to Nora," he said carelessly, managing to have his back to her as he said it. "But, of course, I should like that to be *entre nous*." This was true, but not in its implication.

She had upset him to such an extent that he began to think it possible that she knew something about painting after all, and that there was perhaps more in his own than other people had been able to find. He stood back to look at the level-crossing, trying to take himself by surprise, but he could not.

He said: "I am glad you didn't like the Italian one."

"There is something about Italy which brings out the vulgarity I suppose we all possess in some degree," she said loftily; and he wondered if Nora had told her what an enormous fund of vulgarity had been discovered in himself, and decided that she had told it all.

"As a matter of fact, I have miserable associations in my mind with the very name of Italy," she added truthfully. "The unhappiest thoughts . . . . I try to avoid speaking of the place." She was not only seeking to protect herself from the pains of jealousy, but had shrewdly guessed that to banish Italy from their conversations would suit Esmé very well, too, and give him confidence in their relationship.

"What are your fees for portrait-painting?" she asked, when she had seen relief settle on his face. He is not very good at hiding his feelings, she thought.

127

"I don't paint them."

"I wanted you to paint me."

This time, he did manage to hide his feelings; his look of wistful regret was entirely feigned.

"It is a different genre," he said. "If I were ever to attempt it, it would not be at your expense, you know. I would not have the world scorning me for blurring *your* features."

"Some might think them better blurred," she said playfully.

He looked at her gravely and wondered if there were not a monstrous authority of composition and of colour in the picture she made, sitting against the window, upright, her dog at her feet, the tawny animal against her snuff-coloured gown, the black hair built out to support her winged hat, one long white hand ungloved, encumbered with rings.

His landlady knocked on the door. In order to find out what was going on, she had been obliged to bring two cups of tea. "Such a hot day," she said. "I had the kettle on for myself. Does Doggie want a drink?"

"He can share mine," said Angel. Her look saw the woman to the door. She wanted Esmé to herself and no interruptions.

"You have beautiful eyes," he said, considering her as he sipped his tea. At once, she bent down, set her saucer on the floor and filled it for Sultan. When this was done, she seemed at a loss. She was still flushed from the effects of his compliment and he thought that she could not have had many in her life. He was rather touched, and felt some power over her for the first time.

Before she left, the portrait was a settled project, and sittings had been arranged. She had been anxious to start them the very next day, but Esmé had the cheque to cash, then canvas to buy before he could begin.

"Then will you come to Lulworth Gardens tomorrow and see Nora and look through my wardrobe to choose what I shall wear for the portrait?"

"I want you in that dress, with the dog lying against it."

"Is Sultan to be painted, too?" she asked excitedly. She was pleased at that, though disappointed that she was to wear so drab a dress. She had imagined herself in one of her low-cut evening gowns or with white lace to the throat, or even in what she confusedly thought of as a 'Grecian toga'; but she recognised certain obstinacies in him and having won a victory or two she decided to bide her time about her clothes.

It was growing late and she stood up and tugged Sultan to his feet. She had such a store of treasures to go over on the long walk back, and felt a superstitious fear that too much delight was coming to her too quickly.

When she had gone, Esmé was able to examine the cheque that she had left on the table. She had made it out for three hundred pounds. He took another look at the painting of the level-crossing, then tucked it under his arm and ran downstairs, out into the cool, watered street, on his way to the framer's.

His landlady went up to collect the cups and have a glance round his room. The cheque had now blown on to the floor and she picked it up and examined it with astonished interest.

Nora and Esmé were reunited without enthusiasm on either side. She felt secure in Angel's protection: at least while she was there there could not be talk of Italy, therefore no mention would be made of his desertion, of money owing or jewellery sold. Forewarned as she had been by Angel, Nora could only be terse and sarcastic in a general way. "Is it really Esmé? I had quite forgotten what you looked like. And we are none of us any younger, I suppose."

He glanced at her and agreed. He almost dared to say that her greying moustache gave her a military, a more distinguished air: his private smile at the thought he had withheld ruffled her as much.

"In all these years, I daresay nobody mended your clothes," she added. As Angel moved uneasily as if about to interrupt, Nora said: "If you give me that jacket and Miss Deverell will excuse your shirt-sleeves, I will mend the pocket here and now."

She hoped that she humiliated him by making him hand it over and display a crumpled shirt, stained in the armpits; then she hurried from the room, leaving him, she felt sure, to Angel's disdain.

But Angel was capable only of tenderness, which, far more than admiration and worship, can withstand a great deal: it can absorb disillusion and the day-by-day revelation of frailty, without becoming poisoned or attenuated. He sensed that he had begun well with her. At a time of exhaustion in him, she had appeared prophetically. He had so often taken the initiative in life, without the reserves to back up his actions; he was always withdrawing from absurd forays he should never have set out on. The emotions he had inspired in other people were not peaceful ones, adoration turned into contempt, desire to jealous anger. His life had been hindered by his beauty and the adventures it had permitted him. The adventures had all been expensive of money and of fortitude, and were beginning to be expensive of the beauty itself. Waking sometimes at the ebbing, hopeless time of dawn, he felt afraid of what he was doing with his life and where the life was leading him—my one life, he would think. He would shoulder dread away, turn over and wait for sleep. When the light was strong and the day really there at last, he felt his gay and careless self again. But since coming back to London, he had begun to suffer the moods of dejection during the day as well. In the late afternoons, the horror would swing over him, wherever he was, as long as he was alone. He would long for distraction. On the afternoon of Angel's visit, he had gone eagerly to the window when he heard the children come shouting down the street; it might be something to watch, a thief on the run, a procession, a dog-fight. Angel, looking up and seeing him at the window, could not know how well she had timed her call. Bored with sexual escapades, he began to take pleasure in an entirely new experience: an interest in personality. He had never found women mysterious, but monotonously, blatantly predatory. When he was with Angel, he was obliged to guess; one mystery led to another, she was endlessly involved in them. He began to wonder about her when she was not there, and was surprised to find himself doing so. That out-of-sight was out-of-mind with him had been a common plaint of other women he had known. He discovered that his speculations about Angel passed the time pleasantly. He had scarcely a friend in the world, had been so often obliged to cover his tracks, to make new beginnings; and escape from a woman entailed escape from her milieu; even where he might have done, he had not bothered to keep friendships in repair.

And Angel had brought him back to painting. She had reminded him of it—for his inertia had been as bad as that; he had forgotten it and ceased to trouble, except in the small hours when he remembered that it was the best part of his life.

When Nora had heard that he was to paint Angel's portrait, she was incredulous. "He can't paint at all, let alone a likeness, let alone a likeness of you. He will make you all grey and wretched as he makes everything. Oh, he won't do justice to you, dearest Angelica. I shall feel the shame of it. And it was I who always wanted your portrait painted. Oh, I believe I put the idea into your head. But I had thought of Orpen, perhaps, or Sargent. I had never, never dreamed of Esmé. And to put Sultan in it—he will never sit still, he isn't the sort of dog to *be* in a portrait. You should have a lap-dog or one of those white hounds. Sultan, darling that he is, just doesn't go with evening dress."

"I am not wearing evening dress."

"But people always do in portraits. There, you see, that is Esmé, beginning as he means to go on, insisting on being different from other people. Quite fatal, that attitude has always been."

"Your brother and I are in accord over it."

She could not bring herself to say his name.

Esmé had had his way about the snuff-coloured dress. To Angel, it became associated with fearful delights and nervous tension, and she would begin to tremble as she put it on.

"You must help me to find out how to do this," Esmé said as he put her in the chair by the window and arranged her hand against her skirt. When he touched her, her heart swerved.

They were alone in the room, except for Sultan ranging dejectedly about. Esmé's thoughts were all bent on her; for an hour he was hers. She had never allowed herself to hope for such delight.

"Now your eyes—so!" He put his finger-tip under her chin and tilted her face towards him. A wonderful great bony nose, he thought. I shall make something of that. "Beautiful eyes," he said, as he had said once before. Then he remembered that the compliment had been too much for her, and he turned away quickly so that she could hide her embarrassment.

He had borrowed a pastry-board from his landlady and now pinned some paper to it and sat down to make some sketches.

"Do talk if you want to," he told her, but for once she could find nothing to say. Her lips were tight together and her eyes fixed pleadingly upon him. She listened to the faint, tinny scratching of charcoal on the paper, longed to see what he was making of her, braced herself to face dismay. Sometimes he muttered an irrelevant remark, threw it at her, as a means of communicating with her, or to tide them over the long silence. His narrowed eyes stared at, seemed to devour her features; yet not see her. She faced him gallantly, stared back as steadily as she could, feeling not there, in a way outraged; for how could he look and yet so monstrously ignore her?

His head swayed as if to some music she could not hear— dreamily, hypnotically. She was exhausted and wanted to cry out or to cry. Just when she could bear no more, the dream fell from him, his face changed, he looked at her quite differently, at *her* again, and smiled. Then he put the board against a wall, so that she could not see the drawing, and fetched a bottle of madeira from a cupboard. He filled a chipped wine-glass and handed it to her and poured some into a tea-cup for himself. The cup was white and had a gilt clover-leaf on it and reminded her of the living-room above the shop in Volunteer Street.

Love had laid her waste, so that she was open to other emotions, too, from which she once had been immune. Compassion followed the picture of her old home into her mind: furiously she rejected it, it still had a reality which other places since those days had not. She felt a moment's pity for her mother, glimpsed how much more real it must have been for her, who had lived longer in it and left it at a later age. How imperfectly it must have prepared her for her life at Alderhurst. Angel could see how *that* must have lacked substance: in the end, she had lost the strength of application to the task.

She moved restlessly, as if to evade these thoughts. The wine branched delicately in her, the faintest warmth. I want love only, she thought. Not the other intrusions.

Love and the wine transformed her. As she was *now* he wanted to paint her—not staring him out in defiance, as she had done; but glowing, uncertain, with thoughts crowding in, some of them, he could tell, disturbing.

"I read one of your books," he said, sounding as if it were rather a surprising thing to do.

She blinked, jolted by what he had said. She always supposed that everyone had read all of her books and had them nearly by heart, that they thought about them endlessly and waited impatiently for the next one to appear.

"My landlady lent it to me. I sat up until I had finished it." She drank her wine.

So it is only compliments about her looks which devastate her, he thought.

"It was called *Aspasia*."

She acknowledged this to be the title of one of her novels.

He brought the bottle of wine to refill her glass and standing close to her as he poured it out, said: "I think that the secret of your power over people is that you communicate with yourself, not with your readers." Then he moved away.

She reflected on this, sipped her wine, frowned, then swung on him a look of astonishment. She wondered how he had divined the truth of those trance-like experiences, the act of will by which she projected herself into another world out of which, when the time came, she emerged physically shaken. There were no readers there in that fever.

"Yes, that is true," she said.

He had thought the novel, with its confusion of Greek and Roman deities, its high-flown language, its extravagance, tiresome in the extreme, and he had only ventured on it from curiosity; but some of the white-heat in which it was created struck back at him from its pages; he could understand how less sophisticated readers would be carried away, beyond criticism of all the inaccuracies and improbabilities.

"You are made to suffer?" he asked, then wished that he had not, dreaded a description of the soul wrestling in the toils of creation; could not bear that, he thought.

She touched her breast. "Here," she said. "The most appalling indigestion. I think I breathe badly when I am writing— hold my breath and let it come in gasps. I feel cramped. Then when I stand up the pain begins—it is all right if I can belch. Why do you laugh?"

"You surprise and delight me," he said. "There are so many questions I find myself asking. I want to know more and more before I begin to paint. For instance, which came first in you— the novels or the loneliness?"

She made no answer.

"You tell me things about yourself—your childhood, your girlhood—but they don't match. I simply cannot piece them together. Something is missing. How am I to paint you if I don't know what it is? What, for instance, happened in Italy?"

"I have never been there."

"But what happened *about* Italy? Was it love? I suppose that it was love. It is always that that makes us unhappy."

"I suffered jealousy," she said, and as she turned her head away from him he saw her throat move as she swallowed.

The portrait progressed, and so did Nora's anxiety. Her birthday, after all Angel's hints and suggestions, had been completely forgotten. The day came and passed without a word to single it out from any other, and she went to bed early, feeling deeply hurt. There was a great deal in her life now to wound her: Esmé had been callous; Angel was more so, but with Angel Nora felt the pains of martyrdom more exquisitely. She brooded over her sufferings with a saintly acceptance of them, added each new one to her hoard and wondered if any woman ever was so wretched. She had no weapon of retaliation save death, and this came continually into her thoughts and dreams. "If I were to die, she would be sorry," or "She would realise how much I do for her, what I protect her from." The life suited her devotional nature and at no time did she ever think of leaving Angel, unless it were to die. She gave up her time gladly, but she did not forget that she had given it up. She had sacrificed her poetry, she would recall; not remembering that her inventiveness had already run out when she had made the sacrifice, or that she was not always attending to Angel and the servants: there were long hours when Angel was writing when Nora found it difficult not to be quite idle.

In Lulworth Gardens, though, Angel wrote not a word. She began to enjoy being well-known and a success, she gave parties and went to them and met a great many people and spent a great deal of money. At large gatherings, she was easily recognised on account of her air of authority and the absurdity of her clothes. At small dinner-parties, she was dull and dominating. If, for a moment, she were not the centre of attention, she fidgeted and exclaimed and interrupted. "Angelica Deverell was here the other evening," some people liked to say, but she was not invited twice. That summer, though, there were enough invitations to fill her days, if not Nora's. In the country, Nora accompanied Angel everywhere: in London she was left at home. Angel did nothing to draw her into the gaiety. She kept her in the background: when she could not, she introduced her to people with a tone of exaggerated kindness. "And this is my very dear friend, Miss Howe-Nevinson." Her way of saying this suggested that Nora was her paid companion and she herself a most liberal and fond employer. "We are like sisters," she would sometimes add. The words had once been Aunt Lottie's when she had spoken of her mistress; but Angel did not remember.

Esmé worked hard, not only at the portrait, but at some more of his interiors of London public-houses. He fell in love over again with those subfusc bars, with their ferns and patterned glass, marble-topped tables, immense hat-stands. When he showed Angel what he had done, she praised him as soon as she recoiled. She was not shown the portrait, but she rehearsed the speech of gratitude with which she would try to smother her indignation. "You are my only ally and support," he told her and made all her duplicity worth-while.

Then one day, she went all the way to Chelsea for a sitting and he was not there. "He didn't say anything," said his landlady. "I will wait," said Angel. She waited for an hour, and then sent a little boy for a cab and went back to Lulworth Gardens. Esmé had gone to Goodwood and forgotten all about her.

"We arranged for you to come on Friday," he said, when she arrived again the next day.

Both of them knew that he was lying.

"Then it was my mistake," said Angel.

In that hour in his room she had studied the unfinished portrait, going to the easel again and again to look at it, but remaining baffled. There were dark sweeps of colour, folds of drapery, her hand with a glove; but her face was a blank; the feeling of not being there she always had when he was painting her, was intensified.

Nora spent her days longing to return to the country. Esmé was a threat to her once more: she imagined him running away with Angel for her money, or running away from her, leaving Nora to bear the consequences. She felt dispossessed and lonely in London; no longer sole confidante and constant companion; and she knew that whatever happened between

Angel and her brother there would be no good in it for herself.

Esmé had lost money at Goodwood and had impinged on a set of people from his past life and been snubbed. When he awoke in the early hours of the next morning, he had comforted himself by thinking of Angel, and had been quite magically soothed and able to fall asleep again.

Each day now, Nora pointed out how the season was over; she could always mention someone who had gone off to Scotland or Cowes or Baden Baden, and urge that Angel should give the grand evening party she had so often spoken of and then they could return to Alderhurst. But Angel made an excuse of business still to be attended to. She was writing nothing and the only claims upon her time were the sittings for her portrait and visits to her dressmaker; she was spending extravagantly on clothes. Willie Brace had been wrong in saying that she would always be haunting them with her complaints. She went there once, near the end of her stay in London, with the extraordinary request that to her next book which they were to publish in the autumn should be added a frontispiece and several coloured plates painted by Esmé.

"So it has happened at last," Theo thought and wondered how he could stave off the suggestion.

"London has agreed with you," he said. She was wearing the most bizarre hat with a Hussar's plume. It added so much to her height that the effect was overwhelming and he wondered how he could ever say no to her demand. He was not able to. He hardly went the right way about it in pointing out all the other occasions when her judgment had been proved wrong. She was especially angry at his mentioning her pseudonymous novel, her trap for the critics that not one of them had fallen into. The plan had failed, as Theo had warned her it would. The sarcasm was as bad as before. "If this is not Miss Angelica Deverell," one reviewer had written, "then Miss Deverell had better look to her laurels. Here is somebody who may exceed her in confusions and absurdities."

"The secret was out before the book," Angel had said accusingly. She said so again now. It was impossible to get anything into her head, Theo decided. He wished that she would have an agent to whom he could talk about practical matters. At the mention of costs she would fly into a rage and ask if she were not the best-selling author he had ever had, and would hint that there were other publishers in London, in that very Square indeed. "Not a hundred miles from here," Aunt Lottie would have said. Before Angel left, Theo had promised to see Esmé to discuss the illustrations.

"Nora will write to Hermione to invite you to my farewell party," Angel said, and left him with two events to dread, instead of one.

The portrait was finished and Angel had expressed her gratitude. Sultan was so realistically presented that she was afraid that she was, too. In the middle of dressing, she would stop to study her face, in the triple glasses drawn together to reflect her profile, sometimes catching a strange glance unexpectedly, wondering all the time if she was what Esmé saw. The portrait lacked exuberance and he had painted her in her darkest clothes against a banal background; the empty window behind her, the bare wall, emphasised the suggestion of loneliness. He had been tempted to scrawl a title upon the blank side of the canvas: 'Study In Solitary Confinement'. Her eyes and the dog's looked mournfully out of the picture; Sultan's dully, hers reflectively. One or two critics, long after, were to note this, but at the time people thought the portrait dreary and tactless and wondered why Esmé had not the wit to modify the arch of her nose, the eccentricity of her clothes and correct her slight astigmatism, and if she would not disguise her own pallor, he, on canvas, might have done so. Nora was openly scornful; no one else dared to say a word; no more commissions for portraits came from it.

Angel, at first shocked, soon grew used, from constant looking, to seeing only what she chose, especially the narrowness of her bare hand with its emerald ring. She would gaze at this detail for a long time each day. One of the lesser ancestors was moved from the wall and Esmé's painting was put there in its place; for a reason she would not give, some silk drapery was hung in front of it, hiding it completely.

"Is it Lent?" Esmé asked when he saw this, and was vigorously shushed and hissed at by his sister.

Plans for the farewell-party made Nora happy again. She had a great deal to do and the knowledge that when it was done they would return to Alderhurst where there would be even more for her to do. The invitations had been going out for weeks, in relays of lessening optimism, beginning with dukes and filling in later with baronets and foreign titles. To have been under the same roof as Angel at some time or another, even if at the other end of a long table or in a distant part of a ballroom, was enough to qualify for an invitation; but it seemed that Nora had been right: London was empty; dukes had gone North for the grouse, marquises had disappeared to Biarritz; one countess had even joined her children at Frinton rather than stay any longer in the deserted capital; there was nobody about. Esmé complicated the situation by reading the list of guests before the invitations were sent and scratching out one name after another. "Don't ask him," and "Leave her out—or me, if you please," was all that he would say.

"Why make London your nest when you have fouled it so?" asked Nora.

In the end, actresses had to be invited and opera-singers and one or two elderly men-of-letters; no critics.

In the evening, Hermione's sharp eyes were everywhere. Angel had ordered a bower to be made of a recess at the head of the stairs and here, among potted hydrangeas, she waited to receive her guests, with Nora placed a little farther back and in a darker dress. Angel was in lilac, so low-cut in front that her top ribs showed in rows.

"Magnificent!" said Esmé, and to Nora's annoyance raised Angel's finger-tips to his lips.

At the sight of him, Theo drifted out of sight behind a

screen of pampas-grass. Later in the evening, when champagne had made them both nonchalant, they spoke to one another.

"Your idea about the illustrations," Esmé began. "Awfully sorry, you know, but it's not in my line."

"Never mind," said Theo gratefully. "Just an idea."

"Very kind."

"Where is your portrait of Miss Deverell?"

"Well may you ask. Stuck in the dining-room and covered with a curtain. Why hang it up at all, if it so displeases?"

He was to discover why. After a string quartette had played, and no one, taking Angel's lead, had attempted to listen, the double doors were opened to the dining-room. A buffet-supper, smothered with smilax, was laid on a long table: a boar's head, a salmon, concoctions of lobster hung about with whiskery prawns, timbales and galantines, all masked with sauces and mayonnaises, or half-masked with aspic.

"How delicious!" said the elderly men-of-letters, edging towards the table as they had learnt to do at many literary receptions. Then Esmé saw Theo coming towards him, looking ruffled and concerned. "You must stop her," he said in a low voice. "A horrible suspicion has come to me from something I overheard your sister say. . . . How could she have encouraged her? Did you know of this? I suppose you did."

"Did I know what?"

"That she is going to unveil her own portrait—here, in front of everyone."

"Good God!"

Esmé looked behind him for escape, not in Angel's direction, where Theo wanted him to go.

"You must put a stop to it."

"I can't get at her."

"Shake your head."

"But she isn't looking."

The music of Strauss faded significantly: there was an expectant hush and the literary men looked up from the array of food rather irritably, wondering what was going to happen. Angel, smiling and happy, faced the room, waiting for absolute silence. Behind a screen of potted palms Esmé and Theo backed away out of sight; they went a little way down the staircase where they could not be seen, and sat there side by side, with their hands over their ears. When they heard the music beginning again, they raised their heads and looked at one another.

"Not 'God Save the King'," said Esmé.

There had been an embarrassed murmuring, someone had begun to clap, then stopped.

"What on earth did she say? I hope no one ever tells me. I shall have something to say to Nora. Nothing would ever make me go back into that room."

"I shall have to, and Hermione will tell me every detail of what happened," said Theo. "She will not have missed a single thing."

"It will be all over London. You see, my sister is in love with her; she has surrendered her judgment to love."

"She is devoted to her, I know. . . ."

"She is in *love* with her," Esmé insisted. They had both drunk too much champagne. "In love. In love," he repeated.

"The sooner she goes back to the country, the better."

"Yes," said Esmé doubtfully. He suddenly felt his indignation go.

"I wish my fondness for her would suspend *my* judgment," Theo said.

"I wish mine would, too."

"I shall have to go back to Hermione. I shall say that I got separated from her in the crush and have been looking for her everywhere."

"I shall say that I got taken short."

Then Esmé stood up and walked carefully down the stairs and out of the front door.

Hermione had scarcely missed Theo. She was spooning up jellied consommé, thinking out her account of the evening for Willie and Elspeth Brace. Food was beginning to soothe embarrassment. The unkinder guests were delighted with the evening. The literary men would dine out on it for weeks.

141

"Delicious," they said again and again, and no one could know what they referred to.

"Was it all right?" Angel asked Theo. "People seem pleased." She had been looking for him and he had kept his eyes on his food as if by doing so he became invisible.

"So good," he said weakly. I mean the soup, he told himself, although it had jellied too much, he thought, and was rubbery. Elaborate food was always a little below par, he decided.

"And what do you think of the portrait?"

"It is too crowded about for me to go to see. I must tell you later."

"Do you know where Esmé is?"

"He seemed rather unwell to me. I believe that he has gone home." He thought, seeing her look of anguish: And I hope that he has not gone for ever.

She had wasted her evening, if he was not there. Oh, make it end! she prayed. She was for ever exhorting some unknown power—not God, but some vague enemy, the one who upset her plans and frustrated her at every turn. Make them all go home! she willed the antagonist. Let it be over!

They returned to Alderhurst without seeing Esmé again. They found the garden full of golden-rod and Michaelmas-daisies and spiders' webs. Nora went happily to work about the house and Angel wandered in the shrubbery with Sultan or explored the new roads which were cutting deeper and deeper into the woods and thickets. Her summer, with its exquisite sense of expectancy, was gone and the expectancy was gone, too. She was overcome by melancholy, tormented by her longing for a tender word. Esmé had answered none of her letters; she wondered if he had gone abroad again. Sometimes she dreamed of him: the dreams had an air of reality which stayed with her all day: they enveloped her; she was incapacitated by the improbabilities they contained, and unable to work or to concentrate on anything that Nora said.

Then Sultan had distemper and died, and she was out of all

control with grief. A few days later, Esmé received a distracted letter, on black-edged paper, begging him to come and comfort her, to stay for a few days and take her mind off her loss. He had ignored her other letters, partly because he was too lazy to reply and partly because her behaviour at her party, so bizarre, so menacing, had made him disinclined to meet her again. But this astonishing letter moved him. He forgot that he had thought her vain, mad, outrée, and began instead to think of her being tender and full of supplications.

He had not wanted to become involved in their household, and out of London she and Nora were also out of his mind: yet he found himself writing a letter of condolence (for no one but he could fully understand, she had assured him) and promising to visit them. He had been pretending for weeks to a persistent young woman he knew that he was always in the country from Friday to Monday, and this time it could be true.

At once Angel seemed to get over her grief. He had dreaded her despondency, not knowing that his letter had put an end to it. She met him at the station in a small pony-trap that she had hastened to buy in order to drive him about the lanes without having any room for Nora to accompany them. Her happiness as they jogged back towards Alderhurst was tinged with triumph.

Nora welcomed him with reserve, but she had obeyed Angel about the food, which was excellent and abundant and suited to masculine tastes: there was a saddle of mutton and wing-ribs of beef, a York ham with Cumberland sauce and a terrine of grouse. After meals in restaurants or faggots and chips carried back to his room, Esmé was delighted by all this and made wistful, as was intended, by the thought of the lost comforts of domesticity.

The house was comfortable, although by Sunday it was beginning to seem claustrophobic to him; he felt the ennui of the week-end guest, defenceless, unable to escape, beset by strange church-bells; restless, overfed, and tired from too much conversation. If he were left alone for a moment, he fell asleep.

On Saturday evening, some neighbours had dined: a professor of Greek, who listened gravely to Angel's descriptions of Athens in the fifth century, two ill-favoured women who were dog-breeders, and a clergyman who seemed to have been invited for no other reason than to be demolished in argument by his hostess. After dinner, they were taken to the shrubbery to see Sultan's grave. The dog-breeders thought they had the very thing to take Angel's mind off her loss. "Not to replace Sultan, or to attempt to do such a thing," one of them said tactfully. "Just to give you something else to think about. The only thing to do. You will grow to love him for his own sake."

"What is he?" Esmé asked.

"A wonderful St Bernard."

"Those dogs that have the brandy," Esmé said wistfully.

"I could never love him as I loved Sultan," said Angel.

"Of course not; of course not." The two ladies nodded and agreed, feeling now that the cheque was almost in their hands.

The next evening, Angel and Esmé set off in the pony-trap to look at the St Bernard. The cheque changed hands and the dog was put in the trap where he looked mournfully about him; his face sagged, seemed dragged down; he sighed and blinked his bloodshot eyes. His name, Czar, was engraved on a brass plate on his wide, studded collar.

"We will send on the pedigree," one of the ladies promised. "We will put it in the post."

"Please don't," said Angel. "I love animals for themselves. Those pieces of paper are meaningless to me."

"Heavens, that house!" said Esmé as they drove away. "The choking smell of animals! And all the cushions covered with hairs."

"I didn't notice," Angel said.

It was a heavy, thundery evening; the sky looked curdled, with loose, watery clouds passing below the sun. Angel drove on, away from Alderhurst. She had a poor sense of direction, but she thought that she remembered coming that way home on the night when Theo had taken her in his motor, and at last she was sure. Ahead of them was a signpost and the steep lane leading down to Paradise House. From the high-road they could look across the tops of the trees in the valley. She drew on the rein and turned off the road at a sharp angle to begin the descent.

I hope not more calls, Esmé thought, and he could not help yawning. The dog swung his head up and gazed at him, without curiosity. "You see, he is quite at home already," Angel said. "And who is the most beautiful dog in all the world, then? Who is my precious darling one? Oh, damnation, there's a great cart stuck right across the road."

"Do we *have* to go down here?" asked Esmé, and yawned again and again until his eyes watered.

Angel did not answer him, but waved her whip at an old man who was unloading logs from the cart into his cottage-garden.

"Will you move your cart," she called out querulously.

"There's no road through," he said, coming up the lane towards her. "I would have to take the cart right down and turn it about."

"Then kindly take it down and turn it about. We want to pass by."

"But, ma'am, there's nothing down there—only Paradise House and that's empty and all overgrown."

Angel shook the reins impatiently, staring ahead of her, until the old man went back to his cart, dratting and spitting, and began to lead his horse down the lane.

"Do we have to go?" Esmé asked again and this time she nodded.

At the bend of the road they were able to pass the cart, and Esmé called out his thanks to the old man as they went by.

"A lovely old face," he said.

"I didn't notice," said Angel.

As they descended the slope into the valley, branches shut out the light and the vegetation was more lush; great ferns edged the rutted, grassy lane and there were leaves of a size she had never seen before. They tunnelled through dark foliage and came at last to a gateway. There was no longer a gate, but two posts and deer carved in stone surmounting them. The drive was mossy and the pony stumbled on rough flints that had broken the surface like the fins of sharks. Fir trees creaked and clashed their branches in the wind: there was a resinous, heavy smell and a continual commotion of rooks overhead.

"I think it is all rather eerie," Esmé said and he hunched up his shoulders and shivered. Eerie, said his echo.

Then the trees parted and they drove into a cobbled space before some stables. They had come by a back entrance and the real drive lay ahead of them, a short avenue of lime-trees whose pale leaves had begun to fall over the tussocky grass. The house stood on a slight rise: a grey, Italianate façade with a broken balustrade. The stone above two of the windows had been blackened as if from a fire, and some of the dusty panes had stars of broken glass.

"Shan't we be very late for dinner?" asked Esmé, as she stepped down from the trap, leading Czar.

"I have wanted to see this house since I was a child."

"But why?"

He followed her towards the entrance. The pony was tugging at the coarse grass where they had left him: there was the peaceful sound of creaking leather and ringing bit. "I used to hear about it from one of my relations," Angel said, as she went on in front. "As a child I was always trying to imagine it."

But how different it was from her dreams and from the house she had described in her first novel. The ashen look of the stone was a great shock to her. It was all built the wrong way about and was not big enough or decorated enough, and there were no peacocks. On the terrace, an urn had toppled over and spilt earth in which groundsel and shepherd's-purse had rooted. In a semi-circle behind the house the high woods were turning yellow. There were snatches of rain in the air and it would soon be dark. Esmé thought disconsolately of his dinner; tomorrow he would be returning to London and the good food would all be over. It was dismal to think of going back to Chelsea, to the scrappy meals and the lonely room. He would have to begin working hard again to get some money, for what he had earned from Angel had been melting away. He had hair-raising stories of his phenomenally bad luck, of fortunes lost by a short head or by his own disastrous second thoughts, or information he should never have listened to. But he had no audience for the stories. He knew much better than to tell them to Angel, and there seemed to be no one else. "You and your everlasting horses," the young girl from the tobacconist's always said, stroking his hair as if he were a child. Ah, yes, he thought, there is the girl from the tobacconist's. And new lessons in evasiveness to learn, or leave the district once and for all.

Shutters were drawn across the downstairs windows, but he could peer in through the letterbox into the hall. It was, as far as he could see, hexagonal, with white panelled walls and some empty niches. "For Ming vases, I daresay," he told Angel.

"Do let me see."

He moved aside so that she could look through the letterbox.

"Those niches," he said. "It could be charming."

One side window was unshuttered, and they could see the whole room, with the oblong patches where pictures had hung on the yellowing walls. The fireplace was carved in a silvery fruit-wood in a high relief with roses and ribbons. There was a rusty basket-grate in which lay a dead bird.

The back of the house was more overgrown than the front, and the brick paths and yards were mossy and silvered with the tracks of slugs. A huge boot-scraper rose above a bed of nettles at the kitchen door. The St Bernard seemed quite impervious, ignoring these surroundings, keeping close to Angel and obeying all she said. "He feels at home already," she said.

"But he hasn't *been* home yet," said Esmé.

"I meant here," she answered.

Someone had forced the lock of the conservatory and they were able to push open the door and go inside.

The long shelves were full of flower-pots with the dead remains of plants all strung together in a network of cobwebs in which moths and flies had been entangled never to get free. A handful of rain hit the glass and there was a far-off sound of thunder.

"Will the pony be all right?" asked Esmé.

"I imagined this—the conservatory—exactly as it is," she said triumphantly.

"With all these skeletons of plants?"

"No, no; but facing this way and at this end of the house."

"It must have been empty a long time."

"They lost their money and had to go away. Then there was a fire. No one knew how—perhaps a tramp who had forced his way in. Two of the rooms were burnt out."

"Who would buy it?" he asked. "So hidden away and low-lying and overhung with trees; so costly to keep up, too."

Angel walked to the end of the conservatory and tried a door, but it was locked.

"I shall," she said.

He was too surprised to answer her.

She had found one living thing there among the flower-pots, a great cactus which had surprisingly survived, gross and bladdery; it looked as if it could keep itself going on its own succulence for years to come. She pinched its fleshy pads with curiosity. Then she smiled and said: "It is just like a dream. When I was a child, I used to make up stories about living in this house. People called them lies, because I sometimes forgot what was real and said things aloud which I would have done better to have kept in my dreams; but I was only willing myself towards the truth. All the same, it seems miraculous to me now that it is going to happen. Nothing shall stop me."

"But so much is to be done. Such repairs and rebuilding. You haven't even seen inside. It might be a hollow shell for all you know of it."

"Yes, it might be," she agreed placidly. Then she said:

"Nobody else wants it, but that doesn't lessen my pleasure. When I was a little girl, I once went to a children's party and there was a Christmas-tree—a huge one, to the ceiling—they never seem so big nowadays. It was covered with presents and after tea they were to be given out to us. Near the top was a fan, one of those rounded, wooden ones, perhaps Japanese. It was black, with a scene of mountains painted on it, in rather frosty-looking paint. All through tea, I couldn't eat for anxiety. I wondered how I could be sure that I should get the fan. Then we sat round on the floor and took numbered tickets from a hat. There were nineteen children and I was number nineteen, so I had the very last choice of all. Oh, you can imagine how despairing I was. The first girl went up and chose a paint-box, but that didn't raise my hopes. There were so many dull things on the tree, like handkerchiefs and money-boxes and bags of sweets. As it went on, this torture, and children chose other things, I only felt more desperate. . . ."

"I can't bear it," Esmé murmured.

" . . . and when it came to two away from my turn, I could hardly breathe and I wondered how I could endure losing when I had come so near. The girl before me went up to the tree and I shut my eyes. 'Number nineteen,' they called out. The fan was still there. I shall never forget that moment. I went up and fetched it, and when I brought it back, a girl next to me whispered: 'Hard luck! It isn't even new'. But I was in the seventh heaven. And now I am, about this house. I know that I shall have it. I am older now and better-off and can control things more, without enduring all that nervous strain."

Esmé had been studying her face while she was talking. He thought: I wish that she would write of things like that, instead of all that dishonest nonsense. "What became of the fan?" he asked.

"I can't remember."

"You know, *I* have sometimes had what I wanted and it hasn't been at all the best thing for me—as no doubt Nora has told you."

"I expect a woman can manage to be more single-minded, not so waylaid by love."

"I don't know about love. It seems a charitable word to use in my case."

"But all of this running away," she said boldly. "Did you never want a wife and a home of your own?"

"Unlike you, I dare not let myself dwell on improbabilities. You know I have no money."

"Other people with very little money seem to marry."

"Perhaps I should be too proud."

"You must learn to make money from your painting, as I have with my pen."

"Nobody believes in my painting but you. I have no faith in it myself."

"Then I will have enough for both of us."

It was growing dark outside; in this dim, aqueous light she could scarcely see his face. He was not trying to look at hers, but bent moodily over the St Bernard, fondling its ears. He seemed sulky and dispirited all of a sudden. Then he raised his head, and when he spoke his voice had managed to gather a new warmth. "It was an exciting story. I hope you get everything you want, always. This house and. . . ." He broke off as if he wondered what else there could be that she could possibly desire.

She turned her back to him, examining the cactus plant again, afraid for herself lest the house, just like another childish toy, was to be the sum of her good luck. When he saw this, he went to her and put his arm along her shoulders and turned her towards him.

"Tell me!"

"I comfort myself with material things," she said in a muffled voice, her long fingers pressed to her brow, covering her eyes. He knew then that she was about to risk everything and say what he himself would now have no need to say.

"What other things do you want?" he asked gently.

"Love." The word came with such a gasp that the St Bernard for the first time looked surprised.

"You have love," Esmé said, "But perhaps it is not where you wish to see it. And such love must always be useless to you. But if it comforts you to know, it is none the less very true."

"I don't understand." She seemed confused and leant back against the bench.

"I mean that I love you," he said quietly. "You can keep the knowledge, if you care to and it means anything to you. I didn't intend to tell you, but I am told that women like the thought of hopeless love; the more the merrier, perhaps. A little trophy for you, something to hang on your bracelet— like this!" He took off his signet-ring, kissed it and put it into her hand. "When you are an old lady, you can show it to your grandchildren, and say 'That one was Esmé's—or was it Tom's, or Dick's or Harry's?' Never mind, it will all be forgotten, except that I told you my love when I meant not to, and you had that triumph—meagre as it was against all the others."

She put one palm over the other, the ring safe between them, and wondered what to say. SHe wanted to clutch at some of his words before they faded, but already they were flying away from her. Lightning, when it filled the conservatory, flashed upon something bright in Esmé's hand. Thunder broke with a splintering noise above them. "What are you doing?" she asked.

"There! I have cut our initials in the cactus—as well as I could see to do it. A and E. It is to commemorate an occasion." He clicked back the blade of his penknife and dropped it into his pocket.

"That poor pony!" he said.

It was the only time in her life that she had forgotten an animal. When the rain came, drumming and dancing on the glass roof, she was glad that they would have to stay there longer. He had his hand on the door and was peering into the darkness outside, waiting for the storm to pass over. As it began to ease off, she said in her flustered harsh way: "I haven't thanked you. For the ring, I mean, and for what you said. No words will come. All I can say is that I love you, too, and have for years and shall for ever."

When he turned to her, the look of surprise on his face was wasted, for by now it was quite dark.

PART 4

i

THEY returned to Paradise House from their honeymoon. There was scaffolding over the front—the South side— and patches of new plaster, a smell of paint and putty and a sound of hammering. The balustrade had been mended and the fallen urn put back. Two peacocks had arrived. Angel had sent an order for them when she was in Greece, and Nora received them nervously. They moped on the terrace, which they covered with their droppings; they moulted; they sometimes screamed but never fanned out their tail-feathers.

Nora was worried about everything, especially Angel's increasing extravagances. The house was eating up money, she wrote to her; but Angel never had the letter. They had moved on; for everywhere was so disappointing. Greece was especially disappointing. It was nothing like her novels. There was so much fallen masonry, dazzling and tiring to the eyes; olive groves looked dusty and really there were only pillars to temples. The food was nauseating, plates of black octopus and black olives and black liver-sausage. She had had good food all her life and missed it. Esmé laughed at her squeamishness. They were both tired from travelling and he from seasickness. He tried to hide the fact of his nausea because it prompted her to make long speeches on will-power and morbid imaginings, on abandoning oneself to the rhythm of the boat and thinking of other things, not of oneself the whole time. "The food isn't wholesome and that is why you are sick. It is foolish to blame the elements or the sea. I was wiser than you knew when I refused the egg and lemon soup and that ghastly-looking squid lying in rancid oil." Esmé stuffed his fingers in his ears.

The sea-sickness speech irritated him dreadfully, but there were other annoyances, too. She had brought with her a flowing white pleated garment and in this insisted on being photographed, standing on a plinth. She owed this to her readers, she said. And she collected souvenirs. Wherever they went he was loaded with peasant costumes—which she would put on as soon as they reached their hotel—with baskets and bottles of wine, with pottery, with strings of beads and ikons and plaster statuettes. She could not learn the currency and managed to convey an impression of deep suspicion, frowning at the coins she was given and muttering her distrust. At Rhodes, she boxed a little boy's ears for tipping a live mouse from a cage into the harbour. "Christianity has made the place drab," she said in Athens. At Delphi, she bottled some water from the sacred spring. "It shall be a present for Nora," she said. "To inspire her with poetry." Esmé thought it a cheap enough present. His irritations he worked off by correcting her pronunciation of Greek and, when they reached Venice, of Italian.

Venice—although Italy—was strangely less disappointing. It had the advantage, but was not to have for much longer, of not having been the background of one of her novels. There, Angel bought a great deal of vulgarly ornate glass, more baskets, more peasant-costumes. Esmé had shellfish poisoning and was sick again. Angel had never had any patience with other people's illnesses, and she thought that Esmé was doing his best to spoil her honeymoon, from heedlessness, gluttony or lack of common-sense. They went in a gondola on the Grand Canal in the moonlight, but that again was not what she had imagined. Later, she was to write of such an excursion as the climax of romance. But Esmé was not romantic. "We like different things," he said. "A great pity." He had loved Greece, and her complaints there had exasperated him.

He knew that she became especially watchful as soon as they were in Italy, and he was careful to guard her peace of mind. When they walked in the narrow streets or sat in the great Square drinking coffee, he looked neither to right nor to left. Once she remarked, in a voice irritating with its tone of leniency and condescension, on a girl who passed by them: "*So* pretty!"

"Oh, was she? I didn't see." He half-turned his head.

"A great pity that they so soon coarsen and grow florid," she added.

Like many romantic, narcissistic women she shied away from the final act of love-making. She would have lived in a world of courtship and hand-kissing if she could. Sex seemed to have nothing to do with her. It was a sudden reversal, not a continuation, of the delights of being wooed. She had to become a different person before she could endure it, and she was not always able, even for love of Esmé, to make the change. That desperate communication with herself in which she writes, holds good in love as well, he thought.

She was happiest when she was lavishing love and presents upon him. As soon as she guessed that there was something he wanted, she would not rest until it was his. She did not notice that he was growing sulky, like a spoilt child. The gifts were all so inevitable, and the signs of his gratitude so eagerly looked for. She had a sad way of damaging his enthusiasms, in the way that she had damaged Greece, with her scorn. Jealousy was at the root of her cynicism. He was not to admire anything or anyone but her; not even a fragment of sculpture.

For the most part, their moments of happiness did not coincide, so were bound to be imperfect; but there were times when she was animated and interested and he was pleased to have her company. It was not much to say of a honeymoon, but she seemed oblivious that their marriage had not made a very brilliant beginning. She could be gay and conspiratorial when she was alone with him, and enjoyed the laughter they had together over a foolish young woman, a fellow-passenger as they came up the Adriatic, who had fallen in love with Esmé and was for ever finding questions to ask him about the ship's time or the weather. Angel, basking in Esmé's indifference to the girl, enjoyed the situation. "I suppose there will be countless other young women," she said and she took for granted that they would all be part of the same joke, drawing husband and wife closer together rather than alienating them. Esmé, for his part, was quite glad that she was there to protect him from the girl's tiresomeness.

Even in Greece, they had had some idyllic times, especially when she could forget her distaste of the ruins or her certainty that all the mules were overloaded. They spent a morning wandering on a hillside, looking for tortoises; they ate their luncheon of garlic-sausage and olives and watched the lizards among the stones. Esmé had tried to dig up a mandrake, scooping the earth away with his fingers, and Angel knelt beside him watching. He uncovered the shoulders of the strange root, exposed the smooth, bifurcated body. "It is like an idol," she said. "Or an image for sticking pins into. And will it really scream as you drag it from the ground?"

"That is what we are going to find out."

She leant closer to him, silent and tense. Make it scream! Oh, make it scream! she prayed. There was a loud snap and the root had broken. Esmé pushed the earth over it again. Angel was quite bitterly disappointed. Later, they lay down in the shade and fell asleep. When he woke first, he saw a little snake lying close to her head. As Esmé moved, it slid away under a stone. He was pale and trembling as he pulled her to her feet. She looked at him with pleasure, but deep amusement, too.

"It was lying near your head. It was almost in your hair."

"But I like snakes," she said.

They went back home through France. In the South, the landscape, the vines and cypresses and the flat, crenellated roofs seemed to whirl round in the intensity of the heat. They became anxious to be home, and they thought of Paradise House embowered in greenness, in a mist of rain, as they had often seen it since the first evening. Angel was full of her plans for it, the ones she had made before they were married and the new ones she thought of every day. Esmé was acquiescent. It was *her* money and he took it for granted that she would spend it to his best advantage. Even on his honeymoon he had begun to have a faintly convalescent air and managed to convey the idea that he must not be troubled with trifles.

The trifles emerged as soon as they reached home. The door was opened by a servant they had never seen before. Nora had engaged her while they were away and she stared at her new mistress as if she were hypnotised and looked as if she would take flight.

"Welcome!" said Nora, coming across the hall with her arms outstretched. "Good evening, Esmé," she added, turning to him when she had kissed Angel.

So that is how it is to be! he thought; we shall have to see. Soon after their betrothal, he had asked Angel if there would be room for Nora and him under one roof. "Oh, yes!" she had said blithely. "I could not do without either of you."

"I know how bridegrooms should behave," he now said. "But I cannot very well carry Angelica across her own threshold." I cannot very well carry Angelica, he added to himself.

"*Our* threshold," she said, looking about the hall. "Where is Czar? All the way home, I had in my mind the picture of him coming to meet me. I thought he would come bounding down the steps. There's nothing wrong with him, is there?" she asked with a sudden change of voice.

"No, nothing," Nora said. "Edwina, fetch Czar from the library, please."

The maid hurried away and Angel raised her eyebrows at Nora. "Edwina? How very unsuitable."

"She refuses to change. I had to take what I could get. They told me at the Agency in Norley that girls simply won't work out here. It's too much in the wilds and they are frightened of the walk home on their afternoon off."

Angel had a curiously silencing thought—I was once offered a job in this house myself. But it did not seem to be the same place. She could not—even if she had cared to, and nothing

157

did she desire less—have peopled it with the ghosts of Aunt Lottie's Madam and that other Angelica; she did not imagine Aunt Lottie herself coming home down the lane after one of her Wednesday afternoons in Volunteer Street, brushing Madam's hair in one of the rooms upstairs or looking out of one of those windows and seeing Angel's novel left out there on a seat on the terrace.

Edwina now came back into the hall, dragging the dog by his collar.

"Come Czar!" Angel called, patting her thigh.

He sat down and yawned, then turned his head and looked out of the open door.

"He seems so staid after—after other dogs," Nora said apologetically.

He gave no sign of recognising Angel and bore her embraces indifferently. A poor start, Esmé thought.

"Ah, you put the portrait here, Nora," said Angel, straightening her back and looking about her. "I had really imagined it in the dining-room."

"It can soon be moved," said Nora, wondering how many more mistakes she had made. She had supervised the move from Alderhurst, so that they should come back at the end of their honeymoon to their new home.

"You must have worked truly hard," said Angel, with a puzzling warmth. "How lucky we are, Esmé, to come home and find it all done for us."

Nora's gratitude for this tribute lasted, and fortified her later when they went over the house and Angel exclaimed with vexation at the way carpets were laid and curtains hung.

At the end of the house, on the first floor, a room facing North had been planned and furnished as a surprise for Esmé, and Angel went ahead of them and opened the door to see if all of her instructions had been obeyed. It was her idea of a studio, with all she had ever imagined it should contain: the daïs, the easel, the lay-figure, the draperies. Esmé, when he saw it, could not think of any suitable words. Angel watched him and waited. "It is so splendid," he said, "that I

158

shall be too overawed to paint." She looked pleased. I shall often be able to say true things, in the confident hope of being misunderstood, he thought.

After dinner, Angel went to the library with Nora to sign cheques. She sat down at the table and Nora settled nearby with an 'I told you so' look upon her face. Presently, Angel said severely: "We are spending too much money. There won't be enough in the bank to meet all this. You know what I have had to pay for the house."

"I tried to point that out to you. I have been dreadfully alarmed at the way the bills kept coming in."

"Two dozen dusters! What do we want with two dozen dusters? Surely, old rags would do?"

"I hadn't any old rags," Nora said patiently.

"I could have given you some of my old vests and things if only you had asked. What is this? Two loads of manure? And there must be all that pony's dung lying about. I noticed a great heap of it in the lane on our way down—all flattened by the wheels of the trap and wasted." She signed her name to a cheque for five hundred pounds to Lucille. "I am sorry to criticise, Nora, on my first evening at home, but salmon and duckling at one meal is quite unnecessary. We shall have to do without some of our little luxuries until I have recovered from buying the house."

And since you are now landed, Nora thought, with the biggest luxury of all—Esmé, the luxury no woman can afford.

"I have signed quite enough," Angel said pettishly. "That bank-manager will be angry with me."

"Just the bill for the peacocks," Nora pleaded. "The man wrote such an impatient letter."

"I will write him an even more impatient letter back. Two drearier, mopier birds I never saw. I hate dispirited creatures. Ah, well, I am tired now and I shall go up to bed. My own bed at last, not one full of fleas." She went to the window and looked out at the narrow stretch of parkland, yellow with buttercups and with two oval clumps of elm-trees. Beyond that, the woods rose away gradually towards the horizon.

My first evening here, she thought. "I shall want some book-plates printed," she said to Nora. "Just 'Ex libris' and then 'Angelica Howe-Nevinson, Paradise House.' And some device with peacocks," she added. "I will ask Esmé to do a design."

More expense, Nora thought.

"If Bessie has unpacked, I can give you your present," Angel said as she went upstairs with Czar following. Alone in her room, she felt a sudden panic about money: she had put it away from her when Nora was there. I must keep it all going, she thought,—the house, and Esmé and all I have promised him—balancing it on my finger-tips, racking my brain. She felt disinclination amounting to nausea at the thought of starting another book. There is nothing in me, she moaned aloud, covering her mouth with her handkerchief as if she were going to retch. Perhaps it is all finished. Soon she felt better, and began to wander about the bedroom, looking at the things that Bessie had unpacked. She took the medicine-bottle of water from the Sacred Spring which she had brought with such care from Delphi, uncorked it and drank deeply. Perhaps its magic had ceased hundreds of years ago and had only been for poets in the first place, but it seemed an experiment worth making. She replenished the bottle from the water-jug and took it along to Nora's bedroom.

"You see, I carried it safely all the way from Greece for you," she said.

"What is it?"

When Angel had told her, Nora gave it a peculiar look and put it down on her dressing-table. "I shall always treasure it," she said.

Angel returned to her own room and found that Czar had settled himself on the eiderdown at the end of the bed. Angel undressed and let down her long, black hair. She felt nervous and not herself at bedtime, wondering in an unsettled way if she would be expected to play that ludicrous and alien game of sexual love, in which not only she, but Esmé also, seemed to her to lose identity as well as poise.

Esmé had spent an hour or more going round the gardens, rather fancying himself as a kind of rustic squire. When he came back to the house, he saw the lights in his and Angel's bedroom and went up at once. She was asleep, with her dark hair spread all about her pillow, and most of the rest of the bed was taken up by Czar, who opened one bloodshot eye and looked at him. There was an overpowering smell of dog in the room, and when Esmé tried to pull him off the bed he began to growl. "Oh, leave him, the blessed," Angel murmured, stirring in her sleep. "So very long since he has seen us."

Esmé spent very little time in his studio; he began instead to be absorbed in gardening. All the day, while Angel was shut indoors writing, he was about the grounds, busy in the green-houses or walled garden or clearing the shrubberies. He had found a new way to contentment, and with the help of two boys he began to bring order and beauty to the neglected grounds. He never thought of London. In June, he dressed himself up and went to Epsom to see Durbar II win the Derby: for himself he had rather it had not: then he came home, eager to work again.

They began to entertain a little, although some of the rooms were still shut up from lack of furniture. There were country neighbours who had known the previous owners and who, when they called, declared that the garden had never been so beautiful in all the time they could remember it. Angel was delighted and full of gratitude to Esmé.

There were not to be many happy weeks. In August, war with Germany was declared and by the next spring Esmé had gone to France.

To be at Paradise House was to be cut off from the world where such a war could come about. Sometimes, newspapers remained folded on the hall-table all day. Nora would read them after dinner when she allowed herself what she called 'a breather'; Angel was too preoccupied and Esmé too indifferent.

The impact of war when it came was all the more overwhelming. Nora had for days made sombre prognostications, but Angel and Esmé were used to her forebodings; they looked on them as part of her martyrdom and they thought that she indulged in them and in her warnings about money, with too much relish. They had learnt to cheat her of satisfaction by ignoring her. Thus, when war came, and she was seen to have been right, they still felt disinclined to take the matter seriously. When they were made to, Esmé was sullen and Angel frenzied. She would not have the war discussed. Embowered in their trees, they were to turn their backs upon the outside world. "More fool he," she said, when one of the youths who helped Esmé in the garden joined the Army. "If that is where he thinks his loyalty lies, let him shout for his job back when the fighting is over in a month or two."

"It won't be over for years," said Nora.

Esmé was thoughtful and uneasy. He walked aimlessly in the garden instead of working there. In October, he said that he was joining up. He made this announcement to Angel curtly and shamefacedly, as if he were saying instead that he was leaving her for another woman. She became so hysterical that this might have been the case, reviling him for deserting her, accusing him of moral cowardice and bloodthirstiness; she pleaded with him, her face distorted with weeping; she threatened him that, like the garden-lad, he would find Paradise House locked against him when he returned. When, for the first time, she saw him in uniform she felt shock and estrangement. Nora never forgot the afternoon that he went away. Angel drove him to the station in the trap. She would not kiss him: she blamed him too much for her distress. As he jumped down from the trap, she remained sitting there, with the reins in her hand, her face averted. "Then, goodbye," he said hesitantly, feeling foolish and helpless. He had reached the station-barrier when he heard her calling his name. He turned and was about to go back to her when she shouted "Write to me soon. Tonight," then she jerked the reins and drove away out of the station-yard. He had seen tears running down her cheeks: he felt disconcerted and would not look about him in case other people had seen them, too.

Nora had tea ready, and was watching from the drawing-room window. Angel jumped from the trap and ran up the steps into the hall. She pushed past Nora, who came out to meet her, and stumbled upstairs to her room.

"I never heard anyone carry on like that in all my life," Edwina told Bessie. "Goodness knows how she'd behave if he was killed." Angel lay on her bed and wept until she felt as hollow as a shell; until there were only the outer distresses—the throbbing eyes and brow, the stinging, swollen cheeks, the cramped limbs, the exhaustion—but nothing within. She felt that she had cried herself out of existence, and lay all evening inert, light-headed, refusing to stir herself to eat or speak. The next day Esmé returned. He had thought that she would be delighted to see him again. Touched and worried by the excesses of her grief, he was glad when he had at once been given forty-eight hours' leave. She will have got over the first parting, he thought. Next time she will take it more calmly.

She took it calmly, it was true. Throughout the two days, she was hostile or indifferent. She blamed the Army for sending him back to play upon her nerves when she was weakened with grief. At that time, a love-letter would have restored her more than his presence could.

She went back to her novel and filled its last pages with an onslaught against war quite irrelevant to what had gone before. The pacifist beliefs, about which she became more and more bellicose, were frustrating to Nora for whom war might have meant so much. She could imagine Paradise House as a hospital, with the grounds full of wounded Tommies: she thought of them sitting out on the terrace in their blue suits with plenty of cheerful greetings for her as she hurried by, on her way from one job to another, 'giving out' as Esmé called it. Other women were as busy as could be with bandage-rolling parties and whist-drives in aid of the Red Cross. As far as Nora was concerned, the war had to be outwardly ignored: she studied the newspapers secretly, and if she came upon a name she knew printed in the casualty-lists she was obliged to keep it to herself. Interest could only be morbid, Angel said, and she implied that by forecasting war, Nora was responsible for it.

There was to be no hospital at Paradise House; sewing-parties and whist-drives were out of the question. Angel shut herself up in her room and began to write another novel, an allegory of peace and war entitled 'Irene'.

Her grief for Esmé was not concerned with his safety. She missed him and thought him guilty of deserting her; but she did not try to imagine the horrors of trench-warfare that day after day he had to endure, the demoralising rain and mud, barbed wire, gunfire, the impossibility of seeing any end to the situation but the single, the personal, solution of death. For her, Esmé had truly gone into a no-man's land, and although they wrote to one another it seemed to her that he had suspended existence, a ghost who once had been alive and who yet might return to living. She skimmed through his letters, with their descriptions of a world she found strange and repellent, until she came to the last few sentences with their messages of love, rather reiterated as they were, letter after letter, a formula after which he was at last able to sign his name.

One day, Lord Norley's carriage came down the drive. Angel kept the old man waiting while she sat at her desk, wondering what he could have to say and how she should react to whatever it might be. Without coming to any conclusions, she went downstairs.

"I am so sorry that Nora is out," she told him in a condescending voice. "She has taken Bessie out in the trap to pick blackberries, although what use they will be, I can't think. I hear nothing but groans about there being no preserving sugar. Can *you* get plenty of preserving sugar, Lord Norley?"

"I . . . I expect that we are as badly off as anybody else," he said, "Although I no longer have a very sweet tooth. Don't worry about Nora—I can see her another time. I really came to see you."

"I was sorry that you couldn't be at our wedding," she said.

"Yes."

He looked at her uncertainly. She did not help out the silence.

"I was abroad," he added.

"So I gathered," she said carelessly.

"I should have liked to have seen Esmé before he went overseas."

She thought, so the recalcitrant nephew who must not be lent a penny, who was cast-off and ignored, becomes a hero as soon as he puts on a uniform. What a wonderful thing war is.

"I should like to write to him, if you will give me his address." She went to a writing-table and took up a goose-quill pen. The scratchy sound it made on the paper went on a long time and he listened to it nervously. She is certainly bearing malice, he thought, and he wished that Nora would walk in.

"The ink is wet," she said, handing the piece of paper to him at last.

"You must miss him," he said humbly.

"Yes."

"If there is anything that I could do. . . ."

"No, there is nothing for anyone to do. I have my work."

"The thought of your work makes it difficult to say what I have come for. There must be a loss to literature every time we take you from your desk, but by helping us, you could feel that in your own way, you were working alongside Esmé to win the war. I know that many wives are comforted by that."

She seemed, at first, not to have heard a word of what he had said. Then she alarmed him by saying: "I would not lift a finger to help the war in any way. I don't know what it was you were going to ask me to do, but if it is in that direction I shall refuse. The war has separated me from my husband and was the cause of our first disagreement, and I never allow Nora or anyone else to mention it in my presence."

Lord Norley felt, as Theo so often had, the kind of exasperation that is stupefying. He did not know which way to turn or where he could begin to explain his disagreement, and he left without making his request and without being offered any tea. Nora and Bessie had not returned and Edwina had left long ago to work in a munitions factory. The house was half shut up and there was nothing to show for Esmé's work on the garden; the lawns were shaggy again and tall grasses grew around the urns and the stone seats on the terrace. Every evening, Nora made excuses for the simplicity of their dinner.

"It does well enough for the two of us," said Angel. "And you are always wanting us to economise. Vegetable stew or whatever it is seems an excellent way of economising."

They were certainly spending less. There were fewer temptations, isolated as they were at Paradise House and with Esmé away and so little to buy in the wartime shops; but Nora, who now managed Angel's money-affairs, knew that less and less money was coming in, royalties were dwindling, and 'A Venetian Summer' had been the first of Angel's failures: an extra grievance she had against the war.

Nora was rather pleased and stimulated by having to economise: it put her, she thought, into the ascendancy; it suited her to face the challenge of making ends meet, although the ways in which she tried to do so were too trivial to be of much assistance when Angel was so liable to sudden extravagances. Nora's blackberry-picking, her 'husbandry' as Angel rather sarcastically called it—the gathering in of everything from the garden, the seed-collecting and the herb-drying, the boiled nettles for luncheon, the rose-hip and the rowan-berry jelly—could be more than discounted by Angel's reading an advertisement of a silver tea-service for sale, or a sable muff and collection of ostrich feathers, or even, one day, a suit of mediaeval armour. She began to study *The Times*, the *Morning*

Post and the *Westminster Gazette*, not for the war news, but for something nice to buy. Articles came on approval, and even if she did not really approve it was too much trouble to send them back, especially as they were sometimes difficult to re-pack, like the bronze figures of centaurs or the deers' antlers. It was through advertisements that she began to collect her Persian cats. When three had arrived, Nora begged her to stop; for she could not feed them, she said. Twice a week, she went in the trap to fetch horse-meat for Czar: now she would have to go three times. The cats, all males, fought with one another and upset the peacocks.

"They will settle down," said Angel. "They can have one of the upstairs rooms to themselves."

"And I can imagine what they will make of it," Nora said. "The drawing-room is bad enough."

Angel was fretting about Esmé. Other men had leave; but he did not; his letters were so much less frequent than her own to him; she thought that the War Office confiscated some of them, and others were so dull and guarded that she wondered if they were perhaps written in code. She spent her days writing 'Irene'. After tea she would take Czar for a walk, one or two cats often following after: there would be an uproar from the peacocks on the terrace as they set out. When she came back, she would wander about the house and look into the conservatory to see if the cactus was still safe, still bearing their initials. In the evenings she sat with Nora in the drawing-room, and when she had finished her letter to Esmé she often sighed and complained that there was nothing to do.

We must be the only women in England who can say that, Nora invariably said to herself, thinking of all the busy fingers.

At night, the three women lay asleep in the great house. Branches sawed and scraped above the roof. The valley seemed stifled with foliage in summer and creaking with frosty timber in winter-time. Sometimes the rain hissed down until the garden steamed like a cauldron: for hours after the sky had cleared, the sound of rain falling from one leaf to another would continue. Esmé did not come or write hopefully of coming.

One morning, Nora had a letter from Theo Gilbright, asking her to see him in London if she were ever there, implying that it would be as well for her to make the effort. "My suggestion is confidential," he had written.

Nora had an elderly aunt in Kensington, who was greatly surprised to have a letter promising a visit from her niece. She would have been more surprised to hear Nora describing to Angel how dangerously ill Aunt Jessica was and how she had sent for the family, and that Nora for one would not refuse this last request.

"Will she leave you anything?" Angel inquired.

"A trinket or two, perhaps."

It seemed a long way to go and a lot of trouble to take on the chance of getting a trinket or two, Angel thought. "While you are there, you could go into Gilbright and Brace for me. There are a few things I want looked into. And to Jay's for some glacé ribbon to trim my Leghorn hat." She kept thinking of commissions—and leaves me no time for the death-bed, Nora thought in amusement.

Theo received her kindly. He guessed something of the difficulties of her life without being able to imagine the compensations. She glanced round the office nervously, and seemed reassured by the sight of a row of Angel's novels in a bookcase.

"And how is Angel?" Theo asked. He looked tired and his beard was full of silver hairs. Willie Brace was in the Army and Hermione in the suburbs at work as a V.A.D. He was left in London with a great many worries: Angel was not the least of them.

"She is thinking of buying a motor-car," Nora said, as if this told him what he wanted to know.

"And who will drive it?"

"She is getting a chauffeur, in fact, she had really arranged for the chauffeur before she thought of the car. He can help in the garden as well, you see."

"Is he a very old man?"

"No, he is middle-aged. He was called up, but luckily he had an abscess on the brain . . . yes, I think it was that . . . something, anyhow, which has left him a little odd in the head."

"How very fortunate. Apart from the motor-car, her health is good?"

"She is never ill. I have never known anyone so strong. But she is so restless in her mind. If only Esmé could get home on leave; yet sometimes I think that it might only make it worse for her. I shall never forget the day he went away—how inconsolable she was."

"Miss Howe-Nevinson, would you think that you have any influence over her?"

"None," said Nora honestly.

"Then I don't know what we are to do. I asked you to come and see me—and I realise how justly angry she would be if she knew—because I think I know something of your position there. She confides in you over business matters?"

"I look after them for her."

"So I thought. Then you realise how things are. Her last book—it has been worse than a disappointment."

"Yes, I realise. I thought it was because of the war."

"I am afraid it is because of the book. She will never listen to reason from me. I wondered if she would from you." Nora shook her head.

"Well, then what are we to do? There is a different public now and she does not attract it; her old public is baffled and antagonised by all this pacifism: not only do they not agree with it in principle, but they see no place for it in a romantic novel and I am afraid that they are right. I have said so, but she will not listen."

"She is a great writer all the same," said Nora, lifting her chin high and blushing. "Nothing can alter that."

"She is a writer with increasing commitments, too," Theo said sternly. "Commitments that are not my affair, perhaps; but as her friend I feel great anxiety and some responsibility. Quite frankly, I don't like the sound of her new book: in fact,

I dread its arrival. I wish that she would go back to her old style and give people something to excite them and enliven them and take them out of this wretched present: if she does not, I wonder what will happen."

Nora looked into her lap, like a little girl who is being scolded.

"I am not only speaking as her publisher; but as her friend as well," he said.

"She won't listen to me. I dare not speak to her about it. She hates criticism, and you can't imagine how fiery and obstinate she is."

"I think I can, as well as anyone."

"If the war could end and Esmé come home again, all the bees in her bonnet might stop buzzing."

"And it might be too late."

"We must hope for the best," said Nora.

He thought her extraordinarily placid. He sent for a cab and took her to tea at Gunters; the least he could do, he supposed. She was arch and gay as if she had come to London solely for this treat, and he wondered if she had ever been taken out to tea before; with that moustache, he rather thought not. There were so many officers there with young women that she felt she had edged up to the war as close as she was likely to get.

"Another thing," Theo said, "I cannot have that photograph of her as a frontispiece. That is her latest idea. But why should I bother you? It is most unfair of me. It is I who must tell her. You know the one I mean. She is standing on a sort of plinth, with some drapery blowing about her . . . taken in Greece . . . rather crooked . . . not that it couldn't be straightened; but it just won't do." I suppose I ought not to speak to her like this, he thought. Very disloyal and not her friend's affair anyhow. He just hoped that some of it might seep through to Angel. Nora had fallen silent, and her face was turned at a strange angle, sideways to him, as if she were averting it from someone. She shielded her pale cheek with her hand.

"Will you please take me away?" she asked him, as soon as he stopped speaking. "I feel faint. It is so hot in here."

"Shall I send for some water or sal volatile?"

"Oh, no no! Please, if I could just go quickly and with as little disturbance as possible. I am sorry."

All the way out to the street, she whispered apologies. He called a taxi and went with her to her aunt's house. As they drove towards Kensington, he patted her gently on the knee and said: "You needn't pretend. I saw what you saw. I shall keep it to myself."

"Esmé?" she whispered.

He nodded.

"Oh, dear, what am I to do?"

"Nothing: be careful to do simply nothing, put it out of your mind, for ever; no matter how difficult it may be to do so or however provoked you sometimes may be."

"Oh, I should not speak from provocation; but only if I thought it best for her."

"It wouldn't be."

When they reached her aunt's house, he asked: "Do you think he saw you?"

"I don't know. I looked away at once."

He saw you, Theo thought. "Pretend that he didn't," he said. "Say nothing to him when you meet. And don't worry. They are strange times and people behave in war as they wouldn't in peace."

"But Angel wouldn't see it at all like that."

Neither did Theo. He said: "That is why we must protect her from knowing. I wish that I had not brought you to London. I have worried you and let you in for this shock."

But Nora had recovered. Her cheeks now burnt quite brightly as she shook hands with him and went up the steps towards her aunt's front door.

Much more sadly, Theo got back into the cab. He knew that Esmé had seen them, and hoped that he would trust in their discretion, not lose his head and confess to Angel when there was no need; but he hoped, too, that, knowing himself discovered, he would try to make amends. He will ruin her with his callous ways, he thought angrily.

171

Esmé had been sitting, half-turned away from them, gazing intently across the table at the girl with the fluffy hair and the grey velvet hat. She had shaken her head at him as if he were behaving like a naughty child; then her face grew serious, with a pensive, a sympathetic look; then she blushed. He has not seen me, Theo had assured himself, with a hand on Nora's elbow as he steered her towards the door. They see only one another. At that moment, Esmé had looked up. His glance had skidded past Theo to Nora, whose back was just, but too late, Theo thought, disappearing from view.

ii

"We will pretend that it never happened," Angel said on Armistice Day. Esmé, hunched up on his crutches, looked ruffled and disgruntled. On some days, when it rained, especially, his leg ached more than usual. His trousers were pinned up neatly above the knee where the limb was severed. "If it hadn't happened to me, I'd have done it myself," he had said at the time. "I had just about had enough of flaming France." Now, he longed to walk freely about the garden again: he was not adept with his crutches and Marvell, the chauffeur, had always to be at hand to help him. "My Nannie," Esmé said.

So they were to forget the war, he thought. "I do so hope that I shall not be a reminder," he told Angel, who smiled fondly at him. This fond smile was sometimes more than he could tolerate: it made him feel quite vicious towards her. Now she will pat my head or tousle my hair, he thought. Instead, she came to him and laid her hand on his shoulder. If it weren't for Nannie, I should go mad, he often thought.

There did not seem to him to be anything dim-witted about Marvell; on the contrary, he was brisk and spry; he had used his loaf, he told Esmé, and was still using it, to make for himself the snuggest, most leisurely life he could, camping out in cosy squalor in rooms over the stables, and cooking for himself on a primus-stove: there was a perpetual smell of onions frying or onions fried when Esmé went to see him, as he often did to pass the time. It suited them both to sit and talk about horse-racing; the garden, in which Esmé had once taken such pride, was a disheartening sight. He had come back from hospital to find it overgrown, unrecognisable, and he had lashed out pettishly at some nettles with one of his crutches and called Marvell out to do some weeding, cursing him. They still, if it were a fine day, would fill a wheelbarrow or two with thistles, Esmé sitting on the grass or shuffling along on his bottom like a toddler, and Marvell moaning and gasping about his rheumatism. He was certainly no gardener and was content to break the thistles off at the root. At the first spot of rain, he would help Esmé to his feet and back they would go to the rooms over the stables where he would make some cocoa and bring out the racing papers.

"You ought to make the effort and go one day," he told Esmé. "It would take you out of yourself. Could get to Newbury all right; maybe Cheltenham."

"How the deuce can I go like this?"

"I could take you in the motor and see you were all right. Chum you into Tattersalls, if need be."

"It's an idea," Esmé said. "Quite an idea, Nannie, you artful old sod. I shall have to look into it."

"Well, here's the racing-calendar if you want it. You can take your pick, sir."

When Esmé mentioned going to the races, Nora said: "So you are starting all that again?"

"Well, God! I must pass the time somehow. The hours go so slowly in this drowsy, dopey place."

"You should do some work. What about that fine studio? It seems rather wasted on you."

"How can I paint like this?"

"I get tired of hearing you say 'How can I do this?' 'How can I do that?' Other men manage to. Are you going to make excuses for the rest of your life?"

In the middle of their now frequent disagreements, caution would suddenly silence him. He dreaded provoking her to a dangerous disclosure. If she had seen him in London when he was on leave, was she biding her time, waiting to be rid of him when the best opportunity arose? But he could not think why she should wait, unless it was a feline pleasure for her to do so, to keep him busy with conjecture. One day he would be quite sure that she knew nothing: he even dared to mention Gunters, tempting providence, not able to bear the uncertainty any longer. "Heavenly ices there before the war."

"Have you seen my silver thimble anywhere?" Nora asked Angel. Her voice was so smooth, so casual. Surely she was not changing the conversation: she was scarcely listening to what he was saying—chatter about ice-creams, merely, which could not interest her. But he could not be sure. The next day she had said to Angel, who was talking about hats: "Why not have a grey velvet one? I saw such a pretty one when I went to London that time. It was ruched and trimmed with yellow osprey-feathers." She described just such a hat as Laura had been wearing at tea that day in Gunters.

"Grey doesn't suit my colouring," said Angel. "And I don't approve of women wearing osprey-feathers. They are torn out of the living birds."

"Yes, I suppose it is rather cruel," Nora murmured thoughtfully.

Angel's tranquillity was wonderful. The war had ended for her on the summer's day in 1918 when the telegram had come. She had been sitting on the terrace correcting proofs. Nora was cutting blossoms for her carnation wine, and their scent drifted into the scent of the lime-flowers on the avenue. The perfumes alternated as the breeze changed its direction. It was a humming, buzzing afternoon. The sound of Nora's scissors snipping away grew fainter as she moved farther along the herbaceous border. Angel had looked up at the new sound of a bicycle on the gravel drive.

She took the telegram fearfully and opened it. Nora, straightening her back and turning towards her, saw her read, then close her eyes. He is dead, she thought. He has been killed. She dropped the scissors into the basket and went towards her. As she drew near, she saw a look of rapture upon Angel's face. She held out the telegram to Nora and her hand was shaking. "He is wounded," she said. "At last. And he is coming home."

"Angel by name and Angel by nature," said Esmé who was still a little drunk from before luncheon. From the library window he was watching Marvell putting some large cans of broth into the car. "Or the Lady Bountiful of Paradise House," he added.

Marvell, who was also a little drunk, and from the same occasion, turned and winked at him and then assumed an obsequious expression even more impertinent.

"It is a good thing we are not all as selfish as you," said Nora, who was sitting by the fire, darning Esmé's socks. Which I also knitted in the first place, she thought.

"I bet they pour the stuff down the sink as soon as she's gone."

"You bet too much," was all she said.

Now Angel went down the steps towards the car. She was wearing a tweed cape and carried a basket full of jars of jam.

"Pots of jam now," Esmé said, watching.

I made the jam, too, Nora allowed herself to think just for a second before she brushed the disloyal thought aside.

I bet too much, Esmé thought. If only she knew.

His gratuity had gone long ago. He owed one of his army friends money, a great deal of money. They had met at Newbury and taken a long time on their journey home. Esmé had hoped to make good his racing losses at poker, but had not done so. The friend had made a fairly swift transformation into an enemy, had become cool and sarcastic, later had taken to writing insolent and threatening letters. Esmé now looked upon him with contempt: this made the insolence worse to bear. I really haven't a friend, I suppose, he thought, going through one name after another in his mind; but he meant, I haven't anyone left to borrow from.

The boredom of life at Paradise House was becoming too much for him. The only relief to the tedium had been the days at the races with Marvell, days he could no longer afford. He had sometimes thought of going to London to meet Laura, but to do so would have involved him in a conspiracy with Marvell, and that he shrank from. That morning a letter had come from her to tell him that she was married.

"I wish you would stop sighing," Nora said. "It is so very irritating."

He stopped sighing, and began to tap his teeth with his finger-nails.

"I can't think why you don't do some work," she added.

He did not enlighten her, but stared in silence out at the budding garden. He had half meant to begin a landscape, loving the bone-bare shapes of hills and hangers; but now all the tiresome little leaves were unfolding, blurring the outlines he admired.

Where was Angel, he wondered? Reading her works aloud to some sulky, helpless invalid, no doubt. This new rôle of benefactress had suggested itself to her when she had realised that the country people gave no sign of recognition when she drove by. She did not expect curtsies, she told herself, but those sullen stares puzzled her. She felt her presence at Paradise House resented. The cottage people stood too much in awe of her, no doubt, for she was not just the Squire's wife they were accustomed to, but a celebrity, a world figure. That they would not know how to behave was understandable. With her jars of jam and her beef-broth she set out to show them the way. She began to be a dreaded figure in the neighbourhood. Esmé, from Marvell's innuendoes, could realise how dreaded. The innuendoes wounded him; he was so vulnerable to them that he could sense them coming, he would try to stave them off and, when he failed, would not forgive himself for having let the opportunity arise. But once spoken, the words were allowed to pass: he pretended that he had not heard or had not seen the implication; he betrayed himself and Angel and hated both himself and her in doing so.

Nora snipped off a thread and pulled the darning mushroom out of the sock. She wondered if it would be provoking him too much if she asked him to stop tapping his teeth. Although she had a sense of mastery over him and was sure that he knew it, if she goaded him he might become violent. As a boy, he had once turned her teasing to terror and had swung a croquet-mallet at her shin. At that moment, no thought of the consequences could have deterred him. She had driven him beyond reasoning and had ever after hesitated to do it again. And cripples are noted for their ungovernable tempers, she reminded herself. She supposed that frustration made them savage.

If I could go for a long tramp, thought Esmé, I might shake off all the annoyances. He imagined walking very quickly indeed, shedding one worry after another as he went, breaking into a run, arriving breathless at his destination, but free.

"What time is it?" he asked in a dull voice, not bothering to turn round from the window to look at the clock.

"A quarter to four."

Nearly an hour to tea-time, he found himself thinking, as if he were a child. The thought took him back many years to a nursery afternoon with a sky outside as overcast as this one. He tried to step quickly back from the image, from the suffocation he felt at the memory, at the picture shouldering its way up from the darkness. There had been rain on the outside of the nursery window and the smear of his own breath on the inside; Nora, as now, sitting beside the fire with her sewing or her poetry-writing or her scrap-books or any other of her pursuits which kept her so busy. He had looked out into the deadness of the afternoon, at a monkey-puzzle tree wet with rain against the wet sky. "What time is it?" he had asked and Nora had said: "Look for yourself." But he had not bothered to turn. It could not be less than an hour to tea and there was nothing to do. He had felt burdened by the thought of all the afternoons of his life; yet the boy had been protected as the man could not be; had been unable, fortunately, to see himself thirty or more years later standing at

177

another window but in the same sort of panicky boredom, still thinking that there was nothing to do, and with the extra burden of memory.

He longed for a diversion.

"What time will Angel get back?" he asked.

"Not much before six, I expect."

Any diversion, even death, he suddenly thought; the words formed so distinctly in his mind that he was afraid he might have spoken them aloud. When she comes back, I shall speak to her, he decided. I shall tell her that I must have the money. She has treated me like a child: we will see if it still holds good.

He wondered in a detached way what her reaction would be: he had at last learnt to stand so far aside from his own pride that whatever she said would be interesting to him. He rather hoped for a storm; it would bring his experience of this dull day to a climax: the hours could hardly drag by in quite the same way afterwards: the tempo must quicken. His decision stimulated him. He also felt enormous relief at the thought of telling her, of laying his burden on her. The money now seemed as good as his. He wished that she would come quickly; but he could pass the time better, having something to look forward to. He had made up his mind, and he tried to turn it to other matters, fearful of changing it.

She listened to him with her head bent, as if it were she who was in disgrace. Impatiently he had followed her up to her bedroom when she returned from her sick-visiting. He might have had good news to tell, he was so suddenly eager to speak to her. At least I don't have the trying business of wheedling it out of him, she thought. His technique with confessions was bold. It was less painful to him to begin at the end with the sum total, or even an exaggeration, of his trouble: then, when the listener was staggering from the first blow, he would make his way back towards the beginning, toning down his excesses with mitigating circumstances, an air of candour and self-reproach, a sadness that from the weakness of his character,

178

the effects of his childhood, not much better could ever have been expected.

Angel sat at her dressing-table. She had taken off her hat and was swirling it round and round on one hand, gazing down at it as she listened. Esmé lurched about the room on his crutches. He went over to the window and straightened the curtains, then he banged on the glass to frighten the peacocks down on the terrace. Angel flinched at the noise.

"You see," he said, and he turned on her a look both helpless and ingratiating. "You see what you have married. I wonder that you were ever so silly."

"I have never regretted it," she said stiffly. A little later she asked in a frightened voice: "Have you?"

"But it is *you* who have reason to. It is I who have let you down and I who have had nothing to give. Nora, for instance, might say that I married you for your money."

She was still absorbed in her contemplation of her hat; her fingers smoothed the velvet flowers and touched their beaded stamens. Then she took in a deep breath very sharply, and lifting her head stared at herself in the looking-glass. "I have no money," she said.

She saw his reflection slope back against the window-sill. He glanced down at the carpet and traced a design on it with one of his crutches.

"I thought . . ." he began and then changed his mind about whatever he had been going to say and said in an exhausted tone: "Then I am to be disgraced and done for. I thought that there was only one way out of it and so there is."

"Something must be thought of," she said quickly. "I can get some money." She looked wildly round the room as if searching for it there and then. She knew his moods of despair, so much more desperate since the war, and half-knew that his life contained too little to occupy a grown man: she feared lest he might now decide that it contained too little to justify prolonging it; his dull voice, his hopelessness threatened this. She struggled to put aside her guilt and fear. "I will find a way, I promise you. I should not have been so lazy lately, or

179

so extravagant. This house costs a great deal . . . Nora will tell you. She knows how I stand."

"But *you* wouldn't tell me. . . ."

"What do you mean?"

"You tell me nothing. I am treated like a small boy. You and Nora run the place. It might not *be* my home as well."

"But we run it for you."

"Well, please don't bother to. And, if it costs so much, especially don't bother to."

"I love it."

He knew that he had said too much.

"I feel such a despicable fool having to come to you for money," he explained. "It is my own sorry fault for squandering what I had; that only makes it worse, and no man would want to ask what I just had to ask."

She knew that he had had a little money of his own, and supposed that he had squandered that as well.

"There is so little here to pass the time—as I am," he said. He banged the toe of his shoe with one of the crutches.

She had known this too, and to smother her self-reproach had tried to make Paradise House like a pretty bird-cage full of amusing devices: instead of swings and looking-glasses and tinkling bells, she had furnished the studio, acquiesced in the race-going. He had not come to love his captivity; he had only lost the courage to escape.

"How soon?" she asked. "How soon must you have the money?"

She blushed, which he had rarely seen her do; he felt shocked at the sight, the ugly colour running up one side of her neck and across her forehead.

"It is a question of staving him off," he said. "From now on, until I pay him, can only be unpleasant and may well be worse."

It did not occur to Angel to try to borrow the money; only to earn it, as she always had done. She laid down her hat and then took a deep breath and stood up. She felt strength gathering in her, a physical strength in her arms and finger-tips and a glowing confidence in her heart. She smiled at him, but he lowered his eyes.

"Don't worry," she begged him. "Only tell me this—when you said that there would only be one way out if you couldn't pay . . . what did you mean?" She waited fearfully for his answer.

"I meant that I should have to ask Nora for the money."

She felt great relief and was able to smile condescendingly and say: "Oh, that would never have done. We mustn't ask such favours of other people. Besides, Nora wouldn't have as much money as that. You must just leave it to me. It will be all right. You shall see. I will work day and night to take this worry from you."

He made no movement towards her and had nothing to say. Alert in his sensitiveness, he wondered what other crude words she would have to torture him with. He felt that he must beat her off with his crutch if she came near him. He pretended that he did not know she was waiting for him to reply. After a moment's hesitation she left him. He listened to her hurrying across the landing, and then there was a lovely peace in the room, as if a bluebottle had gone suddenly out of the window.

"Well, we're not having it, that's all. Not any more. You can get that straight."

Angel, on her way to find Nora, heard this strange voice shouting in the library: it was difficult to tell if it were a man's or a woman's. It rasped and rattled with breathy fury. When she opened the door she saw an old lady confronting Nora. She was dressed in black with a white scarf folded across inside her collar; her fists were clenched in grey cotton gloves. On the table beside her was a jar of Nora's gooseberry jam.

"I'm saying," she said as soon as she saw Angel, "I'm saying you can put a stop to it. The poor old man was crying when I got home. It was pitiful to hear. 'You mustn't leave me,' he

said, 'or she'll come back. Don't let her ever come again.'
'She won't come again', I promised him,—'or only over my
dead body.' And you wouldn't have got in this time if I
hadn't had to take some washing back and left the door on the
latch in case his sister looked in. Crying himself sick, he was.
He hasn't much longer to live. I'll see that he has his week or
two in peace."

"What is this?" Angel asked Nora.

Nora shrugged. "It seems that your kindness isn't appreciated."

"And I can make my own jam, thank you," said the old
lady. She took the jar from the table and held it for a moment
to the light. "Look at the colour of that," she sneered. "I'd
be ashamed to own it mine."

Nora put her hands over her ears. "Angel, do stop her,"
she said.

"Angel!" the old lady shouted. "I like 'Angel'. Angel's rich,
I must say. A fine Angel, clarring about with your pots of
jam, pestering people when they're under the weather,
frightening that poor little Doris Nott when she had a tem-
perature of a hundred and three, sitting there reading at her
till she was nearly distracted, some book about heathens, too ...
and her mother too nervous to send you about your business. . . . ." Angel walked across to the door and opened it and
stood beside it. . . . . "Well, I'm not too nervous. Put a step
over my threshold just once more, that's all."

"I am waiting for you to go."

"No doubt you are, as others have waited for *you* to go."

She seemed reluctant to come nearer to Angel, to pass close
to her as she would have to on her way out, and she could
feel the power of so much suppressed fury threatening her.
Her own anger was petering out, but the satisfaction it had
given her was spoilt by the fear that it might have provoked
physical violence. She almost ducked as she skirted Angel at
arm's length and then made up for the indignity by shouting,
once safely in the hall: "Well, I've warned you."

Bessie came hurrying from the inner hall. "See this person

out," Angel said and at once she went back into the library and shut the door.

"The terrible old creature," Nora said. "I felt sure that she was crazy and I was just going to ring for Bessie when you came in. I wouldn't have bothered you or had you upset in this way."

"I'm not upset, but I don't want to discuss it. As you say, she was mad."

"I shouldn't go there again, or to any of them. The ingratitude!"

"There won't be any more time now."

She closed her eyes for a moment and then, as if this had served to turn her mind to something different, said: "I think I shall go to bed."

"Yes, have a rest before dinner, then you will feel quite different again."

"I mean that I shall go to bed to stay."

"You have tired yourself out. Shall I send up a tray?"

Already on her way upstairs, Angel began to take the pins out of her hair, and loop after loop dropped to her shoulders. "I am going to bed to finish my novel," she said. "I won't get up again until it's done. I will have my meals up there and no one need interrupt me."

"But Lady Baines is coming to tea tomorrow."

"You can tell her that I am ill. Say anything you like."

"I don't understand. *Are* you ill?"

"No. It is a vow I have made to myself. I will stay there until I have written the last word."

Nora stood at the bottom of the stairs, her hands clasped anxiously.

"But why this sudden hurry? Surely you could wait until Lady Baines has been?"

"No. Every hour matters now. I need the money," Angel said. She was at the turn of the stairs. Her hands were full of hair-pins and the long black hair hung down to her waist.

It is Esmé, Nora thought. She was half-tempted to ask questions, but before she could sort out her words in their most tactful order, Angel had reached the landing and could not have heard.

Two of the cats leapt up the stairs after her, another squatted down in a dark corner of the hall. Nora clapped her hands at it and shooed it out on to the terrace. She felt suddenly braced and energetic, and with her thoughts on meals, on light but nourishing food—beef tea and fish soufflé came at once to her mind—she hurried through the baize door for a word or two with Bessie.

Day after day, Angel sat up in bed writing. The cats were glad. They liked to have someone in a warm bed where they themselves could lie about and doze. When Esmé went in, as he was sometimes compelled by guilt to do, a dozen pairs of golden eyes would be turned towards him, would blink contemptuously and then close again. Angel would blink, too, but keep her unfocused gaze upon him, her eyes questioning him, as if her tongue were tied, her thoughts elsewhere.

The wet weather trailed away, the sky lifted and dazzling sun poured over the dripping garden. Steam rose from the woods and the heavy silence the rain had imposed on living things was at an end: birds came out to the tips of the branches and began to stake their claims again; rooks woke early, clamorous above the chimney-pots, and there was a stirring in the undergrowth, movement once more, as mice, shrews, rabbits began to emerge; the grass was full of insects and, as soon as Angel's bedroom lights were put on in the evening, moths flung themselves against the window-panes. Rain was shaken from fur and feathers, the boughs dripped until they were dry. Then the heat became settled. It seemed unlikely that it would ever rain again. People in the cottages began to grumble about their vegetable gardens and worry about the water in the wells.

The weather passed Angel by. She was writing about St Petersburg, about fur-swathed figures driving in troikas through the endless snow. The Russian revolution had filled her imagination with the most lively pictures of captivating luxury and arrogance set against a background of vast pine-forests with wolves, and country estates with colourful serfs; cossacks, tuberculous students; music, chandeliers, intrigues, adultery: great tragedy, too, for the beautiful and proud—this, her favourite theme.

When the sun poured too strongly into her bedroom, she wiped her forehead with the sheet—without disturbing the cats—and went on writing. She remembered that in this way she had written so much of her first novel, translating herself, as its heroine, to the Paradise House of her imagination. Now she was a famous writer, living in Paradise House itself and, if not rich any longer, she had at least spent a great deal in the past and still had the means within herself of earning more. She recollected with distaste and pity the girl she had been, and thought with relief of how her life had changed. Beyond all this—the unimaginable good fortune—she had Esmé. Even her day-dreams of the past had not envisaged *him* for herself, although she had invented him, or someone much akin to him, in one book after another. I have everything, she would think, not in gratitude, but in profound wonderment and content.

Esmé took her letters to her one morning. There were still plenty from her admirers; every morning came some from people to whom her books had been a turning-point in their lives, an inspiration or a solace in grief. She read these letters several times and always answered them, with a vague graciousness, in her sprawling handwriting, in violet ink. She imagined such letters going their way, the recipients thunderstruck, felled by gratitude and surprise: they would be passed round and boasted about and handed down as heirlooms. Occasionally, she received the other kind. Clergymen objected to her views. She was accused of corrupting the young. These letters gave her a sense of power and she enjoyed reading them; she could perfectly understand that clergymen would be provoked, and she did not write for children. Letters which merely made carping criticisms, about flowers coming out in the wrong season, Orion appearing in the night sky in August, or some confusions with Greek deities, she put down as the work of literary critics, a part of their general scheme against her.

She laid aside her writing and opened the first of her letters, and the usual look of pleasure brightened her face. "Here is a dear old man," she said. "At times, he writes, my books have rescued him from despair, lifted him to a higher sphere . . ." she peered short-sightedly at the letter. . . . "Yes, 'higher sphere' I think it is . . . how kind of him to write. And what an educated hand-writing." She passed it over to Esmé, full of confidence, and took up another. "Dear Madam," she read, "Since you can only describe what you write of from your own experiences, we must deduce from this fact that you are nothing but a common whore. Please keep your excesses to yourself and spare yours in disgust, Lover of Literature."

Esmé looked up quickly at the sudden stillness. She read the letter through again and began to tremble: her eyes burned and blazed. "Lover of literature!" she gasped. "Lover of scurrilous slander."

"Let me see," he said gently.

While he was reading the letter, she tried to calm herself, to fight down nausea. Then she heard him laughing, softly at first and then he flung back his head and laughed as he had not done for years. She looked at him in amazement which changed to cold disdain.

"So you don't care what is said of me?" she asked when he had finished. "It doesn't matter what is written—the most slanderous, defamatory thing about my personal character?"

"It isn't to be taken seriously," he said hurriedly.

"It wasn't written as a joke; you must see that."

"You aren't upset about it, surely?"

"I feel very sick," she said and her eyes filled with tears.

"My dear Angel, you must learn to be above such a petty thing. It was scrawled by a lunatic when the moon was full. Who else would sit down and take such trouble?"

"I still feel sick," she insisted. Then more calmly, she added: "Yes, he must be mad."

"He or she."

She looked again carefully at the letter, then at the post-mark. London E.C.4 meant nothing to her. "Such illiteracy: do you see the handwriting? The excruciating composition, and the nasty little piece of paper. Oh, but all the same I am upset now. I feel that I can't start my day's work. I am tired already."

"Get up and come out into the garden. You can work there under the trees or on the terrace. Don't waste the sunshine."

"No, I shan't work so hard or so fast as I shall if I stay here. I should waste time by dressing myself and I can eat my lunch more quickly on my own up here. And I have vowed to myself, too."

Every pathetic word alienated him. He grew sulky again with guilt and no longer cared if he comforted her or not.

"I will read the other letters another time," she said quietly, putting them on one side. "Will you burn this loathsome one? We will try to forget it."

He went up later in the day and she seemed cheerful again. Manuscript lay all over her luncheon-tray; the cats slept on some of the pages. The sun beat into the room. She had taken off her nightgown, her black hair was thrust back from her glistening shoulders and her face was damp with sweat. He sat down in a chair by the window and watched her.

"Am I interrupting you? Tell me to go away if I am."

"No, no." She shook her head and went on writing. The blue-black hair lay against her cream-coloured arms; the skin under her armpits was a deeper colour, of a shade near apricot. With his eyes half-closed he tried to set limits to the picture he saw, as if he were going to paint her as she sat upright among the tumbled bedclothes and the crumpled pillows. The raven hair was a wonderful contrast to the gradations of white through cream to warm yellow. He studied the textures of the linen with its grey shadows and her skin with its golden lights. He sat and considered her, trying to see her afresh, wondering what she was like, as he had often wondered when they were first acquainted. Since their marriage, she had become nothing better than a constant irritation: he overlooked her courage, her loyalty to him. In the trenches during the war, she had not seemed a real person to him, symbolising home and warmth and comfort, as wives did to other men. He never spoke of her and few of his fellow-officers knew that he was married. When his time for leave had come, he could not return to her, to what he now thought of as a barren conflict. Once I get back here, to France again, he had told himself, I shall never see another leave. He was hopeless about the future of the war and had only lived from day to day longing for this precious respite from the rain and the rats and lice, the flat, sodden landscape with its splintered poplars and ruined churches, its noise and his fear of it. It was intolerable to think of spending the few good days, the last of his life as he saw them then, at Paradise House with Angel. He had married her when he was in despair, had had nothing to give her and never would have, certainly not love, and he begrudged her, knowing well how she was suffering, his few days away from the war.

I could have spared her those, he now thought. It was a thing I once had to offer. And the chief reason why I cannot feel affection for her now is that I behaved basely to her then.

Nora opened the door. She had come up to collect the tray. She liked to do this herself because she missed Angel's company, especially at meals, which she and Esmé ate in silence. Today, she thought it a good thing that she had come herself. "Angel! Where *is* your nightgown? You mustn't sit there naked, however hot it is. What if Bessie had come up to fetch the tray?"

She was miserably put out at the sight of Angel's nakedness and Esmé's presence. This was part of the life under that roof which she chose to ignore. She stacked the pages of manuscript neatly and picked up the tray. "Please, Angel!" she said. "Do remember what I have said. It is wrong to embarrass servants."

"Oh, fiddlesticks," Angel murmured when she had gone. "What is she chattering about?" She shook her damp hair back from her shoulders.

"Couldn't you have the blind half-drawn if you are so hot?" Esmé suggested.

"No, I couldn't see."

She looked at him for a moment with an expression of fear. "My eyes are much worse," she said. "I have to write so large and look so close to see, but even then they burn and ache and keep misting over." She covered them for a moment with her hands. Trying to be kind to her, he went over to the bed, took her hand from her eyes and looked at her. "Suppose I were to go blind . . ." she began. "What would happen to us?"

"Such lovely green eyes," he said, refusing to be drawn into her anxiety. Then he said lightly: "And why should you expect to see with them as well?"

She smiled, but she knew the truth—that the compliment was only what he paid to escape being troubled. One more worry I must keep to myself, she thought.

She finished her novel before the end of September. It was early evening when she wrote the last word, and she at once got out of bed and began to dress herself. Her legs were weak from having rested so long and she felt stifled and uncomfortable in her clothes. One or two cats took over the warm place she had left in the bed and she gathered up the scattered papers out of their way. She felt a reluctance to leave this room and face the strangeness of downstairs again. When she was half dressed she went to a window and leant out. It was a cool and colourless evening. One of the peacocks dragged itself along the terrace, looking sick to death. She was unlucky in her pets, she often said; though Esmé felt it was the pets themselves who were unlucky.

The parrot had died; the marmoset long ago had caught pneumonia and perished, with agonies of shivering and teeth-chattering and little pleading noises; Sultan had his grand memorial over at Alderhurst; various cats had simply disappeared; she had tramped the woods calling for them, but they would never be seen again. Now this peacock seemed unable to support itself upon its legs. As she leant out of the window watching it as it trailed feebly about below, she heard two shots from the distant woods a long way away; in the still evening she heard their echo running round the valley. The sound emphasised the stillness. No one seemed about. She wondered where Nora and Esmé were, and, feeling suddenly as if she had been deserted when she most needed company, she hurried to finish dressing. The end of her work, to which she had advanced so determinedly, so eagerly, came with a sense of anti-climax. She had emerged from it at last, to a perfectly dull evening with nothing exceptional in the least likely to happen, no fanfare of trumpets, not a glass lifted in salutation, or even any sensation within herself other than tiredness and a certain shrinking from the world.

Bessie was in the hall when she went downstairs. She was brushing up feathers from a torn little bird that the cats had brought in: she straightened her back and said good-evening suspiciously, as Angel passed. So she has finished swinging the lead, Bessie thought, thankful that there would be no more trays to be carried upstairs.

Nora was in the library, writing, but she did not know where Esmé was.

"You ought to get one of those artificial limbs," Marvell told Esmé as he pushed him through the woods in his bath-chair.

"Those *what?*" Esmé asked contemptuously. "Oh, for God's sake, don't run the damn thing straight over these tree-roots. It jars my leg that isn't there."

"Very sorry, sir," said Marvell, pulling a face behind Esmé's back. Esmé knew perfectly well that he was doing this. Venus Wood was on the other side of the valley, but they made their way there most evenings at this time, along the rough track, Marvell puffing and groaning as he pushed and Esmé snapping at him, enjoying their strange companionship all the same. They made an odd picture to the few people they ever met, boys out bird's-nesting, men going home from work to the half-dozen cottages scattered in the valley, women collecting kindling wood. Marvell wore an old panama hat stuck with jays' feathers, Esmé carried the guns across his knees.

The duck-shooting had been Marvell's idea.

They had discovered the lake in Venus Wood one evening when they had lost themselves on their walk. The stretch of water, tarnished in the evening mist and reflecting the high trees which rose from its edge, was almost sinister in its silence and its unexpectedness. Nothing was stirring there; it was so enclosed, so windless. But as they stood on the bank, looking about them, they became conscious of a faint disturbance in the air, as if a breeze were blowing up; it was a far-away commotion, a gathering volume of sound. As it grew louder, it resolved itself into the beating of wings and the crying of the wild duck as they flew in over the tree-tops to the lake. At once, notions of wholesale slaughter came to Marvell's mind.

A rotting punt was half out of the water among some rushes, and this Marvell had later managed to repair. Like schoolboys, they could think of nothing but their new enthusiasm and, with Angel in bed and never wanting the car or wondering where they were, they were free to do as they pleased. When the boat was ready, Esmé had gone with Marvell to buy the guns in Norley.

Then, at the very time when their plans were all made, with the boat ready and the guns obtained—but not yet paid for—Angel had finished her novel and was to be up and about again. It had been her custom to wheel Esmé about the grounds for an hour before dinner, accompanied by Czar and several of the cats. He could only think now that at some moment during their boring perambulations the ducks would come flying in over the trees, alighting on the surface of the lake, the elephant-grey lake, dozens and dozens of them ready for slaughter, and he would not be there to see.

And Lady Baines was to balk his designs even more.

She came to luncheon the next day in her maroon-coloured Fiat with its fringed and buttoned upholstery, silk tassels, cut-glass bottles, vase of roses and maidenhair-fern. The chauffeur's livery matched the motor car.

191

Lady Baines was Angel's nearest neighbour, she had declared on her first visit, ignoring the dozens of cottages, the doctor's house, the Vicarage, which lay between Paradise House and her own home. "No one between us and Lady Baines at Bottrell Saunter," Angel told people, doing the same.

Widowhood had increased Lady Baines's authority. She was nearing sixty, and for many years, since her husband died, had given most of her time to what she called 'public work', in spite of the fact that it was largely settled in secret— 'settled nicely', as she would say, having pulled all the strings, had a word with so-and-so, written notes, summoned underlings to her presence. When the time came for the public meeting itself, her antagonists, ready to be crudely defiant to her when she opposed their schemes, would be flustered to find that she had nothing to say: instead, an attack would be launched from a quite unexpected quarter, from some nervous school-teacher or verbose trade-unionist; support would come from all parts of the floor, for Lady Baines's notes had been sent far and wide; she had had a word with so many people and told them to have more words with other people and they would hasten to obey. Party politics meant little to her: she saw them as a sign of weakness, in fact. On the Bench and on County Council Committees she was indomitable and inflexible, using herself as her standard. She set an example, and when other people fell short of it there was a sickness in the community which she was prompt to deal with; broad-minded, humanitarian, her work for unmarried mothers, sexual perverts and adolescent delinquents was energetic and forthright and discussed by her always in the most explicit and technical of terms. She knew about life and nothing shocked her. In her bearing and manner, with her expensive, dowdy clothes, her fine pink-and-white complexion and her love of gardening, she was most people's idea of a typical elderly Englishwoman. She had, though, come from Boston, Massachusetts, as a bride; but that was long ago.

"You're getting fat, Esmé," she said as soon as she came

into the drawing-room. "You'll let yourself get out of condition. You need more exercise."

"How can I take exercise, like this?"

"I had a cousin who lost a leg in Africa . . . had it snapped off by a crocodile. Ridiculous man. Making a laughing-stock of Christianity, everybody thought . . . I forgot to say that he was a missionary. But ridiculous or not, he faced the situation with courage." Esmé winced. "He never gave in. He got himself a wooden leg and he started to play games, a thing he'd never gone in for much before; cricket, you know, with a runner, of course, when he was batting."

"Of course," murmured Esmé disdainfully.

"Polo, ping-pong, croquet. . . . ."

"How wonderful!" Angel said briskly, to put an end to the catalogue.

"Archery, tricycling. . . ."

"How very grotesque!" said Esmé.

"Another thing," said Lady Baines. "Until your wooden leg arrives . . . and I must remember to get you an address . . . until then, what is wrong with sedentary exercises?"

She sat down on the edge of a chair and stretched one leg forward; with her hands on her hips, she began to bend and chant, "Over to the left, straightening, down to the right." Her toque slipped down over her forehead. "Trunk bend to the right, trunk bend to the left."

Bessie came in to announce that luncheon was ready, and seemed spellbound.

"Have you got all that, now, Esmé?" asked Lady Baines. "Another one for the pot-bellied. Grow *tall*. . . ." She put up her chin and quickly straightened her hat. "Stretch. Shoulders back. Buttocks clenched. Now draw in the diaphragm. Hold your breath." She held hers for what seemed an unconscionable time. Bessie withdrew and stood in the hall with her hand over her mouth. Nora and Angel looked at one another uncertainly, Esmé, with loathing, at Lady Baines. "Exhale!" she shouted triumphantly, when she had done so. "Now luncheon!"

But luncheon was not any better. They listened queasily to her descriptions of incestuous cottage-life about which she had been making some inquiries. When the veal pie was brought she asked for the crust only.

"Have you ever *seen* a calf led to the slaughter?" she asked Nora, who was glad to say that she had not.

"I have only seen soldiers," said Esmé, but no one paid any attention to him.

Angel could remember the cul-de-sac leading off the Butts in Norley: Abattoir Lane, it was called; the panic-stricken beasts were driven into it, herded together, lowing and baying, making frenzied attempts to escape. But Lady Baines was describing it vividly, even the inside of the slaughterhouse, for she had made it her business to do the full inspection.

Nora looked at her plate in disgust and remorse.

"Beautifully tender," Esmé said, to annoy Lady Baines, to show how little her words influenced him.

"If we had to do it ourselves, or even be present always when it was done, there would not be one of us who was not a vegetarian," she was saying.

"And poor little beans, too," said Esmé, "shredded to bits and dropped into boiling water."

"I love animals," Angel said slowly. "I hate violence."

"I was sure it was only thoughtlessness," said Lady Baines. "And so you have finished your novel? And what is this one all about?" Without waiting to be told, she said: "I ought to write a book myself one of these days." She implied that it would be a long time, however, before she had not some better way of occupying herself.

"How *blunt* she is," said Esmé wearily when she had gone. He could see that Angel was preoccupied about something.

The duck-shooting had to be secret. Angel's thoughtfulness had led to this. "I see that I shall have to revise our ideas," she had said at dinner after Lady Baines's visit, and she refused to eat the fish or the ham savoury. "All animals are the same, after

194

all. I keep thinking of my darling Czar being treated so brutally, the cats snared like rabbits or the peacocks shot like pheasants. I blame myself for what I have done—corpse-eating, as Lady Baines so rightly describes it. I am sure that we can live very well on vegetables and eggs."

"But what will Czar live on?"

"He can live on eggs as well."

"Poor eggs!" said Esmé. "What fiendish brutality!"

As soon as dinner was over, Angel went to her desk and began to make notes for a pamphlet she would write, a letter she would send to *The Times*, a lecture she would give. She was burning with her new indignation and eager for the crusade. And now for the first of the great vegetarian novels, Esmé thought. But he was glad to see her busy writing. The next evening, when she was still doing so, he was able to go to the lake with Marvell. At dinner they had had cheese-pudding.

"I am sorry we couldn't go for our turn round the garden," she told Esmé. "I had to write while it was all in my mind."

"It didn't matter, Marvell took me."

"Where did you go?"

"Through the woods a little way."

"Then that was all right," said Angel.

What we need, Marvell and I, is a retriever, Esmé thought, looking with contempt at Czar who was in a dejected mood after his first vegetarian day.

Esmé's terrible moment had passed. Angel had given him the money, made her bright and soothing speech, smiled her fond smile. He had been able to pay his debt and the threatening and insulting letters had now ceased; but he was wounded in a way he prayed to forget, and he shied away from the reminders.

"Those weeks of writing so many hours a day have strained your eyes," Nora said, as Angel peered at a letter she was reading. "You are getting quite a frown. Why not see some-one? Perhaps you should wear spectacles."

"I don't believe in them," Angel said. "They make muscles lazy. Work is good for every part of the body."

But she often covered her burning eyes with her hands, and when Esmé saw her do this he always looked quickly away.

Theo was happy about her new novel: it broke into a canter at the first sentence, he wrote. It raced away. It was in her early style, full of swagger and exaggeration. He hoped that, with the war forgotten, she had rediscovered her romantic vein, given up her preaching, her irrelevant thunderings and denunciations. He did not know yet what damage Lady Baines was doing.

"Marvell gets less and less done," Nora complained. "The garden's a disgrace. He leaves that boy to work on his own. There is no supervision. He himself just disappears. What does he do all day?"

"I'm afraid I take up a good deal of his time," said Esmé, with a look of simple candour.

"If you got one of those self-propelling chairs or one with a motor to it, you could take yourself out and let Marvell get on with his work."

"Rather tricky to manage in the woods with all that undergrowth and the tree roots across the paths."

"You needn't go to the woods."

Angel thought Nora's was a good idea and she sent for the invalid chair at once. Marvell was not very pleased when he saw it; it would lessen Esmé's dependence upon him, which might in time lessen his own power to arrange his life as it most suited him. He was now sometimes obliged to stay at work while Esmé went down to Venus Wood alone.

When he went without Marvell, Esmé often left his gun behind. He was sometimes quite content to sit there on his own or to lower himself into the punt and paddle it out into the middle of the lake, watching the sky and water changing colour. He preferred the solitude to Marvell's shiftings and whisperings as they waited to open fire. He was better able to feel and observe the nature of the strange and isolated place. He was drawn to it: it had for him a hallucinatory quality and came often into his dreams, sometimes in a way which disturbed him. I won't go there again, he would think hurriedly, just at the moment of waking.

He liked to sit quite still and guess how long it would be before the moment when he would first hear the ducks coming in. It was almost apprehensively that he strained his ears; something so inevitable about their coming gave him a sensation of dread. He tried to imagine an evening when he would wait in vain, and he believed that if ever there were such an evening he would go home very much disturbed and never visit the place again.

When the short days came, the ducks were earlier, flying in in the afternoon, sometimes when the sun seemed to be slipping down through the branches of the trees, with its pink light all over the surface of the water and the frost-rimed bracken at its edge.

It would be dark before he was out of the woods, his hands dead with the cold and his limbs stiff. Marvell, a little huffily, would greet him; in spite of his crossness at having been left out of the expedition, he usually had some little treat for Esmé, something to warm him up, some cocoa and a bacon sandwich; once, as Esmé was now starved of meat, a pot full of pigs' trotters, in their gluey juice.

"Poor little pigs!" Esmé said.

"I don't think!" said Marvell.

The winter passed and Venus Wood remained a secret between them. Angel and Nora were both occupied with producing pamphlets and attending meetings. Vegetarianism led to so many other enthusiasms and indignations, to campaigns against vivisection and vaccination, the muzzling of dogs, the use of pit-ponies. Nora was given new chances for martyrdom. Duties called her from opposite directions at the same time: there was always some pleasure she could deny herself, as on one evening when Angel set out for a meeting at Lady Baines's. At first, Nora thought that she could go and then she was sure that she must not.

"I shall have to stay; although I should have loved the outing. I don't seem to have had a breather all day; but Bessie is baking bread and she will never knead it enough if I am not here to watch over her."

Marvell had the car on the drive and was just running a leather over the windscreen when Angel and Nora came out of the house.

"The evenings *are* drawing out," Nora said. "Last week it was dark at this time."

A shot sounded far off and the noise ricocheted about the valley.

"I am always hearing this," said Angel. "What does it mean, Marvell?"

He passed the leather slowly over the glass, seemed to consider and then said: "Poachers, I shouldn't be surprised."

"How dare they? In my grounds, do you mean?"

"It sounded like it, madam."

"Then I shall have them punished for trespassing and plundering, slaughtering harmless creatures. I won't have it, Marvell."

"No, Madam."

"It's your business, you understand, to make sure that it's stopped."

"I'll see to it tomorrow."

He held the door open and she settled herself in the car. "I shall be back at six-thirty, Nora."

"Give my kind regards to Lady Baines," Nora said wistfully and turned back to the house.

When the meeting was over, Marvell drove Angel back through the dark lanes. "Quite a nip in the air," he observed, but received no answer.

As soon as they reached Paradise House, Nora came running down the steps.

"Esmé hasn't come in," she said. "I think Marvell should help us look for him." She had flung a coat over her shoulders and her teeth were chattering. "It's been dark for so long and I've been round and round the garden calling until I'm hoarse."

"I'll go straight away," Marvell said. He took a torch from the car and set off at a jog-trot. "I've been to the stables," Nora shouted after him, but he ran on without replying. The light from the torch swung from side to side, striking the boles of trees. He ran without hesitation and he did not waste his breath with calling.

Angel had said nothing. She stood on the drive, seeming irresolute, as if not quite certain what the commotion was about. Then a great sense of danger dawned in her. She flung her muff down on the steps and turned to Nora, almost thrusting her away from her. "You go to the orchard and call."

"Es-mé, Es-mé," Nora began to shout immediately as she set off. To hear her own voice seemed to give her courage.

Angel followed Marvell. She felt instinctively that he had chosen the right direction. She had no light and kept running into the trees; brambles snatched at her ankles and caught her skirt as she stumbled forward, her hands stretched out before her. She thought that she was lost in the darkness, and after a while she stopped and tried to find her bearings, and then she heard footsteps and saw a light zig-zagging between the trees. Marvell was coming back. She managed to call out to him once, her voice harsh with terror.

"Madam, turn back; we must get help."

She could not move or speak. The torch-battery was running out, the light dimmed, then it failed altogether.

"Venus Wood lake," Marvell was saying, but his words seemed nonsensical to her. "His wheel-chair there on the bank and the boat turned over on the water. Oh, madam. . . ."

"What boat?"

"There's not a sign or sound; the water just as still and black as the sky and his crutch floating out there on it. Something terrible wrong, I would say. Poor madam!" He made a movement towards where he could sense but not see that she was standing, but she had suddenly started forward.

"Don't go there, I beg you," he said. "You come along back to the house with me and we must send for the police."

She was plunging on through the trees away from him, in the direction he had come.

"Oh, don't go to that dreadful place," he shouted after her.

Half-running, she blundered on. The trees blocked her path like obstacles in a nightmare, seeming to move forward in her way. She began to call Esmé's name as she ran, and the sound of her distracted voice made Marvell's heart turn over. When she came to the edge of the lake she fell silent. It was not so dark there where the trees parted, and the water looked smooth and polished, unmoving. For a moment she was too afraid to call or make any sound: it seemed to her that her slightest breath might precipitate disaster. Then she began to whisper his name over and over again: as her panic grew, her voice rose until she was screaming hysterically. She tried to blot out everything with her cries. The sound rang round and round the lake and frightened birds flew off the tops of the trees, their clattering wings like derisive applause from hundreds of clapping hands.

PART 5

i

THE memorial—Esmé's memorial—was built on rising ground beyond the house. It could be seen from the lime avenue; people approaching by way of the drive were confronted by the untidy gap in the woods where beech trees had been felled. Nature had hastened to fill in the space temporarily with fire-weed, now bracken was beginning to encroach upon the granite obelisk; rabbits nibbled the grass under the iron chains which railed it off; the stone was splashed with the droppings of rooks and wood-pigeons.

The memorial itself had never been finished. Angel's further plans to embellish it with a flight of steps and a marble seat carved with Esmé's name had never been fulfilled. Word had come to the stonemason that her credit was not good in the neighbourhood, and he had decided to send in the bill for the obelisk itself before risking more materials. Now, fifteen years after Esmé's death, a part of the money was still owing. The mason did not consider, as Angel did, that a signed first edition of one of her works was a generous substitute for half the sum. She was, as the years went by, inclined to try more and more to settle her accounts with anything but money: dismayed and indignant tradespeople received copies of her novels or old photographs of herself; they invariably returned them, but by that time the account had been written off in Angel's mind: she herself was calmly satisfied that justice had been done. Consequent rudeness she ignored; they were part of the general unrest, the prevalent philistinism which had brought about so much wretchedness, socialism, income-tax, the decline of her own fame and, lately, a recurring threat of war.

Few people came to Paradise House; those who did almost fought their way through weeds to the front door. Lady Baines drove over once or twice a month from Bottrell Saunter and, apart from the vet who was always being summoned to dose a sick cat, the doctor was their most frequent visitor. He called nearly every week to attend to Nora's gout.

"How can she have gout?" Angel had asked when the illness was first diagnosed. "A glass of elderflower wine's the most she ever takes."

"Heredity," the doctor said wearily. He knew what he was up against—Angel's impatience with Nora for being ill and her impatience with him for saying that she was.

"Gout!" she said furiously when she returned to Nora's bedroom. "Some fine relations you must have had." Brewery folk, she thought, as Aunt Lottie would have done.

Aunt Lottie had died in peaceful retirement, but a year or two before her death she had paid a week's visit to Paradise House. The invitation was given in a spirit of condescension and accepted from curiosity. Angel looked forward to making the most of the situation in which, in the face of all that Aunt Lottie could ever have imagined or desired, she was the mistress of Paradise House, sleeping, no doubt, in Madam's bedroom, and Bessie up in the attics where Aunt Lottie's place had been, where Angel herself, if she had not had other plans, might have found herself, too. Motives, on both sides, were spiteful and the visit was stimulating for that reason. Angel was as over-bearing as she could be and Aunt Lottie remained resolutely unimpressed. It was horrible to see the dear old place in such a state, she said, and she wouldn't have come if she had known. Madam must be turning in her grave.

"You should have seen it when I took it over," said Angel. "Burnt out, broken down."

"Best to have let it be; best to have let it fall down and put it out of its agony. Why throw away good money, just to be left with this great mockery of a place?"

At every turn there was something different to deplore.

"All these horrible dirty cats, the smell is dreadful. I'm sure they're all breeding like rabbits. And what does that Marvell do the whole day long to be letting these weeds clutter up the terrace? Madam's rose-garden, what a mercy she's not here in my place to see that." It was the burden of her conversation, that Madam's death had been propitious indeed: all the same, she dwelt on the picture of her revolving in her grave at the sorry decline of her old home.

Angel was complacent. She knew that her aunt was retaliating as best she could; but the fact was indisputable that something had come about which she could never have believed possible, and Angel was not ending up in prison or the workhouse, as her waywardness had always indicated, but at Paradise House itself, however ruined and run over it might be.

"You ought to sell it—not that you could," her aunt often said.

"I intend to stay here for the rest of my life."

"The timber would fetch something," Aunt Lottie said, ignoring her. "Cut your losses and build yourself a nice little bungalow, a small place that you could manage to keep clean."

Paradise House was not clean. Even with most of the rooms shut up, Bessie could not manage it, old as she was and with such haphazard help as she got from the cottage people in the valley, who could not come if it rained or if their children fell ill, and when they did come were too much infected by the air of neglect in the house to do much work. Nora was now so often laid up, and Angel, as Bessie said, never took a duster in her hand.

"What happened to that girl—Angelica?" Angel asked Aunt Lottie. Old inhibitions persisted and her voice was surly.

"Girl! Well, my goodness, her own daughter's expecting her second." But she had not grown up in Angel's mind, and never would. "She married a very nice gentleman, a barrister, but things aren't what they were for them. All the wrong people have come to the top these days and the real gentry have to reduce and cut down. It's hard for people like that, I always think, and Miss Angelica wasn't brought up to do a great deal for herself."

Angel imagined her struggling to put on her own stockings.

Theo had retired and the business was run by a nephew of Willie Brace, who seemed blandly impervious to Angel's threatening letters. She would not admit the thought that her fame had reached its peak and passed away; instead, her great vanity grew; she was entangled in delusions. She insisted that there was a conspiracy against her, that she had made powerful enemies by her outspokenness: indeed, she was able to look round her and find with the greatest difficulty enough friends to count upon the fingers of one hand: Nora, Lady Baines, Theo, perhaps, who sometimes wrote letters to her or sent a book which he, always mistakenly, thought that she would like to read. To make her list up to five, she would have to include the scoundrelly Marvell, with whom she enjoyed a cantankerous day-to-day relationship—she, trying to beat him into sub-mission—he, eluding her with craft. There was also a young man who called occasionally to look at Esmé's paintings. He had discovered one or two of them in London and tracked down the rest of the collection at Paradise House. Angel was suspicious and insisted that they were not for sale, but she felt sensations of tenderness towards him. That he was an art critic might have affected her differently, but his enthusiasm for Esmé's paintings disarmed her.

"Do you see?" he asked her, as they stood in front of her portrait. "The wonderful economy in colour and composition?"

"I always thought the hands exceptionally well done."

"And in portrait-painting something a little extra is asked for. The work cannot be judged quite from the usual standards; for the point is that there must be some likeness—the imagina-tion is fettered."

She raised her hands and glanced at them. They were shiny and crinkled nowadays, discoloured and with veins on them as thick as worms. To her, they were still as smooth and white as in the painting. "Something tragic and solitary about the pose and setting, the eyes yearning ... perhaps I embarrass you?"

"I am never embarrassed," she said coldly.

"In most portraits of women, the attempt to catch the true expression fails; instead of looking mysterious they appear as smug as the Mona Lisa; a warm smile turns into a smirk; far from appearing sad, they seem merely harassed."

"That was my dear dog, Sultan," she said.

The other paintings were put up on the easel one by one and murmured over. The young man, whose name was Clive Fennelly, was dressed in a navy-blue suit; his black shoes were dusty; he was determinedly citified in his appearance. His dark eyes seemed too luminous in his pale face, his greasy hair was receding already at the temples. He looked unhealthy, but there was something about him, perhaps his voice with its intimate tone and adenoidal drawl, which was sexually attractive to women. Angel was especially conscious of such an attraction—from fear of its ultimate meaning—as with Esmé when she first had known him. She sensed a promise of tenderness, the quality she always searched for and so often brusquely rejected, not knowing how to deal with its effect upon herself, suspicious of the emotions it aroused in her.

"I love this house," he said. They came down the stairs from the studio into the hall. There was a shaft of sunlight over the floor in which a cat lay crunching a dead mouse. "So cruel!" Angel murmured wearily, turning her head. "God's fault: not mine," he heard her say. She sat down for a moment in one of the empty niches in the wall. Once she had planned to set statues in them, but had long ago forgotten.

"This house and you in it," said the young man. He was completely sincere. The space, the quiet, the strangeness captivated him; it was so unlike the neat villas, the golden privet hedges, the shaved lawns of the suburbs where he lived. The wildness and beauty were enhanced for him by Angel herself in her dress of faded, streaky red, her coiled-up hair with not a grey thread in it, her eccentricity which seemed to him so typical of the decaying aristocracy. He was to be allowed to come again and to take photographs of the paintings for an article he would write, but on no account were they to be entrusted to him or anyone else in London, not to be bought or borrowed or looked at.

When he returned it was half-way through August and the house was full of dusty sunshine. He drove in his open car along the lanes to Paradise House. In the fields on either side, the braided ears of wheat were a pale colour against the blue sky; the elm-trees almost black. From the sunny landscape, he descended into the over-lush greenness of the valley where water trickled over stones, the earth smelt of mushrooms.

The front door stood open and a peacock stalked out of it as Clive Fennelly came near. Bessie crossed the hall, drying her hands on her apron. "Madam's in the courtyard. You are to go round," she said. "Shoo that saucy bird off as you go, if you please, sir."

Clive clapped his hands rather nervously at the peacock as he passed by, and did not like the look he got from its round eye.

In the grass-grown courtyard he could hear voices. In a wash-house, he found Angel bending over a mangle; her long wet hair was between the rollers, and Marvell was turning the handle. Water splashed down on to the stone floor.

"I am nearly ready," said Angel in a muffled voice. She could see only the visitor's feet in the doorway. When Marvell released her hair from the rollers, she swept it back over the towel on her shoulders, straightened herself and held out a wet hand in greeting.

"Thank you, Marvell," she said, walking away with Clive. "He always washes my hair and it dries much quicker that way," she explained. "It is really rather thick and long. We will go up to the studio and get things ready for you. My dear friend, Miss Howe-Nevinson, who was ill when you last came, is much better this morning and getting up for lunch."

All the morning she watched Clive at work. She paced about the studio, brushing her hair, and when it was time for luncheon she went down with the towel still on her shoulders and her hair spread over it. Because Nora protested, she determined to keep it down all day.

All through the meal she and Nora quarrelled, Angel irritably and Nora with many gentle reproaches. Clive, sensing the enjoyment both had from this, was not embarrassed. It is what will be missed, he thought, when one of them dies and leaves the other all alone. Worse, in a way, it will be, than losing a husband or a wife; perhaps this is a more consoling relationship.

"But if Bessie makes mint-sauce you say you prefer onion-sauce," Nora said. "And if I order onion sauce, you ask for red-currant jelly. I'm sure I don't know where I am."

Her illness seemed to have emboldened Nora. She spoke her mind more freely and had found out what a pleasure that could be.

Angel refilled Clive's glass with wine and left Nora's empty.

"I should think I might have onion sauce *and* mint-sauce and red-currant jelly, too, if I want them," she said.

"The table looks like a grocer's shop already with all the pots of this and that. Mr. Fennelly must think us very strange."

Mr. Fennelly went on eating his mutton.

"I should like some more wine, please," Nora added in a quiet, aggrieved voice.

Angel filled her mouth and, chewing slowly, looked dreamily out of the window.

"Angel, I said that I should like a little more wine."

"*You* fetch the red-currant jelly and *I* will give you some more wine."

"But why not ring for Bessie if you are so set on having it?"

"I reminded her of it when I saw her laying the table. She said there wasn't any."

"Well, if she said that there isn't any, then there isn't any."

"August—and all the red-currant jelly finished?"

"Mr Fennelly will be tired of hearing about red-currant jelly."

"No, no, not at all," he said quickly. "Most fascinating." Angel glanced at him suspiciously. "I didn't realise it was a seasonal thing," he added.

"I make it in June," Nora explained, "and in the ordinary way it is a bad year when it doesn't last right through until the following June. Fifteen pounds I aim at, and a long and tedious job it is. This year, however, I was in bed with gout when the fruit was ripe. Not much gets done when I am not about.

"Gout runs in her family," Angel said.

They are like naughty children, Clive thought.

After luncheon, Angel took him for a walk.

"I should like to have come," Nora said, "but I have to try to clean some of the silver."

"Yes, you ought to rest your foot," said Angel.

It was the time of year when the peacock shed his feathers and, as they walked along the terrace, Angel gathered them up, turned them so that the light struck the gold and bronze and blue, stroked her cheek with them as she talked—a strange figure to Clive, in her long, faded red dress and with her black hair hanging down her back. Cats followed her, arching themselves and cavorting about the hem of her skirt, bewitched by her presence. After a while, as Angel led the way out of the garden and up the slope towards the obelisk, one cat after another lost interest and flagged, felt themselves drawn too far from home, or were distracted by scramblings in the bracken. Two young Abyssinian cats remained, going lithely on up the hill, their wide tufted ears pricked forwards, their coats, ticked like a hare's, shining in the sunlight.

Clive Fennelly took out a handkerchief and passed it over his face. He thought that Angel, despite her own eccentricity of dress—was it an ancient evening gown or fancy dress?—and her hair falling to her waist, might object if he were to take his jacket off. The two cats went purposefully ahead, knowing this walk, he guessed; he and Angel, who now beat time with the bunch of feathers to some music which only she could hear, followed them. Trees parted, and the obelisk, so preposterous in its conception, now showed above them on the skyline. Prime Minister he might have been, Clive thought, or some discoverer of the North Pole; not an unknown minor painter of erratic talent and, from what one gathers, the very slackest of habits.

Every time he tripped over a briar or stumbled on a mole-hill, he felt that she must be deploring the pavements on which he usually walked, and perhaps be imagining with clear contempt the crescents of cosy houses, all so unlike her own house, the flowering trees, the neatness of the suburbs where he lived.

"There is one of my late husband's paintings in the Norley Art Gallery," she remembered to tell him.

"And also an immense Watts presented by you."

"Ah, you have seen it? That was Lord Norley's choice, you know. I merely gave the money. It was not at all the sort of picture that Esmé or I ever cared for."

"I wondered about that."

Breathless, he turned to look downhill, to give himself a rest. Below them, the walled garden was now visible. They could look right into it, at the tangled growth and broken glass, and see the rotting fruit lying on the paths; in the quiet of the afternoon a frenzied buzzing rose up from the wasps that clustered over the bruised windfalls or tunnelled into sleepy pears. Heady, the smell of the fermenting fruit. He could imagine the steamy heat down there where neglected peach-trees grew in the dusty glasshouses: the fruit at luncheon had been bored into and speckled by insects and picked up off the ground, he guessed; not off the trees.

The two cats turned and waited, seeming impatient. Angel resumed the climb and they trotted gladly at her side. When they came to the top of the hill, she sank down upon the spongy turf amongst rabbit-droppings and thistles. Clive sat down, too, and the cats stretched out, yawning.

Paradise House was in miniature now, a model laid out upon a tray. The stables were arranged about a square court-yard, and a minute Marvell could be seen, crossing to the pump with a bucket in his hand. From far away came the hoarse donkey-cry, the wheezing and coughing, as he jerked the pump-handle; water gushing into the bucket flashed silver.

There was no other view, only the tops of trees spreading away into the haze.

"Down there my husband was drowned; the lake is hidden in the woods," Angel said. "Such a short time we had together. I think of other marriages and how they dwindle, and hang fire, and fall into neglect, and I am thankful that although ours was so soon over it was as perfect as it could be while it lasted."

She suddenly pulled her gown down off her shoulder and began to scratch some spots; flea-bites, they looked like to Clive. "As perfect as could be," she repeated. "I wanted this place to be a memorial to that and to him. While he lived here he was completely happy. It is something to know that. It has had to be a comfort to me all these years that I have been alone."

"To have his sister with you must have been a comfort too," he suggested.

"Ah, Nora!" Angel smiled, as if at some wry reminiscence. "Poor Nora! Yes, I suppose it has meant something to have her here and to do what I could for her; but she is very old-maidish, you know: her little arguments are often hard to bear. Spinsters fall into such eccentricities." She spat on her hand and rubbed the flea-bites. "You must have noticed at lunch-time, for instance, the silly, pettifogulising little ways. How unlike her brother she has always been!"

Clive thought of the different stages of loyalty to the dead—the weak and imperfect dead. The first stage of having to withstand doubts, forget faults: then the next stage of acknowledging the faults, facing the doubts, learning to accept the dead ones as they were and settle down and live with the acceptance. Angel had never reached the second stage. She did not believe that Esmé was not made perfect by his dying. Yet, there was a suggestion of tenacity in her idealising. "She is fiercely loyal to my brother's memory," Nora had told him when they were left alone for a moment, and had spoken as if great ferocity were necessary. Angel had settled for perfection, had vehemently achieved it in her mind and was now at peace. The dead belonged to her as no one living could have done.

She was watching the cats, so absorbed that she had forgotten Clive. They had discovered a spring trickling downhill through the grass and, like two children, they experimented with it, seemed to discuss its dangers, with heads cocked and eyes alert: one put a curving paw into the water, as tentatively as if it were scalding hot; the other sniffed and shook drops from his whiskers. Their curiosity was then diverted by a passing fly: the water suddenly bored them and one yawned and turned its head, showing a pink triangle of opened mouth, ribbed roof to it and petal tongue. With starting, glancing movements the other advanced upon it, trying to work up a fantasy of peril and recklessness: hissing, paw raised, like an heraldic beast, the threatened one waited: they fell upon one another; rolling and struggling, went downhill, scuffling like hares with their hind legs. At the height of battle, tenderness checked them, they stopped fighting and began to lick one another peaceably. When Angel called, they came to her; but made drama even of that, weaving their way sleekly through the grass, jungle creatures now, softly treading, menaced, they pretended, from all sides.

"When I was a child, I could not have believed how happy my life would be," Angel said, gathering the cats on to her lap, where they plucked at the threads of her skirt with outstretched claws.

"To have such creatures share one's home! What a privilege!" she said, kissing their warm paws.

He thought of the chairs in her drawing-room, the brocade on which the cats had sharpened their claws, and of the curtains they had torn to ribbons.

Perhaps she saw nothing as it was, everything as it should be, though doubtless never had been; thought she retained whatever her hands had once touched: fame, love, money. Like a fortune-teller in reverse, he knew what she had been, and could tell what she had had by her assumption that it was all there still. The wrecked gardens seemed not to grieve her, as

211

they obviously grieved and irritated Nora; the prodigious collapse of Paradise House he could foretell; the stains already running up the walls, brickwork at the back held together only by matted ivy, floor boards rotting, plaster crumbling.

"A great place to keep going," he said, looking down at it.

"It is not a difficult house to run. Old servants get lazy, though," she added. "In fact, we had better go down again soon, so that I can tell Marvell to mend the car. Otherwise, he will leave it until the morning, and keep me waiting when I want to go out."

When she stood up, she trod on the hem of her dress and ripped it undone. They walked round the outside of the iron chains, to view the obelisk from all sides. It was the same from all sides. Nothing was written on it.

As they went down the hill, other cats came to meet them. "I will pick you some peaches to take back to London," Angel said, for she had begun to feel great affection for this young man and wished to spin out his visit. The door of the walled garden fell off a hinge as she pushed it open. Clive walked gingerly behind her, dodging round the waspy fruit, starting with horror when a toad shifted under a rhubarb leaf. The glasshouses were stuffy and he hoped that other toads—or worse—were not lurking there. "Tell me if you see any peaches," Angel said, peering short-sightedly among the leaves. "If there are none, then Marvell must be selling them. I long ago suspected it. Is that one?"

It was over-ripe, half-covered with a wrinkled skin of mildew, but she made him pick it. "You can cut the bad bits out when you get back to London," She held out her skirt in front and he dropped the fruit into it when it was gathered— some as hard as apples and with skins like green felt, some bruised and brown. "When you eat them this evening," she said, "you will know that they were still growing on the tree this afternoon."

He put his hand into the leaves, a sensation he disliked very much, grasped the only good-looking peach he had so far found and the only one he could imagine himself eating, and felt a sharp pain in his thumb. The wasp crawled round the fruit.

"Now what's wrong?" asked Angel. "If you are stung, just suck your thumb hard. I daresay Nora can find something to put on it when we get back to the house. She is a great one for fussing round. Don't leave the peach there after all that." Again the leaves brushed at his wrists; he shooed away the wasp and picked the peach. "That's a good one," Angel said. "Nothing like Paradise House peaches." As they made their way out of the garden she had her skirt bunched up in one hand and held the peach in the other as she ate it.

"Do pick up any pears if you want them," she said. "I know what London fruit is like."

They found Marvell in the courtyard.

"Have you been busy with the car?" she asked him, guessing that he had not.

"No, madam; to my mind the axle's gone, and that would be beyond my jurisdiction. It's no more then anyone could expect, the drive all stones and tree-roots."

"I want you to hurry and get it mended. I must drive over to Bottrell Saunter in the morning."

Bottrell Saunter! My God! thought Clive, standing by, sucking his thumb. He had had rather a lot for one day and his head was aching.

"Now, madam, if you could just get but a glimmer of sense in your head you'd understand that the car will have to go away. It's a garage job, a broken axle."

"You are supposed to be a chauffeur; you should fix it. I take no interest in mechanical things, so don't bore me any more. Just have it ready in the morning."

"It won't be ready . . ."

"And when it is done, you had better see to the drive. If it needs tidying up, then tidy it; don't come and worry me." She switched off her anger and gave Clive a warm and gentle smile, as if to underline the contretemps with Marvell and show that it was only with *him* that she was forced to be impatient. As they turned to go, her face became stern again and she said: "And will you stop stealing the peaches. I know what you are up to."

In a frenzied voice, he called after her: "And that's the last time I'll wash your hair for you, madam. You'll see. It can get crumby with nits for all I care."

"And now for Nora and her wasp-sting remedies," said Angel. "I have brought you a wounded man," she called, as she ascended the steps; her skirt, full of mouldy fruit, held out before her.

"What pleasure can he get from life at his age?" Angel said. They were discussing Lord Norley—their last hope—as they so often did. "However old is he now?"

"Ninety-seven, if you please," said Nora. "A vein of obstinacy in him. Esmé had it too. But even if he died to-morrow it would be too late now, it couldn't help us in this present difficulty."

The war had finally made it impossible for them to go on living so largely on credit. They found that they could not dodge from one shop to another for their rations: it seemed that some bills must be paid, or supplies would be cut off.

"It wasn't a very pleasant thing for a tradesman to do, to send such a letter at this season. It could be quite enough to spoil our Christmas altogether. Seventy-five pounds! Yes, it shows a fine Christmas spirit, I must say, to mention it at this season. And such a hypocrite, too. I can picture him singing hymns and carols, 'Goodwill to all men' and so on." Nora gave a sarcastic laugh. "Then he retires to his back-parlour to write threatening letters to elderly ladies."

"I think 'elderly' is rather premature. But it is an impertinent tone for a tradesman to use" Angel said placidly.

"And what proof have we that this bill is right? To spend seventy-five pounds would have taken us years and years. 'To Goods' indeed. 'To account rendered.' It means nothing. I am only surprised that he drew the line at seventy-five pounds. Why not a hundred and seventy-five, or *two* hundred and seventy-five?"

If she says 'Three hundred and seventy-five' I shall scream, Angel thought. "I can sell my emerald ring," she said quickly to stem the mounting hysteria in Nora's voice, but she only managed to change its course.

"Why *should* you? In the end, what shall we have left?"

Marvell came in to 'do the black-out' as he called it. He climbed onto a chair and fastened the shutters across the insides of the window.

"Don't come so early," Nora told him. "We could have seen for another half-an-hour by daylight. We mustn't be so wasteful of electricity."

Above her, light shone from a grubby, cobwebbed chandelier. The edges of the room—it was in the library that they were sitting—were in darkness.

"We can't infringe the laws," answered Marvell. "I must do things when I think of them."

"I want to go into Norley in the morning," Angel said.

"We might just do it on the petrol. I'm not promising."

The war was a personal annoyance to Angel, but nothing more. The passionate bitterness of that other war had faded and was forgotten: in this, there was no one to be taken from her; she had no case against it and did not care. The only people she knew were old; all that was happening in their world were small discomforts or fears that death might come a little sooner than they had bargained for, and in a different manner from what they had hoped.

Marvell was old, too, and relentlessly rude; but was a part of her life. They had sharpened their wits on one another for years; he had seen her through her grief at Esmé's death: she was most bound to him when she was admonishing him, being admonished; and she struck off his anger purposely when she was bored, though knowing that his was always the last word.

When he had drawn the shutters and gone, they heard Bessie shuffling across the hall to bolt the front door; chains rattled, she made a good job of it. They were shut in then for

215

the night, though it was only tea-time: no one would come.

Under the light, they sat on opposite sides of the table, Nora sorting through a boxful of bills, Angel writing a letter to Theo. There is a peaceful communion between two people working together at the same table: the clock ticked, the logs shifted on the fire and Angel's pen scratched across the page. An old blanket covered the table; the bare wood had been cold to Nora's wrists and she had chilblains.

Bessie brought tea in on a tray and they made room for it at one end of the table, spread the bread and margarine with jam and ate it as they read and wrote. There were no interruptions save from the cats, who sometimes mewed from outside to be let in or from inside to be let out. Then Angel went at once to open the door. They spoke occasionally, but almost as if to themselves. "I shall tell Theo what I think of that Willie Brace's nephew," Angel said. "He wouldn't like to see us starve, I know, or to discover how I am cheated."

"*Did* we have coal delivered here in June?" asked Nora. "I certainly can't recall it, if we did."

"Your household books seem all confusion," Angel murmured.

"Yes, I am sure that you could do them better,"

"Oh, no, no! Too late now, anyhow. I could never straighten them out at this stage."

Sometimes an aeroplane beat its way overhead, throbbing and droning across the valley, and Nora always listened nervously until it had gone. "Ours" made a different sound from "theirs", she declared. She could always tell. "Nonsense!" said Angel. "He is deliberately boycotting my books, that nasty Brace fellow. Because I have spoken my mind to him from time to time. No respect, either. It was rash of Theo to retire and a sorry day for me when he did. I wasn't treated like this in *his* time."

"Give him my kind regards," said Nora. "He must be a very lonely man these days."

They both thought for a moment sympathetically about Theo's loneliness, disregarding their own. Hermione had

216

died before the war. "And *I* know what it means," said Angel snubbingly. "Though my marriage was always perfect and theirs anything but that. All the same, there is a sense of loss."

Sometimes Nora felt herself almost too provoked. Your perfect marriage, she thought scornfully. I could tell you something about that.

"Yes, he is a poor old man," Angel said. For some reason, she visualised Theo sitting hunched-up and wretched in a fireless drawing-room, no lights on and sirens wailing. "I will invite him here and give him a rest from the bombs for a day or two," she said.

Nora's thoughts swept over her larder shelves. There was still a tin of butter from Australia, she remembered. Some old admirer of Angel's books had sent it from the backwoods, where only, it seemed, they were ever read now. The tin of meat which had come at the same time had been thrown into the dustbin and retrieved from there by Marvell. "Thank goodness for the prunes," Nora said. "I dreamt the other night that I cooked a whole pan full of them with salt instead of sugar and Rosita Baines already on her way to dinner."

"When?" Angel looked up from her writing with a puzzled, unfocused look.

"In my dream . . . I was saying."

Nora's catering dreams bored Angel dreadfully and she rarely listened. Although Nora knew this, she could not forgo the pleasure of telling them, or repress the resentment she felt when they were ignored.

"I wish you would take my advice and have your eyes seen to," she told Angel. "I don't think you realise how bad they are. You peer at the page and your writing goes all slantwise and I'm afraid your eyes do, too. I don't like to say this, but it gives you such an odd look and I think you ought to know."

"Umpity, tumpity, lumpity," Angel muttered.

"What did you say?"

Angel mouthed as if she were shouting, but kept her voice low. "I said that there is nothing wrong with my eyesight.

I get so tired of repeating everything, Nora. I wish that you would try to listen. Much worse just lately, I've noticed. Of course, if you are getting deaf, you can't be blamed, but I wonder if it isn't really a lazy habit. Mr Fennelly was remarking on it when he was here." She got up and put another log on the fire and, as she did so, took a quick look in the glass above the chimney-piece. Nothing wrong with her eyes, she was quite sure. She picked a cat up from the hearth-rug and held it against her shoulder for warmth. "Strange that I haven't a single grey hair yet," she said.

Nora was flurried and huffy and would not answer.

In the morning, Marvell drove Angel into Norley and she sold her emerald ring. She was a little grieved to part with it, but as she drove away from the jewellers, she thought: "At least I had it once, and that is so much better than never having had it at all."

The shop-windows were full of frosted Christmas trees and stars and paper garlands. She remembered the blobs of cotton-wool her mother had once stuck all over the window of the shop in Volunteer Road.

"When you come to the Butts," she suddenly told Marvell, "I want you to take the turning into Volunteer Road, by the brewery."

"That's a terrible slummy part, madam."

"Just do as I say and drive slowly."

The heavy and sickly smell of malt pervaded the neighbourhood; a dray clattered out over the cobbled entranceway. So little here had changed, no more than a name or two over a shop-front. The Garibaldi, the Volunteer looked just the same, with dirty brick-work, facings of glazed tiles and windows engraved with the words 'Saloon' and 'Ladies Only' and 'Jug and Bottle.'

"Straight on!" she said to Marvell. Yet when they came level with her old home, for some reason she could not look. She turned her head, as if otherwise she might be observed and all the secrets of her heart exposed, and glanced instead at the scene she had often looked out upon from their first-

218

floor window—the terrace of grey and yellow brick houses, ledges of slate over the bay windows, the lamp-post to which the children had tied their skipping ropes. Then the danger-place was passed. They drove under the railway-bridge where bus-tickets and rags of old newspapers blew about in eddies of grit and dust. "In the beginning was the Word," was the message on a poster outside the chapel beyond the bridge.

"Turn left, up the hill," said Angel.

Here, the terrace houses had small front-gardens. Something disturbing stirred and rose in Angel's mind, came to the surface with two names: Gwen and Polly. Her powers of recollection, through long, deliberate disuse, were poor; but there was more here than she wanted, and she thrust the memory back, with a sensation of having narrowly escaped from some threatening and depressing thing.

Curiosity and her triumph at her long-ago deliverance from the horrors of Volunteer Street had started her on this explora-tion; driving through the streets, knowing nobody, caring for nobody. I am Angel Deverell, she had thought. A name in the world; a world, too, in which Norley is perhaps the drabbest, shoddiest spot.

The ancient car and the strangely dressed figure sitting in it were not unnoticed: one or two people glanced as they went by, and these glances she took to be signs of gratified recog-nition. These passers-by would go home and tell their families whom they had seen. Such a gentle mood of complacency she wanted threatened by no Gwens and Pollies, and she soon smothered that remembrance: they had grown old now, she thought, those two ghostly girls; or were getting old, rather, as she was herself, and would have done nothing with their lives, pottering, shopping, passing time; were perhaps at that moment lost in the queue outside the butcher's, where the corpses of sheep (as Angel described them to herself) hung, split in halves, inside the window.

At the top of the hill they passed The Four Cedars, now a Nursing Home.

"Slightly more salubrious up here," Marvell said.

219

On the drive home, Angel was silent. She closed her eyes and leaned back, filled with relief and satisfaction at the way she had ordered her life. Before they reached Paradise House, she fell asleep. Marvell turned into the mossy drive and said: "Well, we've done it. The petrol's lasted. But that will be the last of the gallivanting for a while."

He drew up in front of the house and opened the door. "We're here, madam. Grub up!"

Angel opened her eyes and stared at him. "How dare you wake me?" she said. "You could see perfectly well that I was tired and sleeping."

"And hear," he agreed.

"Close the door at once and leave me in peace."

"Must be time for dindins, madam."

"Close the door. And your impertinent mouth as well."

"Sorry madam. Just as you wish, madam. Pleasant dreams."

He slammed the door and sauntered away, whistling. Angel composed herself for sleep again, but the drowsiness had gone, and she was hungry. Obstinately, she stayed there a little longer, her eyes closed tightly and a stern expression on her face.

As soon as Theo arrived, he began to wonder if he could bear to stay.

It was Spring before he found that he could tear himself away from the bombs. Air-raids were bad, but Angel with her heart full of grievances would be no better, might offer less respite.

Marvell had met him at the station and, driving him to Paradise House, was full of disloyal confidences. Angel had a cough. She thought that she was as strong as a horse, but she had always had a nasty chest on her, to his mind. Nora had had an attack of gout but was now downstairs with her foot on a stool. She kept a walking-stick beside her and knocked away any cats who came near. "*That* stirs up Madam's disputatious gases, if you please. I thought blows would follow, with the gouty one getting the worst of it. Me, supposedly pasting up some wallpaper which had come down with the damp. A lot of furbishing's been going on on your account."

Theo, wondering how to stop this over-shoulder conversation, said nothing.

"Poor old souls, after all," said Marvell. "You'll see some changes, sir. Nothing but skin and bones, Madam is: going a bit nutty, too."

"I have grown rather deaf," said Theo. "I find it a strain trying to hear what you say, so I will close my eyes for a while."

He kept his eyes shut but, when they turned down into the valley, he was aware of the sudden darkness. He felt apprehensive and wondered what he should find, what ordeals lay ahead. Angel's letters, wildly abusive about his old firm, had contained hints of poverty and even starvation. To these, Marvell had added his own suggestions of illness and lunacy.

The house was damp from the winter's rain and fogs. He thought of his comfortable rooms in the house in St John's Wood, of his leather chair drawn up to a bright, fluttering fire and whatever he felt like drinking on a wine-table within reach. Windows rattling from bombs seemed nothing, now that he was faced with the decay of Paradise House.

Angel was in the library, and the fire she sat beside was of hissing, dribbling logs. The lap of her purple dress was covered with white cat's hairs. Nora was opposite her, with her swollen foot propped up on a stool. She was unravelling some tangled wool. "Gain a minute," she had said to Angel who was doing nothing but nurse a cat. Odd little Nannie-phrases came to her lips from time to time: to her, they were familiar and consoling, but Angel only stared as if she did not understand.

Theo was welcomed with fussy motherliness by Nora, and by Angel with regal condescension. They were ageing in different ways, he thought. The edges of Nora's face were blurred and uncertain, her body had sunk into shapelessness, her colour softened; but Angel was more angular than ever—

skin and bones, as Marvell had said—her hair was still startlingly black against her pallor; an air of neglect and grotesqueness about her intensified by her clothes, which were always, nowadays, the remnants of past grandeur—this evening, an old gown which clung about her limply because the velvet was damp, had been hanging in a wardrobe where fungus might grow any day.

"I am sorry I couldn't come to meet you myself," Angel said.

From time to time there was a terrible sound in her chest, as if some ancient clock were gathering itself, ready to strike.

Theo was brought some home-made wine by Bessie, and the two women sat watching him drink it.

"We will have dinner in here, please, Bessie," Nora said.

"Yes, of course, miss."

Angel was 'madam', Nora 'miss'.

"I hope you won't mind, Theo," said Nora. "It is so difficult for me to get about from room to room with this foot."

"And there's no fire anywhere else," Angel said. "I haven't been into the dining-room all winter. As it is, we burn logs faster than Marvell can saw them up."

"The coal situation is difficult," he agreed, though he wasn't much interested. His own house-keeper seemed to manage very well.

"Especially difficult about *paying* for it," Angel said severely. "That's the pressing part. And how is that young nephew of Brace's getting on?"

"I have nothing to do with the business now," Theo said uneasily. "I imagine pretty well, though."

Angel said "Ah." She seemed to be biding her time. She had fallen back into her old idle way of admiring her hands and she sat smoothing them and turning them about. "And Mr Delbanco?"

Theo had not thought of that old friend for years. He said: "Mr Delbanco died some years ago."

"I thought he must have done. I never hear anything of him from that young Brace. When I inquired, he couldn't

222

place him at all. 'It is a little puzzling,' I told him, 'since he is head of your firm—the power behind the scenes, as he was always spoken of'."

"As time went on, of course, he did less and less, his power waned. And you?" he asked bravely—for it had to come. "Are you working hard?"

"I will not write for an ungrateful world." This she believed. Not that her inventiveness had died, her imagination at long last tired. She thought that the reluctance she felt now to sit down at her desk and begin work was due to the fact that, like many a great artist before her, she was rejected by a world grown Philistine. "Let them all blow themselves to blazes," she told Nora once when they were speaking of the war, which was not a forbidden subject as the other war had been. "There is nothing in them for us to worry about." She was often violent about people, as are so many animal lovers.

"Or an ungrateful publisher," she said now to Theo. "Where would he be now if it were not for me, I wonder?"

"I think we should let Theo have his drink in peace," said Nora.

"I am not interfering with his drink. I am telling him about his partner's nephew."

Bessie came in to lay the table, and Nora gave her so many instructions about the cooking that to Theo the dishes were old but intractable friends when at last they were brought in.

"No wine, Theo, I am afraid," Angel said. "You won't need me to give you the reason why."

He was tired from his journey and had looked forward to going to bed, but now he was beginning to suspect that the sheets would be damp. He was too old for these venturings. Angel and Nora thought that he looked old; his face had fallen in at the cheeks and temples and his skin was shiny and intricately wrinkled. The beard that once had been so fiery was sparse and silver; he looked a different shape altogether. As if his skeleton were coming to the surface, thought Nora with a shiver.

At this time of the evening, the cats began to play about

the upstairs passages. They thundered up and down the bare corridors, and Angel listened with the indulgent smile which no person but Esmé—whom it had infuriated—had ever received from her.

Theo had often thought that it was just as well that Esmé had died: it could never have been kept up, Angel's legend of their perfect marriage. The flaws must in time have become as obvious to her as they were to everyone else. Esmé's indifference had curdled into resentment and malice; crippled and hampered as he was, he must in time have broken or broken away. A figure from long ago, he seemed now to Theo, sitting eternally on the stairs at Angel's London party, both confounded and derisive. So long ago, there was another occasion—Theo had almost forgotten it—of callous betrayal. But there was no need to worry now. The risks, he thought, the knife's-edge her peace-of-mind was once balanced on.

The telephone-bell echoed startlingly in the hall, for, as Theo had noticed, the house was very bare of furniture. The massive chests and tallboys, with their ormolu and marquetry, which Angel had bought when she was young and rich, were no longer to be seen, and he wondered uneasily if they had been sold.

"Nora can't help shouting when she telephones," Angel explained. "She has grown very deaf."

"I hadn't noticed."

"She doesn't realise it herself, and of course I try to keep it from her."

Nora returned. She sat down and took up her fork and pushed some stewed apple about her plate, looking thoughtful, knowing that Angel was waiting and edgy with curiosity. Then the pain of not telling became greater than the desire to tease. "He is sinking," she said. A look of peace and complacency passed between them.

"Are you going?" Angel asked her.

"He is in a coma."

"If he wouldn't know you, there's no sense in making the journey. You can't be expected to go there just to comfort the servants."

"Quite."

"He is in good hands."

"The best. Mrs. Warren's, for instance. She has been with him for as long as I can remember."

Angel frowned. "I hope you haven't underestimated her, Nora. She has the advantage of having *been* there, week in, week out, you know; and he dependent on her as he must have been."

"I never underestimate anyone. And I pride myself that I know a little about his affairs and intentions."

"If you only know a little, you have no cause for pride. Nora's uncle," Angel said, turning to Theo, who was wishing that cats liked stewed apple; then he might have slipped some down to the blue Persian sitting at his feet. "Lord Norley. He has had a stroke and is dying."

"Another old man on his way," Theo said, feeling depressed.

"We never talk like that," Angel said briskly. "A bomb can fall on young or old these days." She appeared gratified that the young were in it, too: this seemed to even out the dangers of being old. "Lord Norley is a different matter. He has been unconscious for days. He is as good as dead already."

"Or as bad as dead," said Theo, who did not understand the situation.

Next day, Lady Baines came over early to luncheon and they spent a peaceful hour sitting on the terrace in the thin, spring sunshine, cleaning the cats' ears. Canker was discovered in one, and fleas in a litter of kittens.

"Fetch a sheet, Marvell," Angel called to him. "Say 'please'," he muttered to himself. He was spraying weed-killer indiscriminately about the garden.

"No, a blanket would be better," said Lady Baines. "They can't hop off a blanket so easily."

Theo was disconcerted by the sight of what was brought out from the house: was sure that it was the blanket from the library-table, and hoped that it would not be returned there afterwards.

The kittens were caught and smothered with powder and the fleas dropped off them on to the blanket where Lady Baines, with sharper eyes than Angel's, was quick to kill them.

When it was time for luncheon, she was ready for it, she said. She set her hat straight on her head and, with her tweed skirt covered with flea-powder, went to the library with a good appetite.

"A good morning's work," she said to Theo. "So satisfying." He was itching all over and hoped that the cause was his imagination. He would be glad to get away—from the cats, the fleas, the damp, and these three eccentric women. He had always been glad to get away from Angel; she tired and exasperated him; but he had never been able to replace his first impression of her with any other. At that first meeting, long ago in London, she had seemed to need his protection while warning him not to offer it: arrogant and absurd she had been and had remained: she had warded off friendship and stayed lonely and made such fortifications within her own mind that the truth could not pierce it. At the slightest air of censure in the world about her, up had gone the barricades, the strenuous resistance begun by which she was preserved in her own imagination, beautiful, clever, successful and beloved.

"Ah, carrot flan," Lady Baines exclaimed. "But where," she asked, her glance attracted away from the dish which Bessie offered, to an oblong of unfaded wallpaper between two windows, "where is the William and Mary escritoire?"

"It has gone to be treated for wood-worm," Nora said.

And I suppose, Theo thought, that all that silver they once had has gone to have the dents taken out.

"I should have left that for a month or two—well, that is what *I* was once advised by a man in Wigmore Street. In September; I am sure I was told that, when the grubs are nearer the surface of the wood, d'you know? I am surprised that anyone would dream of dealing with it in the spring. Where did you take it?"

She was indefatigably, almost crazedly interested in other people's trivial affairs.

"A place in Norley," said Nora.

"I shouldn't have trusted anyone local, not after that escapade about Major Cubbage's commode. Well, I hope they will be ruthless, that's all."

Theo wondered why wood-worms were excluded from her compassionate attitude to other creatures, and remembered that she had pounced quite gleefully on the fleas: he supposed that it was a question of size and that she would say that she had to draw the line somewhere.

"Of course, at one time of the year, but I can't recall which it is, they come out of their holes and fly about," said Nora. "If one could catch them then. . . ."

"Fly?" cried Lady Baines. "And how, pray, my dear Nora, can worms fly?"

"I think they are really beetles, you know."

The carrot flan was finished, but the argument continued in the most tiresome way. Yet was it worms and beetles that they were really bothered about? wondered Theo. Nora was growing quite shrill and kept glancing at Angel; seemed to be saying: "There are some things your clever friend *doesn't* know." Lady Baines was deliberately calm, as if she could afford to be so, being in the right.

"I will settle it once and for all," Angel said, and she threw down her napkin and got up. "There is Esmé's insect-book somewhere."

The library had few books. At the dark end of the room there were some shelves behind glass. When she opened the doors, mustiness was released, a smell like stale pot-pourri.

"I am sure I read . . . don't *you* agree with me, Theo?" Nora asked, nervous now at the thought of being faced with proof, the printed word. Which way would it go? She had been quite positive that she was right, but as soon as Angel took the book from the shelf, doubts disturbed her. Had she been thinking of something else all the time?

227

"We shall soon see," Lady Baines said soothingly. She lifted a hand gently and turned towards Angel.

A piece of paper, an old letter, had fluttered from the pages of the book, and Angel stooped and picked it up. The glass door of the bookcase swung open too wide; she closed it and began to read the letter. Theo looked at her. They were turned towards her, expectantly: Nora, with the tips of her fingers on the edge of the table, leaning forward anxiously; Lady Baines's hand slowly sinking as her pose changed from that of calm to one of concern.

Angel then folded the paper and put it in her pocket. She came back to the table, gave the book to Nora, and sat down. She was still and steady: by being frozen with shock was able to keep erect; but her bearing was precarious: movement or any warmth might loosen her, and collapse was only held off, not an impossibility.

"But this is only about *moths*," said Nora, ruffling the pages of the book. At the sound of her voice, Angel's eyelids dropped and then rose, but she made no other movement.

"Is something wrong?" asked Lady Baines. No one answered her. When Bessie brought the coffee, Angel poured it out. Her hands were steady, Theo noticed; but some dreadful destruction within her had become apparent on her face, and her eyes were surrounded by darkness; he could see a raised vein pulsing on her forehead. They were all caught in the silence, though one after the other made feeble efforts to break it.

Even disastrous news could not rouse her. Nora was called to the telephone and came back wringing her hands, but with a bright smile on her face. "He is rallying," she said. "Mrs Warren says that he opened one eye and seemed to be looking at her."

"Ah, yes," said Angel. From time to time she coughed her shattering cough, but when she recovered she was silent and still again.

As soon as Lady Baines put down her coffee-cup and began to look round for her gloves, Angel rose to speed her on her way. Theo and Nora were left in the library. Nora took up the book from the table, blew some dust off it and tiptoed across the room to the bookcase. They waited anxiously, listening to the hiccoughing noises as the old car was started up. Long after it had gone, the sound of it came back faintly now and again as it turned a curve of the drive: they waited for Angel's footsteps across the hall; but she did not come. She was out there on the terrace, re-reading the letter, Theo guessed.

"If it was anything . . ." he began to tell Nora and then stopped, thinking he heard Angel at last returning. Walking slowly and stiffly, as if she were asleep, she came to Nora and gave her the letter.

"That is where your foolish chatter about worms and beetles led me," she said. Although her voice was harsh, it was a relief to them to hear it again. Nora, reading, looked frightened: then it was Theo's turn; Angel nodded towards him and Nora passed the letter over. It looked a lost, pathetic thing, like all old letters; the moment it had matched had gone so long ago. One edge, which had obtruded from the book, was brown; damp had faded the ink; the paper was seamed, as if it had once been crushed up in anger and then smoothed out again.

Theo read:

"Dearest Esmé,

"You will be surprised to hear that I am married. I hope you will forgive me for breaking my promise, but it was one you had no right to ask me to make. We could never have been together again and I have come to realise this lately, not hearing from you. I know how weak you are, too weak to take one single step forward, or away. You must not blame me now for taking a step myself. There is so much of life for me to live and I must do the best I can and in my own way and who knows may be happy in the end, though never I know in the way we were happy together on that last leave.

"My husband does not know of your existence. It is better to start afresh and forget, so I am sending no address and you will understand that you must not try to write. I . . ." but here a tear, perhaps, or just the damp, had obliterated the rest of the sentence, and there was only the name 'Laura' and a scribbled postscript: "Please destroy this."

If only he had! Theo thought, feeling tired and unable to decide how to behave. It was necessary for him to say something, but he could not sort out words in any useful order. He could see a picture instead: Esmé and the girl in the grey velvet hat. The long-ago betrayal set against the tea-time sounds of cup against saucer, laughter, social voices. He had forgotten, for so much had happened since, so much that had mattered to him more. After Esmé's death the betrayal had seemed to become a fainter threat, and then gone out of his head altogether.

"He didn't ever *have* leave," Angel said desperately.

Nora ducked her head and brought her necklace up over her chin in a nervous movement: the string broke and jet beads scattered into her lap and rolled across the floor. Eagerly, and in spite of the pain from her swollen foot, she went down on her knees to gather them up, glad of something to do.

"*Did* he have leave?" Angel asked. "Did he, without telling me? Then he came home after all; he told lies to me and *pretended* that he was so badly treated and that they couldn't spare him? And came back to England, to someone else. *Did* he?" She suddenly shouted at Nora who, now on all fours, looked up in terror.

Oh, please, good Lord, Theo began to pray.

"No," said Nora, seeming to repeat a lesson she had off by heart. "No, of course not. So untrue." She shook her head vigorously.

"Then what?" Angel sank down into a chair and began tremblingly to cry. "I can't ask him," she sobbed. "He can't explain to me."

"But he *could* explain," Theo said. "Something simple and reassuring it would be, I've no doubt. Leave he did not have."

"Certainly not," said Nora.

"There are the *words*," said Angel.

230

"If we can read them," Theo said. "Such a cramped-up, sway-back, illiterate hand, and the ink all faded away."

"But 'leave' it says."

"I think this is some old letter from before the time of your knowing Esmé." Theo could be grateful that the letter was undated—if not for much else. "You mustn't begin to grieve now about Esmé's wild oats. It is so long ago, and not concerned with you at all."

He looked very knowing when he spoke of wild oats, though he had never sown any himself. "Would Esmé have kept such a letter for a moment if it could have been what you suggest?"

"I can't ask him: I can't ask him what it means."

"I don't suppose you ever remember him opening that book in all the time you were married."

"I am sure that he did not," said Nora. She dropped a handful of beads into a glass goblet on the chimney-piece.

"He was always interested in moths," said Angel.

"Oh, when he was a boy; yes," Nora agreed.

"But it says 'leave'. You can't explain that away. That last leave, those are the words. So there was more than one, then?" Her voice rose waveringly to a shriek.

"Esmé never had leave," Theo said quietly. "So there is a mystery here."

"How could you know if he did or didn't?"

"Yes, I could know," Theo insisted. He covered his eyes with his hand and tried to think. "I am the one who *would* know; but it is so long ago and my memory plays tricks on me. But that I put in a word for him, I do recall—his C.O. was some vague relation of Hermione's, I believe. Oh, I didn't do it for Esmé's sake, so much as for yours. I knew what you suffered from that separation."

"Why didn't you tell me this?" Angel looked suspicious, but expectant, too, as if she were ready to believe that he could rescue her.

"I waited for the reply to come: when it did, I was disappointed; said nothing; soon forgot the matter."

Nora was staring at him with her mouth half-open, and he tried to shake this expression of disbelief off her face by pretending to see another bead under her chair.

"Then why does it say 'leave', if there was no such thing?" Angel had clutched at the straw he had offered and was going to use it if she could to rebuild the fortress; but as she backed away from the truth she felt compelled to repeat that question over and over, like a child saying 'good night, good night,' fearfully mounting a dark staircase, staving off peril with words.

"What it said I couldn't tell from such blotted and faded handwriting," said Theo. "From what I know to be true, though—of the facts of the case as I remember them, of Esmé himself, his character, his love of you—I am sure that it must be another word altogether."

"It looks like another word to me, certainly," Nora said without thinking.

"Well, shall I throw the letter away?" Theo asked. "You can soon forget it. Your memory of Esmé will answer it; if he cannot himself."

"Yes," Angel said. "Thank you, Theo," she added.

Does she believe me or not? he wondered. If she did not just yet, in time she would. He tossed the letter on to the fire, as Esmé should have done many years ago. When he did so, Angel looked away.

Wretched, feckless ghost, Theo was thinking irritably of Esmé. With his half-kept secrets; though he must long ago have become dust, he still had the power to destroy her. There was not much else left of him for anyone to remember—his half finished memorial up on the hill, the small collection of his paintings in that morgue-like studio, and Angel's love, as crazed and persistent as ever it had been. But it is as much as is left of anyone of us after so long, he decided. Perhaps a great deal more. As we grow older, we are already dying; our hold on life lessens; there are fewer to mourn us or keep us in mind. I am on my way already and taking the last of Hermione with me as I go. He was utterly depressed.

The blackened paper on the fire arched up and fluttered, with a frail, tinny sound, in a sudden draught from the chimney.

"Another half-an-hour and we can have a cup of tea," Nora said. "And now here's Silky Boy, Angel, come to cheer you up."

The Abyssinian cat stalked indifferently past Angel and made for Theo, whose knee he leapt upon, dough-punching in an hysterical way and drawing loops of thread out of his tweed trousers.

The afternoon went tediously by, with Nora fussing and Angel pre-occupied. Just to drink a cup of tea broke into the boredom wonderfully. Then that was done and there was only dinner to hope for. Angel was beginning to accept what Theo had told her: how, he could only marvel at. But he could see that there were moments when the facts, as they seemed indisputably to be, leapt at her: the truth took her by the throat; then her hand would fly up to her cheek and her eyes stare. Her suffering at such moments was too sharp to be endured: she could not live with such a kind of truth. With Theo's help and Nora's acquiescence she had begun, oyster-like, to coat over, to conceal what could not be borne as it was. The letter was not mentioned again.

The next day Theo went home. He was glad to go. He had done what he could for her. He was never to see her again.

To Lady Baines it seemed that Angel was deteriorating along with her dwindling fortune, but it was a decline of which Angel herself was quite oblivious. She was not so much living in the past as investing the present with what the past had had. To herself, she was still the greatest novelist of her day, and not the first in history to receive less homage than was her due. No one bought her books, and only the middle-aged or elderly had ever read them: she did not know that she was now a legend of which the young had only vaguely heard; risqué, their grandparents, in quaint fashion, said her novels were. The young were not tempted, for such démodé naughtiness does not attract. Lady Baines herself, no great reader, could remember hiding *The Lady Irania* beneath her pillow and being much taken up by the characters in it; they were large enough to satisfy her love of life and her liveliness, though they were bold, absurd and over-serious: her friends in Boston, and later in the Home Counties, were not.

When she met Angel for the first time she had noted the same qualities in her and found that they amounted to eccentricity. Whatever else had happened to Angel, she was still as bold and serious and absurd as ever she had been, but, unwillingly, Lady Baines began to be aware of pathos, too. She was not a subtle woman, and perhaps it was poverty that underlined for her that pitiableness in Angel which only Theo, and once or twice Esmé (who had tried to shut his eyes to it), had ever seen.

To Lady Baines, Paradise House in decay had none of the romantic appeal that it had for Clive Fennelly. Her own house was full of respectful servants, the garden neat with clipped hedges, bedded-out plants and raked and weeded gravel. She thought that Marvell, so insolent and dirty, should long ago have been pensioned off. Angel, though as arrogant as ever, seemed to be drifting into indolent ways, dreaming away her time, hunched over the fire in some tattered old gown, her hair half-pinned up, her eyes hooded by drooping lids. Sometimes, when she was not alone, she seemed to withdraw herself from a conversation, and her lips would move as if to some soundless monologue of her own. When she spoke, as often as not it was an irrelevant remark breaking in upon Nora's polite small-talk; it would seem to come from nowhere and to be unanswerable, yet she expected her train of thought to have been followed. Sometimes she would give way without inhibition to violent and noisy coughing. Nora, wincing, would say reprovingly, "Oughtn't you to *take* something?" meaning, "Oughtn't you to try to stifle it; or go out of the room?" Angel ignored her.

As a girl, she had dozed and day-dreamed through the long

lonely evenings while her mother was at work in the shop, and now she had fallen back into that habit. With her feet propped on the fender, a cat in her lap for warmth, she would drowse and dream, and the more she rested the more difficult it was for Nora to rouse her.

A letter from Lady Baines managed to do what Nora could not, and brought Angel up from her chair, gasping with anger, incoherent. Then she began to cough, clutching the edge of the chimney piece, bowed over, shaken. At the end, when she turned to face Nora, her eyes were brilliantly green and her cheeks and forehead flushed.

"Let her never come here again," she said, beginning her tirade at the end; for the explanatory part of her anger had gone on while she was coughing and she had already reached the summary. "That's a fine thing from a friend. Erstwhile friend, I *should* say. Presiding over the countryside, condescending at meetings with her parvenu American ways. Too many mixed marriages tainting the great English families . . . I would say so to her face. She has aped our ways very well indeed; but this will always happen with people who are pretending to be what they are not—the performance is suddenly shown to be what it is, they make an unexpected mistake and their true vulgarity comes into sight. As now."

Nora had been making little interrupting noises for some time, but now when Angel stopped she could think of nothing to say. " 'Nouveau riche,' is the word for her," Angel said smartly. Two words, Nora thought, dazed. "She has bought her position with a cheque here and a cheque there. I think money must be her god. Lady Midas Baines we must remember to call her in future; that is, if we can bring ourselves to mention her."

"What has she done?" Nora could at last ask.

"She has only offered me money. You may read the letter."

Nora took it and while she read Angel told her what it contained. "She is worried that we have fallen on hard times; suspects—I gather—that we have sold the William and Mary escritoire." As we have, thought Nora. "Hints, or so I fancy, that she would have liked to buy it herself. Perhaps she would like to look round the house and name other things we have that she may covet; she can snatch the chairs from under us, and the table, too: we can eat our meals off the chimney-piece and use the floor-boards for our beds. Why not, since we are fallen on such evil times? An emerald ring in a shop in Norley reminded her of mine and then that I no longer wear it. I must put on my tiara next time she comes to luncheon—though she will never come inside this house again. Do you see that she will lend or give whatever we need, for 'we are old friends', as she says. Old friends may be humiliated and insulted. It is no doubt what they are for. Is that the gist of it?"

"The letter is not quite as you say," Nora began. "It is full of good intentions, though I agree. . . ."

"Full to the brim. I will 'good intention' her." It might have been Aunt Lottie speaking, the trembling anger in her voice was so like that which Angel, with her high-flown ways, had long ago provoked.

For the rest of the day, the storms broke at intervals, pieces of her mind were hurled about the room, and the anger went on all the time in her breast, sometimes exploding in paroxysms of coughing or of words; speeches precipitated, often beginning half-way through a sentence, into the midst of Nora's gentle monologues.

" . . . And then", Nora was saying, "it seemed that it was mid-winter all of a sudden, and I was decorating a tree for Christmas, only it wasn't a Christmas tree at all, but our old Nurse, Esmé's and mine. I was just going up on tiptoe to fix a star to her forehead. . . ."

"She calls me a pauper, forgetting who I am," said Angel. " 'Perhaps you are unaware', I shall say. Have you seen my cheque-book, Nora?"

When it was found, she at once wrote a cheque for sixty pounds—which was all the money she had—and addressed it to a charitable society of which Lady Baines was the president. Marvell was called to take it to the post immediately and was ordered to be ready with the car at eleven o'clock the next morning.

"I should like to go over now," said Angel, "and demand an explanation of her; but it will do her good to get the letter first. It would be diverting to see her face when she receives the cheque."

"And it is best to sleep on your wrath," said Nora vaguely.

Angel lay awake on it instead, and the sun came up on it. By morning, she was swollen with unrehearsed speeches. At eleven o'clock, dressed in some moth-eaten chinchilla, she went out to the car.

"Now don't be late," Nora said anxiously, coming to see her off. "Remember that Mr Fennelly is coming to luncheon and bringing his article about Esmé."

"Don't worry. What I have to say to her will be short and sweet."

"Did you . . .?" Nora leant through the car-window and whispered.

"Yes, yes," said Angel impatiently. All the same, they were not half-way there when she had to stop the car and get out. Marvell leant his elbow on the steering-wheel, looking grimly ahead of him, while she went trailing through brambles into a little wood at the roadside. She's a weak-bladder one if ever there was, he thought. Nice for me, I must say. It's a masterpiece.

"All right now?" he asked, as she came into view again.

By the time they reached Bottrell Saunter, exhausted by anger and her wakeful night, Angel had fallen fast asleep.

"We're here, madam," Marvell said as he stopped the car before the house. He looked round and, seeing how things were, got out and stretched his legs for a bit. A maid had opened the door and he went up the steps to have a chat with her. Lady Baines was in bed with a chill, but sent a message that Angel was to go up to her.

"It would be more than my position is worth to disturb her now," Marvell said. "Last time I woke her up, there were proper tantrums. Instant dismissal the next time, she threatened me with."

The maid looked at him with distaste and went back to her mistress. An impasse had been reached. Lady Baines, propped up in bed, had tidied her hair and was waiting; Angel, sitting bolt upright in the car, slept on. Marvell, enjoying himself, strolled about the garden, looking at the rose-bushes with an air of professional contempt, pretending to be pinching off blight where there was none. The maid, keeping an eye on him, lingered in the hall, flicking a feather-brush about the banisters. A second message was brought down from Lady Baines; but Marvell only pursed his lips and shook his head.

"Then I shall go out and tap on the window to her," said the maid. "I can do it quite respectfully, if you can't. The doctor is due at any moment and Madam must have her chest rubbed before he arrives."

"You can rub Madam's chest till you're both blue in the face, but you're not laying a finger on that car."

He spread his arms wide apart as if he would fend her off physically.

"The rudeness!"

"You do your duty: I'll do mine. Leave it at that."

He sauntered away, sat down on a seat among the flower-beds and lit his pipe. Another maid drummed her knuckles on a window-pane and frowned at him and made scolding gestures which he ignored. He smoked his pipe peacefully and basked in the sunshine while he watched the white doves walking on the roof. A gardener was down on his knees before the herbaceous border with a barrowful of weeds beside him. Poor sod! thought Marvell. The weather-cock glinted as it veered round in the gentle breeze; the trees looked as polished as the windows of the house; monstrous begonias lurked beneath their own leaves and a spray turned giddily, casting water out over the lawn. From inside the house came pleasant, domestic sounds, voices mingling with clattering, chopping, splashing in the kitchen; a vacuum-cleaner hummed away upstairs; someone ran a duster over the keys of a piano-forte, up the scales, down, then all among the black notes. It was as different as could be from Paradise House.

Angel slept on, and when he had finished his pipe and knocked it out, Marvell gave what he meant to be a mocking bow to the maid at the window and went softly back to the car and drove off as quietly as he could. A pleasant morning, peacefully exciting—and plenty more to come, he thought, when the forty winks is done.

More did not come till they were back at Paradise House. Angel, waking up, was hard put to it to sort out where she was. The wrong vista seemed approaching. She groped for the solution, and for her lost anger which had been laid aside while she slept.

"Perhaps you don't remember, madam, the last time I woke you up I got what for. I try to keep pace with my orders but it's change and change-about with you the whole time." Her anger—more than half of it she had meant for Lady Baines—stimulated him. "Not to wake you up, and not to be late for lunch, I was told. I pondered what to do. Whatever I did wouldn't be right, I could see that."

Clive Fennelly had arrived already and, unaware of the situation, came hastening from the house to greet her.

"You thundering dunderhead!" said Angel. "You block-head!" She turned to Clive as she spoke, and bowed. Her joints cracked as she stepped out of the car, as if they were angry, too. Clive followed her into the hall. "That fool!" she shouted, as Nora came from the library. "He will have to go. He has made me look a figure of fun, and to my worst enemy. How can I go back now and say what I must say?"

"Couldn't you write?" Nora suggested, when she had heard the story.

So Angel wrote all the afternoon, bending shortsightedly over the page, waving away all interruptions, whilst Clive sat by with his manuscript on his knee. When at last she turned to him, she looked exhausted. Some of the fury was transferred to the letter; some by its very heat had been burnt out; but there was still enough to last a lifetime. She did not apologise to Clive, who had come all the way from London, at her request. "Wonderful!" he kept thinking. "She is quite wonderful. There is no one like her in the whole of Northwood. One could dine out on her for weeks." Yet he did not and never would! He kept her carefully to himself, almost as if from superstitious reasons.

At tea she was in a gracious mood, talked to him of Esmé and promised to play the piano to him afterwards.

"I think the damp has got into it," Nora said. "It sounded very twangy the other day when Silky Boy was walking on it."

"We can but try," said Angel sweetly. "And now let me glance at your essay, Clive."

He wondered where they stood with regard to Christian names. When she called him 'Clive', he thought that she expected him to call her 'Angel' or 'Angelica' in return: but if he did so, she might think him impertinent; and, if he did not, would be quite likely to imagine the difference in their age implied. For this reason, he always wrote to her on post-cards. She spoke of him to Nora as 'Mr Fennelly', and so put Nora in her place.

She took his essay to the window, straining her eyes to read it. " 'A literary painter,' " she said. "I like that very much. That would have pleased Esmé." It seemed to her to be praise indeed; but Clive looked away, blushing. "This about concentration must come out. Esmé had *great* powers of concentration." She read on. "What is this? 'His discoveries were limited'? Ah, Mr Fennelly, how little even you have understood him."

Clive, having lost his Christian name again, watched sadly while she went to her desk and began to cross his words out, and write others in.

"What is chiaroscuro?" she asked. "It is not derogatory? 'Exquisite,' yes. 'Tender', yes. 'Feminine'! Come, come!" She scratched out the word. "There was nothing feminine about Esmé. A woman could hardly, I think, have painted those scenes inside the public-houses."

The dismembered manuscript was handed back at last, and they went to the drawing-room, where evening sunshine

240

poured in through the long, dusty windows and the wall-paper sagged and hung down from the plaster.

"Now that the war is over we can have the house re-decorated," Angel said, sitting down at the piano. Clive went to the window and, while she strummed and improvised, he stood in the sun and looked out at the tangled garden, feeling that he was under a spell. He loved her, almost as if he had invented her—bad fairy, wicked stepmother, peevish goddess, whatever she was.

"Do sit down, Clive," she said, her harsh voice raised as she played a series of discords.

He perched obediently on the window-seat. In the rose-garden below hundreds of striped caterpillars were devouring the ragwort.

"Yes," Angel said, resting her hands for a moment in her lap and gazing round the room. "The whole house shall be painted and be made pretty again. You shall help me to choose the wallpapers. We will have a gold and white stripe in here and a plain crimson in the dining-room."

She began to play again, more softly, as she planned this new grandeur for Paradise House. But where was the money to come from? Lord Norley lingered on: from time to time, he opened one eye and looked at Mrs Warren. "A drag on the rations," Marvell said to Bessie.

When Nora came into the drawing-room, Angel stopped playing and said: "Nothing wrong with the tone of this. A very nice piano, I think. We must have it tuned and polished and send it to Rosita Baines. I expect her covetous eyes have often rested on it."

PART 6

i

SNOW muffled Paradise House, went up in drifts to the lower window-sills. Each morning Marvell had to dig his way in to see to the fires. The cats could not or would not go out and Angel had ashes carried in for them and put in the empty grate in one of the unfurnished rooms. "It smells like the tiger-house at the Zoo," Marvell grumbled. Before dark he went back to his stuffy room to fry a bloater or dig into a jar of pickled onions. The three old women were alone in the house. The snow sealed them in. By morning the drifts had been renewed, Marvell's footprints across the yard covered over: on all the frosted windows ferns delicately grew; icicles hung from the gutterings.

Nora's hands were swollen with chilblains, but Angel seemed unaware of the cold; her shawl would slip from her shoulders without her noticing; often she let the fire go out as she sat dreaming by it.

"It would happen at such a time, the snow," she said fretfully one morning. Lord Norley had died at last and left a large part of his fortune to Nora, and Angel was impatient to go out and spend some of it. Death duties, bequests to charity, Mrs Warren's annuity, other remembrances and kindnesses, tokens of gratitude, and old servants provided for had taken more than enough of poor Nora's money, she said. "And what use is blood if it is not thicker than water?" she asked. "It will not warm *us*. But Mrs Warren, for instance, can now be idle for the rest of her life, and every old crony who ever raised his hat to him has a nice fat cheque to jog his memory of the occasion; charity begins at the uttermost ends of the world, it seems."

242

As the snow continued, birds that had always before been chary of the house with its swarming cats came nearer, for shelter and the hope of food; they printed their dagger-like footmarks across the terrace and scuffled the snow upon the window-sills. Against the whiteness of the garden the stone walls of the house were as dark as lead; smoke rose from two of the chimneys and discoloured the pale grey sky. The days seemed long, the evenings longer. They passed the time with plans for travelling when the spring came.

Angel's cough grew worse, but she seemed heedless of it; after each attack she would calmly wipe her eyes and settle herself more comfortably in her chair. She refused to see the doctor and, when he called upon Nora, shut herself up in the ice-cold drawing-room until he had left, playing the piano or looking out at the buried rose-garden, at the sad monochrome landscape; weeds, roses, were all gone, only thorned branches broke the snow, looped across the whiteness like barbed wire. Once, she met the doctor unawares, before she could reach the drawing-room door. Emboldened by Nora's anxiety, he said that he thought she would be well-advised to have him examine her chest. Her indignation—as if at a suggestion of the utmost indelicacy—brought on more violent coughing than ever. She fled up the stairs away from him.

Marvell engaged the doctor in conversation before he left. He had been making some show of clearing the drive so that the car could be turned round and he was glad to lean on his spade for a moment or two and talk to another man for a change. Angel roamed up and down the corridors, chafing her hands more from impatience than the cold, and Silky Boy, her favourite, ran beside her.

She felt unwell and restless, with a sensation of disease; there was a bitter taste of anxiety in her mouth and she could not reason with herself or still her apprehensions. She heard the doctor's car going slowly away, and the shadowy house was caught up in silence. "It is all precarious," she thought suddenly; then wondered what the words meant and why they had come into her head.

She talked more than usual at luncheon, trying to stifle the persistent dread she felt, and afterwards, when Nora went up to her room to rest, she was too agitated to sit alone, and she put on a heavy cloak and went out into the garden to find Marvell. The stillness was very strange: there was no sound but that of the crisp snow breaking as she trod on it; she could see her breath fly from her mouth and a few soft snowflakes drifted about her and settled on her hair. Silky Boy followed her, picking his way with suspicion and distaste across the snow.

Marvell, not expecting to be discovered in such weather, had taken the afternoon off and was snug in his hovel, cleaning his gun.

"You have finished work for the day?" Angel inquired.

"What am I supposed to do—mow the lawns or go out and pick strawberries? The sky's full of it. You've got no business venturing out with that chest. I was talking to the doctor about you only this morning. 'Madam's cough is chronic,' he said. Those were his words. Bed and physic is what you need; not trapesing about in the cold."

He held the gun up to the light and squinted along its barrels.

"How dirty you keep your quarters," Angel said, looking scornfully about her. I am frightened, she suddenly thought. But there was nothing to be frightened of; not even poverty now. I have come such a long way, she told herself, and done all that I wanted and there is nothing to fear.

"If you don't take care of yourself, someone must," Marvell was saying. He put the gun back in its case as tenderly as if he were laying a baby in a cradle.

She remembered Esmé calling him 'Nannie' and smiled.

"You are getting fussy in your old age," she said.

"You're no chicken yourself."

He watched her slyly, to see if she would ignore this or fly into one of her rages and once more give him notice to leave. Instead, she said simply: "We are all getting old," and sighed; unlike herself, he thought, and regretted what he had said.

She was fidgety and full of sighs.

"Who is this?" she asked, picking up an old photograph from the littered overmantle.

"My auntie," he said, narrowing his eyes, watching her.

"And this?"

"Myself." Unnecessarily he added: "As a baby."

"Quite a nice baby," she said indifferently.

"Thank you, madam."

Snowflakes were coming faster out of the darkening sky, large ones stuck to the window-pane and slowly melted.

"Now, you get off back," Marvell said. "This will go on all night now it's started. I suppose I'd better come over with you and make up the range for that dotty old woman. You can put this over your head." He handed her a newspaper. Rather unwillingly she left the little room and the two of them set out towards the house. When they spoke, the flakes flew into their mouths. Angel held the newspaper over her head and walked slowly with the snow in her face so that she kept her eyelids lowered. Sometimes she stumbled and he would say "Steady now!" and hold her arm for a moment.

When they came to the house, from habit they parted; she made her way slowly to the front door; he trudged off to the back entrance.

Nora was waiting in the library, full of reproaches. "You're wet through," she scolded. "Whatever possessed you?"

"I felt lonely," said Angel and the words surprised herself.

"You should go straight to bed, I think."

"Oh, no, no, no. The house is like a prison in this weather."

It had often seemed that to Nora, but she had not said so.

When Bessie came in with tea, they were both standing like children, looking out of the window at the whirling flakes; faster and faster they came; the world seemed demented with the hurrying snow: but by the time it was dark it had settled to a more relentless rhythm. Tracks made during the day were obliterated, and then, too late, Angel remembered Silky Boy.

"He didn't come back with me," she said, getting up quickly from her chair.

245

"He must have gone in the back way with Marvell," said Nora.

They searched the house, calling along the corridors, Angel rapping a spoon upon the edge of a tin plate; they flung open one door after another and made insane enquiries of the other cats.

"He mustn't stay out in all this snow," Angel said.

"He will soon come mewing at the door, you will see."

"You know how delicate he is."

In spite of Nora's protestations, she unchained the front door, stepped over the ledge of newly-fallen snow into the thin, cold air, calling and coughing. In the shaft of light from the house the whiteness outside was dazzling, the steps were a smooth unbroken slope. Her own footprints of the afternoon had gone, and the cat's shallower ones must have been covered long ago. She stood there calling "Silky Boy" over and over, and Nora stood in the hall calling her.

"All day I knew that something terrible would happen," Angel said, when at last she gave up and shut the door. "It was because of that that I went out this afternoon."

"Your going out *made* it happen." It will make something else happen, too, Nora thought, looking with anxiety at Angel's too-bright cheeks.

There was another long vigil at the front door before she could be persuaded to go to bed, but she was glad to lie down when at last she did; her forehead beat and burned and the heaviness of her limbs seemed too much for the insubstantial bed to bear—the bed flying as light as a bird through space.

In the night she awoke and heard the cat crying out in the garden. Like a mother whose anxiety is suddenly over, she felt as much angry as relieved. I knew that he would come, she thought, as she flung back the bedclothes and stepped rather dizzily down on to the cold floor-boards.

At the head of the stairs she was overcome by vertigo, clung to the banisters and was afraid to look or step down. She sensed the dim well of the hall as a void into which she was being fatally drawn; taking each stair as a fresh hazard, she groped her way down.

After days of silence, the night had grown noisy. Wind had sprung up, buffeting the house, tugging and sucking at the doors and windows. Outside, the trees creaked as if giants were swinging from the branches.

She ran her hands over the cold walls, groping for the light switches and, when she found them, she thought, so that is what the hall looks like in the middle of the night. Its ordinariness was strange: it was just waiting for the morning.

When she opened the front door the wind rushed in. Snow had stopped falling. The sky was shabby like rubbed suède, with stars scattered untidily. Across the wedge of light, the cat walked towards her; prankish though full of guilt; his tail, his glance wavering; snow in his whiskers; his small mew both peevish and grateful.

She was beyond scolding him; wondering how, with her head so fiery and confused, she could resume the journey back to her room. As she began to climb the stairs, the cat, quite arch and benign now, sprang after her, shaking the melted snow from off its fur. She reached her bed at last and drew the cold covers over her, and the wet cat sat down on her pillow among her tangled hair and began methodically to clean its frozen paws.

What had happened in the night Nora could only guess from the unchained front door, the light left on in the hall and Silky Boy asleep on Angel's shoulder. Angel herself could only turn her head on her pillow and murmur in her delirium.

Marvell, when he was sent for, was like Angel with the cat and, beside himself with fear, could find only words of abuse. He had never worked as he worked that morning until the doctor came: trying to dig a way clear for the car relieved his feelings. The last hundred yards the doctor had to come on foot, sinking sometimes knee-deep in the drifts. Marvell went out to meet him: they fought their way towards one another

247

like last survivors in a polar region, and Marvell was shouting above the screaming wind before ever he could be heard. "It wasn't for my want of telling her, the pig-headed idiot. 'You've no right out,' I said: 'you know your chest as well as I do.' Now what's she landed herself with? Pneumonia it is, I can tell you, doctor, sir. 'It's pneumonia,' I said, 'and you can take the blame yourself.' 'You've got fussy in your old age,' was what she told me and 'Someone's got to fuss,' I said. The bloody stubbornness of her, and I'll tell her to her face. I'm not one to mince my words with her."

For a moment or two, they pushed their way through the snow in silence. Then Marvell said: "She's as strong as a horse, you know," and tears began to run down his face.

In the night, Silky Boy, banished by the doctor, crept back to Angel's bed. Nora, sitting by the fire, in her day clothes, had not the heart to take him away, for Angel turned her cheek towards him with a look of peace and comfort on her face. Or so it seemed to Nora, trying to find signs that she was conscious of anything at all.

The fire burnt dully and sometimes the smoke was turned back into the room, as if the damp chimney could take no more of it. After a while, when Angel's breathing sounded more even, Nora turned out the light and, sitting with her gouty foot up on a stool, tried to snatch at some sleep herself. She was disturbed towards dawn by Angel gasping for breath and trying to raise herself up from her high pillows, and Nora dragged herself across the room, knelt beside her and laid her wet cheek against her hand.

Angel felt nothing. The room was utterly strange to her; it shifted and turned about and she was enfolded in blackness; not a glimmer of light from any direction helped her to realise her whereabouts.

There should be a window somewhere, she thought in terror. If she could understand where she was, she might remember who she was; but she was lost, isolated, without identity. It suddenly occurred to her that she was dead: her heart thundered in her body and Nora felt the sweat trickling down the inside of her arm, running from her wrist into the palm of her hand. Then to Angel it seemed that she was not so much dead as back at the very beginning. It is to be done all over again, she thought. It would be morning soon and the drays would rattle across the cobbled Butts and into the entrance of the brewery; the factory sirens would sound and men would begin to go to work down Volunteer Street.

Nora sponged the sweat from her forehead and then leaned close to her as her lips moved.

"Where are you?" she said gently, as if to a sleepy child. "Why, you are at home, with Nora and naughty Silky Boy, at Paradise House."

The panic lifted. Angel was overwhelmed with relief. She realised that it was not to be gone through again; after all she was at home, in her own bed, with her own life behind her. "I am Angel Deverell," she said and the words were very loud and triumphant and echoed round the room. Nora heard nothing for nothing had been said. She held Angel in her arms until she knew that she had died. The cat sprang off the bed and went to the door, mewing to be let out. He looked at Nora and yawned; but it seemed a feigned yawn, as if he were frightened, and pretending to be bored instead.

The snow, as if it had done its worst, thinned and melted. Nora, who could not go to the funeral, sat in the library with her leg up on a stool and a drawerful of papers on a chair beside her. She had watched the hearse and the old car drive off; Marvell, in ancient livery, which he had not worn since the days when he had taken Esmé to the races, and Clive Fennelly, who had suddenly arrived, having read the obituary —'An Edwardian Novelist'—in *The Times*. Lady Baines had sent a wreath, which Nora had pretended not to see.

She will not like that, she thought, as the coffin was carried out to the hearse. To lie in that graveyard among dead bodies.

Odd thoughts swarmed in her brain. She was a little tipsy from some brandy Clive had given her to drink before he left the house. Sometimes, particularly at the moment when the cars had driven away and a cloud of yellow petals had scattered from the wreaths on the top of the hearse, she could hear a sound as if stakes were being driven into her head. She tried to be busy with the drawerful of papers, old manuscripts and letters, but she wished that Clive would soon come back. Bored with her grief now, her mouth pouched and swollen from weeping, she brought up great sighs, as if each must come with her last breath, the last she ever cared to take.

When Clive returned, some irrevocable change came with him. She could not believe that the dreadful thing was finally done, and at first she recoiled from him as if he had had some guilty part in it.

"Who was there?" she asked timidly after a while.

"Your doctor; a Lady Baines, so Marvell tells me; Marvell and I." He tried to make it seem as big a congregation as he could. "Some other people I didn't know," he lied.

"Rosita Baines is not one to be kept out of anything," Nora said. "It was kind of you to come, though," she added quickly. "What a strange ending! Once I imagined her being buried in Westminster Abbey, as Heaven knows she should have been."

"You won't stay here alone?" he asked, trying to end that train of thought.

"No." She looked round the room as if it were a person she was soon to escape. "When I am better, I may go abroad. I have money, you know, from my late uncle, and I may do as I please."

Then she leaned over and took some pages of writing from the drawer and handed them to him. "I found a will this afternoon; she must have sketched it out a long time ago and never finished it or had it witnessed. She was never business-like and wouldn't be persuaded ever to discuss dying. It was distasteful to her, you know."

Clive took the papers and began to read the rough draft

250

of the will scrawled in acid green ink. "I, Angelica Howe-Nevinson, widow of the late Esmé Howe-Nevinson, Esquire, of Paradise House in Hampshire, declare this to be my last will and testament, hereby revoking all other wills made by me, and bequeath everything of which I die possessed to my dear friend and sister-in-law, Nora Howe-Nevinson. I appoint as executors the same Nora Howe-Nevinson and in conjunction with her, Theodore Gilbright Esquire of Bloomsbury Square, London, publisher and life-long friend, who is empowered with authority to deal with all copyrights of my literary works and of all correspondence from me to other persons, which he shall preserve from publication. The manuscripts of my works I bequeath to the British Museum."

Clive looked at Nora and then back at the papers. "It made me sad to read it all," she said, "though I was sad enough before."

"That the executors," he read, "shall set aside a sum of money to preserve Paradise House as it stands at the time of my"—the word 'death' had been crossed out and 'decease' superimposed—"to be retained as a public memorial and true record of my life."

"There *is* no money," Nora said.

"To my chauffeur, William Marvell, my motor-car," he read aloud and Nora shrugged. "The garnet bracelets she leaves to Bessie went a long time ago," she said.

"When was this written, do you suppose?"

"Perhaps soon after Esmé died."

"And her publisher, this Gilbright?"

"He is an old man now, too old to travel."

"What will happen to the house?" he asked.

"I shan't be here to see."

He remembered other ruined houses he had sometimes discovered in the depths of the country, often blackened and burnt out, or just abandoned, and he had found them fearful and haunting places. At Paradise House, the neglect had started long ago. With Nora gone, no one would come to take on the prodigious burden of its decay. It would be engulfed in the valley, closed over and smothered by the encroaching branches: out-of-doors would creep indoors; first, ivy thrusting into crevices, feeling its way through broken windows and crumbling stone: bats would fly in through the empty fanlight and hang themselves from cornices in the hall; fungus branch from the walls in fantastic brackets; soft cobwebs drape the shutters. The tenacious vegetation of that lush valley would have its way there in the end.

"It is no place for you," he said gently, laying the papers aside.

There was a sudden stamping in the hall and Marvell came in with a trug filled with wet logs. Melting snow dripped off his boots on to the carpet. He stacked the logs beside the fire and brushed up the hearth.

"You had a cup of tea?" Nora asked him.

"Yes, miss."

"We must try to be brave now. In time we shall get used to it, you know." She felt that some such remark was asked of her, but her lips trembled as she made it. Her wintry grief budded into small hard tears again.

Marvell looked grim. He tried steadfastly to ignore her words, which seemed aimed to break him. There is nothing left to get used to, he thought, as he took up the empty basket and went out.

THE END